A FORGOTTEN SEASON

For
Gerald Hagan

Also by
KATHLEEN CONLON

*

APOLLO'S SUMMER LOOK
TOMORROW'S FORTUNE
MY FATHER'S HOUSE
A TWISTED SKEIN
A MOVE IN THE GAME

A FORGOTTEN SEASON

*

KATHLEEN CONLON

THE
COMPANION BOOK CLUB
LONDON AND SYDNEY

THE COMPANION BOOK CLUB

The Club is not a library; all books are the property of
members. There is no entrance fee or any payment beyond
the low Club price of each book. Details of membership will
gladly be sent on request.

Write to:

The Companion Book Club,
Odhams Books, Rushden, Northants.

Or, in Australia, write to:

The Companion Book Club,
C/- Hamlyn House Books, P.O. Box 252
Dee Why, N.S.W. 2099

Made and printed in Great Britain
for the Companion Book Club
at The Pitman Press, Bath
600 872661
582/366

Chapter One

'ARE YOU A good scholar?' the Major said. 'Are you a conscientious pupil?' His eyes were ancient and pale and had the milky beginnings of cataracts forming over them, but still how keenly they surveyed one. He pulled her closer. Imprisoned between his two arthritic knees, she would have wriggled – had she been a wriggling sort of child. His cheeks resembled the physical map of Britain that she studied in Geography: delicate tracings of red and blue upon a sallowish-green background. She could think of no modest reply, and his fierce questioning gaze was too close to be borne. She looked over the transparent rim of his right ear to the flocked wallpaper and her mother said, 'She does very well at her lessons,' in the besotted tone that made the child's toes curl.

The Major pinched the flesh of her cheek between a yellow forefinger and a calloused thumb. 'She's pretty,' he said. But that was old news, ancient history. That was the reason Aunt Dolly draped her oval mirrors and her pier-glasses with tablecloths. Vanity sent you directly to Hell.

'Pretty, and a good scholar too.' The Major fumbled in an inside pocket and produced a silver threepenny bit, placed it in her hand and folded her fingers over it. Its edge dug into her palm, which was unpleasantly

5

moist. If he would let go of her hand she could wipe it down the side of her frock. But he held on. It was a familiar routine. Every time he visited he would sit down on a hard-backed chair, grip her between his knees, encourage her to recite the nine-times table or a passage from *Hiawatha*, and then hand her a silver threepenny bit as a reward for demonstrating her diligence. Afterwards they would eat sandwiches, and maids of honour tarts, which were the Major's favourite, and then they would walk in the park and listen to the click of wood against wood from the bowling green and the Light Cavalry Overture from the bandstand while the Major recalled German bands and quavered his way through 'Wine, Women and Song', and she wondered how many members of the German bands had fallen under the Major's fire on Flanders Field where the poppies grew. For the Major's wars were in the history books; wars that were commemorated in sepia on the sitting-room wall. 'Why should England tremble?' her father called those photographs.

The Major had been her grandfather's friend and she had often heard her parents speculating as to whether, in view of the discrepancy in rank, the Major was a real major. Or was it some sort of courtesy title? Or adopted in order to con the lifesavings out of elderly widows in Eastbourne? No one knew. It was all so long ago, and now the Major lived alone in Alderley Edge and talked about Omdurman and Passchendaele and mustard gas and his dear late wife, and hummed a little Strauss in the park on blue and violet evenings.

He took her arm and tucked it through his own, and squeezed and patted it in the familiar staccato rhythm as they walked stationwards, past the Garden For the Blind and the drinking fountain and the pavilion behind which rough common boys held competitions to see who could pee the farthest. He exhorted her to

6

attend to her lessons, to fear God and shame the devil, and told her that from little seeds did great trees grow. She scuffed the toes of her sandals one against the other. At ten years old the space between her ears was stuffed with maxims: 'He who lives on hope dies fasting. Want must be your master. Don't care was made to care. As ye sow so shall ye reap.' Aunt Dolly recited at least one of them daily. They were the rules. If one abode by them one would be safe.

They heard the approach of the steam train. She bent down and turned over the tops of her white silk socks until their red stripes were in perfect alignment, postponing the terrible moment when the porter would hold open the door of the compartment and the Major would turn to kiss her. His mouth was dry and puckered, and one was aware of ill-fitting dentures joggling up and down against his gums. He took an age to scramble into the train and wave his freckled hand, an age of agony before she dared to wipe her mouth and spit great gobbets of saliva into the glaring geraniums outside the booking office. Miss Tibbs in Sunday School often read them the story about Jesus curing the blind man with his spittle. The child would then stare hard at something to distract her thoughts: the copper jugs of anemones, or sweet peas, or chrysanthemums (depending upon the season), or the plaque above the lectern which depicted a four-masted schooner and said, 'Our ship is afloat on the fast-flowing wave.' There was a picture of Jesus too. He wore a purple robe and had symmetrical golden rays emanating from his head. Jesus was like Miss Tibbs: nice, but boring. Her mother said that Miss Tibbs had missed the boat. (The one that was afloat on the fast-flowing wave?) The child knew only that Miss Tibbs was a good woman and lived with her ancient father in a privet-darkened semi-detached which housed an obscene carved edifice known as a commode. Every week she led them in 'Jesus wants me for a sunbeam,' and the child quaked as she sang it, envisaging an afterlife of endless Sunday afternoons, a yawning chasm of eternal boredom.

So the Major, at least, provided respite from all things religious. And at Christmas she sat at the back of the church hall while little girls in starched frocks went forward to receive improving literature as prizes for good attendance.

It was literature that beckoned her homewards after the Major's train had steamed off to Manchester. Children's Classics, abridged – with garish illustrations of the Little Mermaid walking upon knives and Black Beauty escaping from the flames and Uncle Ebenezer Balfour aiming his blunderbuss at the head of Alan Breck. What could they have abridged? Certainly there was safety if one chose it: Pooh and Ratty and Mole and various little women but, a hopeless addict, she searched out those others from between the thin India-paper pages. They were very definitely una-bridged: Blind Pew and Mrs Rochester and Captain Hook. They menaced her sleep, blundered and stag-gered from between rows of clothes in the wardrobe, groped and cackled in the dim flicker of her nightlight, woke her to the sound of her own screaming. Still she sought them out. They gripped her imagination as Jesus never could.

That was her affliction, she knew: Too Much Imagi-nation. That, and a predisposition towards diseases of the respiratory tract. All summer she conjugated French verbs and read *The Secret Garden* with the rest of the class and copied out 'When the pods went pop on the broom, green broom' from cards with appropriate pictures; the winters were given over to Mrs Rochester and company, and fevered images staring at her from behind the black wire mesh of the fireguard, and the

8

hissing of a steam-kettle, and her mother pouring Lucozade and sighing and coaxing two M & B tablets the size of half-crowns down her throat.

It was a dual existence: the clocks went back, and the camp-bed came down into the sitting room and tins of kaolin bubbled continually in a pan on the gas-stove while her parents did alternate night shifts observing the course of her fevers, and the words 'pneumonia' and 'crisis' and 'delirium' hung in the cotton-wool air around her head. Her yearly survival was a miracle, when, at the going forward of the clocks, she took her first trembling step outdoors, her scarf wound round her chest in the form of a St Andrew's Cross and secured at the back with a safety-pin.

Ten was the testing time. If she could survive until she was eleven she would live forever. And so to walk through the rhododendrons in the park with the Major, suffering his small expressions of trembling affection, was perfectly fitting. He had survived the blasts and the gas and the shrapnel, and though every month he seemed a little less alive, he clung on tenaciously; he knew, as she did, that if you were special you did not die.

She ran downhill from the station, past the boys under the railway arch with persecution alive behind their dull eyes. She was a stuck-up kid who wore a panama hat with a blue band and rode a brand-new bicycle to Burlington Court where they walked in twos around the garden and never said 'Pardon' or 'Pleased to meet you'. She seemed to move faster than either her legs or her lungs could take her, her feet skimming the paving stones, privet hedges and fuchsia bushes and overhanging clumps of golden rod flashing by in a continuous blurred amalgam.

'Why do you run?' her mother said. 'I've told you not to run. Why do you always run?'

9

On the sofa, she doubled her body over, head down to her knees, reaching deep into her lungs for breath. She was unable to answer: I run because I am afraid; of the boys under the railway arch, of the way that the shadows fall, of what might have happened to you during my absence.

An answer was unnecessary, anyway. 'Running, with your chest the way it is,' her mother said, as though conducting an experiment to find out how many different ways there were of expressing the same sentiment. Conversations in her home were words exchanged between persons of different nationalities who had lost the phrase-book. Her mother said something, and, if pressed, the child replied, but always between the question and the response lay a ditch of incomprehension. School demanded another sort of foreign language. She was learning to master both; it was simply a matter of articulating the right words in the right order – the meaning of the words didn't seem to matter too much as long as they followed one another in the approved manner. The real language, the true one, that consisted of interaction and relationship and progression, was all inside her head.

Her father inclined his ear toward the fretworked rising sun on the front of the wireless. The volume knob was turned to its fullest extent. The choir of Holy Trinity Somewhere in Hertfordshire boomed and shrilled: 'Pavilioned in splendour, and girded with praise.' Her father joined in, beating time on the arm of the chair with his tattooed hand. The tattoo said 'Norma'. Her Mother, whose name was Nancy, said, 'What a racket,' and moved her face very slowly and deliberately away from him towards the window. She was turning the cuffs on his shirt; her needle, gleaming, went jab, jab through the material. Her father frowned and switched off the wireless, snap. He was a gentle, jovial man afflicted with increasing deafness and its attendant paranoia. The child was not sure whether communication with him, using the real language, might have been possible; the deafness, which had been narrowing his horizons since before she was born, precluded any investigation.

'I don't think he'll last much longer,' her father said. 'He'll be pushing them up before long. Poor old sod.'

'Don't say that word.' Her mother grimaced as if in physical pain; she hated vulgarity. 'I can't say that I'll be sorry. He's had his time. He's getting to be a nuisance. On and on. Overstaying his welcome. I know that he was a friend of your father's, but enough's as good as a feast, and if it's a little windfall you're hoping for I'll bet he hasn't two pennies to rub together.'

They were talking about the Major. The child was shocked, as always, by the evidence of their disloyalty. An hour ago her mother had been urging bread and bramble jelly and the last maid of honour upon the Major, smiling a smile that started and ended at the corners of her mouth, saying 'Come again soon. We look forward to it, don't we, Jack?' And now here she was, running him down as always, wishing him dead, in a manner of speaking.

'All these peculiar people,' her mother said, snapping a length of thread between her teeth, feeling in her work-basket for the darning mushroom, blinking her tired eyes, 'I'm sick and tired of them. Why don't we know anybody *normal*?'

Chapter Two

RONNIE WAS A peculiar person.

It was he who woke them next morning, thumping away at the back door until his knuckles were skinned. Her father was supposed to be having a lie-in. She heard him say, 'For Christ's sake,' and go thudding down the stairs. 'It's young Ronnie,' he called back, and then, 'Well, what is it, lad? I can't tell a word you're saying.'

Ronnie had adenoids. Everyone did. But Ronnie's were too big, or infected, or something. The doctor said that he should go into the Princess Alexandra Ward and have them removed, but Mrs Spencer couldn't spare him. She said the Farm School should have seen to all that.

'It's all right, I'm coming,' her mother called, and the child debated whether to relish the warmth of her bed or to get up and participate. Spencers' dramas were ten a penny, but invariably worth observing, in the manner of other people's dramas. She picked grains of sleep from her eyes, put on her knickers, and her vest, which had a lining of Thermogene sewn into it, pulled her liberty bodice and frock over her head in the same operation, fastened her sandal straps, and went out on to the landing. Her father was coming back upstairs. He was wearing only his pyjama bottoms, and his

12

stomach, which was matted with black hair, hung over them. She averted her eyes. 'My God,' he said. 'that so-and-so family. Half-barmy, every one of them. I'm going to bed. If you mother's daft enough . . .'

Ronnie was sitting at the kitchen table. Her mother was frying bread at the stove. 'Have you had anything to eat yet?' she asked him. It was a superfluous question, but he paused for a few moments before he said no. She placed four slices of fried bread on the china plate painted with cornflowers, and you could almost hear the digestive juices running as he eyed them.

The child sat as far away from Ronnie as was humanly possible at a small kitchen table. The noises he made! And his nose! And the strange sounds that issued from his mouth whenever he spoke! He was exactly the kind of child that her mother warned her to avoid at all costs. Why then was it that her mother looked at him with something approaching fondness, or pity? Misplaced surely, since Ronnie was a Bad Boy who had been Sent Away.

He drank hot sweet tea with both hands clamped round the mug. His eyes, above the steam, were wide-open and anxious.

'Don't worry,' her mother said. 'She'll last till we get there.'

'She'll clout me,' Ronnie said resignedly. 'She said to come straight back.'

Ronnie was Margaret Rose's step-brother or half-brother, she was unsure of the precise degree of consanguinity; she knew only that Margaret Rose's mother was Mrs Spencer, and Ronnie's mother was a lady with orange hair and bloodshot eyes who had created a terrible disturbance at the Spencers' some five or six years since; she knew that Ronnie was thirteen years old and on holiday, or parole, or whatever, from the Farm School, and that Mrs Spencer and Margaret Rose detested him. She could understand their point of view: he had bandy legs and permanent sores on the backs of his hands, his hair was cut very short and had the same texture as the things her mother scrubbed the pans with, his handkerchief – if he had one – never kept pace with his catarrh. He looked scrofulous; she'd read the word in a history book, and had little idea what it meant except that it sounded as though it applied to Ronnie Spencer.

Heat was already building up, in the paving stones, the gate stumps, the green-fluted gas-lamps and the blistered paintwork of Mr Fiorelli's Ice Cream Parlour. 'It's going to be another scorcher,' her mother said, gazing at the bland blue sky as though the weather was a personal affront, like rationing and the Major's longevity and the way next door's cat did its courting in her back garden. The child kept at a safe distance from Ronnie; one never knew what one might catch. This necessitated walking in the gutter. Ronnie didn't seem offended, just stumped forward, bandily, with his brush-head down and his hands thrust deep into the pockets of his much-too-long shorts.

If she had been asked to think of a suitable alternative abode for Mrs Rochester or Blind Pew or the Hunchback of Notre-Dame, or any other of her nightmare figures, she would have chosen, without hesitation, Number Thirty-two Jubilee Villas. It differed in no way – except for a faint air of neglect – from its neighbours; all were pebbledashed, bay-windowed, equipped with narrow gardens back and front, coalsheds and defunct outside lavatories and wooden porches with scalloped edges over their front doors; but every rust-coloured brick and leaded-light window and

14

wooden scallop was invested with the menace and dread and fascinated wonder that the Spencers personified and aroused in her.

'A lot of fuss about nothing again, I expect,' her mother said, as they made their way past the dustbins to the back door. The lid was missing from one of the dustbins and a thin tabby cat made repeated forays into its depths. Margaret Rose's frilly pants hung from the washing line. 'If that child was ever really ill,' her mother said, 'they wouldn't know what'd hit them.' She knocked at the back door, which was ajar, wrinkled her nose at the disordered kitchen: Mr Spencer's patent-leather shoes on the sink next to a half-empty packet of grape nuts and a saucer containing a quantity of Rodine, with fungus.

'Come through,' Mrs Spencer called, in the voice that made you think that she'd once been on the stage, or had wanted to be.

And so they went through, into the front room where, on a sofa, in the manner of a secular pietà, were grouped the Spencers: mother and father and child – apple-of-the-eye, miraculous-fruit-of-aged-loins, most perfect child.

Mrs Spencer exhaled a great lungful of breath, said, tremulously, 'I'm so glad you're here. We just don't know what to do. She's been in agony.' She rearranged Margaret Rose's head on her bosomless chest.

'Agony,' echoed Mr Spencer. He sat with his hands folded on his knees. He wore a blue-striped shirt without a collar, and there was greyish-white stubble on his chin.

'What is it? What's the matter?' her mother said, divesting herself of her coat. Ronnie had disappeared, bunked. And who could blame him?

'Earache,' said Mrs Spencer, running a hand through Margaret Rose's luxuriant black curls. Everything

15

about Margaret Rose was on too large a scale: her dark hectic eyes, her thick-lipped mouth, her over-abundance of hair.

'Have you called the doctor?' her mother said, parting sections of dark curls to get at the shell-like source of the trouble.

'He won't come. He says bring her round to the surgery at nine-thirty. We can't wait that long, can we, love?'

Margaret Rose moaned quietly. Mr Spencer reached out a hand so that it met his wife's hand in the rumple of their child's hair. This did not facilitate her mother's attempt at investigation.

'Olive oil,' she said briskly. 'Heat it in a teaspoon and drop it into her ear. It'll ease the pain.'

They both stared, round-eyed, as though she'd suggested performing major surgery with the cutlery.

'Have you got any?'

The child shifted her feet irritably, waiting for the command to run back home and fetch the little greasy bottle from the top shelf of the medicine cabinet, but Mrs Spencer said vaguely that she thought they had some *somewhere*, but she wouldn't like to swear to it. 'Do you know, Mr Spencer?' She always called her husband Mr Spencer. The child was reminded of the Micawbers; there was something faintly Micawber-ish about the entire Spencer life-style; one could imagine dunning tradesmen at the back door and moonlight flits to furnished lodgings. In fact, one didn't *need* to imagine, one knew.

Mr Spencer got up and lumbered after her mother into the kitchen. Mrs Spencer rocked Margaret Rose's head to and fro, and crooned under her breath. The child sat down on a hard varnished chair beside the sideboard and thought what excruciatingly bad taste the Spencers displayed in their sitting-room furnish-

16

ings: soiled lace doilies supporting plaster vases, and a beer tankard that played the Drinking Song from *The Student Prince* when you lifted the lid, a series of little jugs that said Scarborough and Filey and Llandrindod Wells, a framed photograph of Mrs Spencer wearing a black leotard at her eurhythmics class eons ago, innumerable framed photographs of Margaret Rose at various stages of development, and the picture that hung from the mustard-coloured dado above the fireplace, the picture that made her flesh creep as much as the nightmares about Mrs Rochester: The Four Horsemen of the Apocalypse representing War, Famine, Pestilence and Death. Pestilence was like scrofulous: one didn't need to know the meaning; the sound of the word was enough.

She ran the fingernails of her right hand under those of her left hand in a vain attempt to remove the semicircular rims of dirt that had collected there during the night. She squinted round the edge of the sofa to see whether Margaret Rose would raise one putty-coloured eyelid and wink. She didn't doubt that Margaret Rose's earache was genuine, but she was certainly putting it on a bit. She always did. That was why Doctor Mackenzie wouldn't come round any more. He'd had his fill of earaches and stomach aches and splinters in the finger. One day Margaret Rose would have raging smallpox and he'd say bring her round to the surgery at nine-thirty.

Margaret Rose, however, didn't wink. She seemed to be asleep. The only sounds were a clattering from the kitchen as her mother and Mr Spencer tried to locate the olive oil, and Mrs Spencer's rhythmic sighing and crooning. She could see Mrs Spencer's reflection in the spotted looking glass with its faceted edges – there was a tiny Mrs Spencer in each facet. She stared, forgetting that reflection worked both ways, but Mrs

Spencer was absorbed. When you said the word ugly you thought of Madame Bonney – who told your fortune behind a bead curtain at the end of the pier: left hand for what you were born with, right for what you made of it – with her hooked nose and ill-fitting frizzy wig. Mrs Spencer's faded features were regular enough, her extreme thinness had probably once been called slenderness, her hair, though it was looped and rolled and dusty-looking, was fine in texture. Nevertheless, you looked hard at her and the word that came into your mind was ugly. You looked at her ordinary face and, somehow, you knew that, just like those awful concentration camp women, she was capable of beating anyone – Ronnie – to within an inch of his life, that if she disliked you and you were at her mercy there would be no quarter given, that every scrap of love and affection at her command was concentrated exclusively upon Margaret Rose. Certainly Mr Spencer was not a recipient.

He came back into the room, his big white hairless hands flapping and empty. She remembered those hands from when he taught her to ride her bicycle on the recreation ground, hands that held on to the back of the saddle, close to her navy-blue school knickers, and never let go, not even when she wanted him to, when she could ride.

Her mother carried the olive oil, a candle in a candleholder, a box of matches and a teaspoon. She set them down on the mantelpiece and, with a non-too-gentle hand, swept Margaret Rose's hair away from her ear and secured it there with a kirby grip. It reminded one of some sort of religious ceremony: the lighting of the candle, the pouring of the oil – a few drops fell and hissed on the bars of the electric fire – the heating of it. As soon as the spoon containing its panacea was brought within six inches of Margaret Rose's ear she came to life and began to scream like a hundred demons. After a bit the child slid down from her chair and left the room. It was embarrassing. She hadn't yelled so much even when they'd put all that penicillin into her bottom.

Ronnie was in the kitchen. He was wolfing down a bowlful of the grape nuts that had lain so dangerously near the rat poison. Every time you saw him he seemed to be eating. It never occurred to her that he might have to grasp the chance whenever it presented itself. Because she felt that her nose was being pushed out, because she resented the unnecessary rumpus in the next room, she decided to be nasty to him. He was a sitting target, a born victim. Margaret Rose said he still wet the bed.

'I expect you've got worms,' she said. And then heaved, because she could picture them, white and writhing in his insides.

He grunted and continued to eat.

There was a milk jug on the table, covered with a piece of muslin that was weighted down with coloured beads. The milk smelt fusty in spite of it. She flicked at the beads with her forefinger, said, 'Why did they send you away to the Farm School? What did you do?'

He made a series of noises which she translated into: 'I kept running off. Away from me mam.'

'Where *is* your mam?'

'In Manchester.'

'Why are you here now, then? Why aren't you in Manchester?'

'I'm with me dad for the holidays.'

Holidays. She wondered if he understood what that word was supposed to mean 'How can he be your dad?' she said. 'If he isn't married to your mum? Mrs Spencer isn't your mum, is she? Your mum's that lady who kicked up such a fuss ages ago.' Phrases came into her

19

head, phrases that had lodged in her brain from the time the orange-haired lady had stood in the Spencers' front garden – they had lived in Salisbury Avenue then – and shouted: 'You can have him now. I've had a bellyful. He *is* yours you know – I've had blood tests – whatever you might tell your other fancy women.' 'Did they get a divorce, your mum and dad?' If only he'd stick up for himself, she thought, if only he'd retaliate, I wouldn't need to do this. I could say the truth then, which is: I think you're repulsive, Ronnie Spencer, but I'm dreadfully sorry for you. 'Do they chain you up at the Farm School?' she said.

He jumped to his feet, shouted, 'Bloody shut up,' threw his dish into the sink, and dashed out of the back door. She could hear his plimsolls going flap, thump, as he careered past the dustbins and out into the road.

She felt shamefully elated. Did Margaret Rose feel the same way when she pulled back his bedclothes to expose the yellow steaming patches? Did Mrs Spencer experience it when she took the strap and beat him until she was out of breath? This delight in viciousness certainly had no place in the private image or even the public one: the child who said, 'Please pass the butter' and waited to be spoken to before speaking.

'She'll live.' Her mother came into the kitchen pulling on her coat, followed by Mr Spencer. He seemed much relieved. He rubbed his hand across his chin. She couldn't understand why his stubble was white like hoar-frost, when his hair was as smooth and black as his patent-leather dancing shoes. He attended the Palais de Danse every Saturday evening, and sometimes, when in expansive mood, gave demonstrations around the furniture in the sitting-room with a reluctant Mrs Spencer.

He bent down until his eyes were level with hers. 'How's the brainy one today?' he said. 'How's Einstein?' He tweaked the bow at the back of her dress. 'We're a proper bobby-dazzler today, aren't we?' She looked down her nose and over his shoulder. He was an idiot. And the hands that tweaked and patted reminded her of large white predatory insects.

Her father was cleaning his shoes and awaiting his breakfast. 'A lot of nonsense,' her mother said in answer to his raised eyebrows. 'Earache. They didn't know what to do.'

'I could tell them. Spoilt little madam.' He banged the shoe-brushes together. 'Why do you run round there every time she sends for you when you know there's nothing wrong?'

'Somebody's got to go,' her mother said, cracking eggs into the frying-pan. 'They can't cope. They haven't a clue.'

And going round there, answering cries for help, allows you to feel so very superior, the child thought, arranging knives and forks on the checked tablecloth.

'What a set-up,' her father said. His fried egg was underdone; strings of glutinous yellow-white yolk hung from his fork. He made a sideways diving motion to capture them in his mouth, wiped his plate with a crust of bread. She felt ashamed for him. If you did that at Burlington Court they made you stand in a corner until the headmistress came round and lectured you on table manners. Her mother ate daintily: little bites of toast and sips of tea. Her mother had been well brought up and had broken her parents' hearts when she married. 'What all these women see in him, I don't know,' her father said. 'I wouldn't touch him with a ten-foot pole if I was a woman.'

Her mother made winking and nodding signs in the child's direction. Her father screwed up his eyes in an attempt to interpret them. Also attendant upon his deafness was the misapprehension that the whole world was hard of hearing, that if he spoke in a slightly lower tone than usual, the child would not be able to catch what he said. It reminded her of when she was little and used to close her eyes in the belief that no one could see her.

She looked at her father, at his thinning hair, his tattoo marks, his messy eating habits. If she could have chosen a father, it would have been Monsieur Paul Emanuel out of *Villette*, or Sir Percy Blakeney, or Claude Rains in *The Phantom of The Opera* before he got the acid in his face and had to wear a mask. However, one couldn't choose, and when she thought that, for instance, Mr Spencer might have been her father, she could only give thanks to heaven for the one she had. Spoiled or not, *imagine* being Margaret Rose. How did she endure it?

It had no effect, apparently, upon Margaret Rose's natural exuberance. She came round at four o'clock that afternoon. She was wearing new red leather shoes. They were to compensate for endurance of a different kind: physical agony bravely borne. She had recovered at lunch-time.

'You kicked up an awful fuss,' the child said disdainfully.

Margaret Rose put her hands on her hips and fixed her with a dark brown protuberant stare. After a few moments she reached a triumphant conclusion. 'You're jealous,' she said joyfully.

This was self-evidently true. The child pulled a handful of leaves off the hedge and stared into the middle-distance. Margaret Rose pointed her toes. Red shoes seemed the acme of desirability. 'I'm going home, then.' At the gate she paused, turned her head, fired her last salvo: '*And* I'm getting a new bike.'

22

Chapter Three

'A NEW BIKE,' she said. 'A Humber with a dynamo and a tool kit. A big proper bike.'

'Oh yes,' said Miss Mingay, rapping Margaret Rose's index finger quite hard with her pencil. The metronome on top of the piano beat out its monotonous message. It reminded the child of the Chinaman on Aunt Dolly's mantelpiece, perpetually nodding.

'Oh yes,' Miss Mingay said. 'But you know, Margaret, the word isn't "bike". What is it, Veronica?'

And automatically, the child answered 'bicycle'. Routine. One didn't talk about 'phones' or 'fridges' or 'bikes'. Margaret Rose didn't know that; she was as thick as a plank.

'You're doing very nicely,' Miss Mingay said, smiling. She turned her head. '*You* need a great deal more practice.'

Outside, among the crazy paving and the night-scented stock and the plate-sized paeonies in Miss Mingay's garden, Margaret Rose pulled tongues and put her fingers to her nose. The child leaned against the gate which said 'Braemar' in wrought-iron lettering, her music-case at her feet, waiting patiently for the performance to end.

'You're a pain in the neck,' Margaret Rose said. 'Everybody's little pet. Just because you're always ill and forever sucking up.'

The child bowed her head. The first part of the statement was indisputable; but it wasn't because she was always ill or forever sucking up. It was because she was every average adult's idea of an acceptable child: quiet, polite, intelligent and diligent. It was the easiest thing in the world to formulate a code of behaviour that would please the adults. Only someone as stupid or as self-confident as Margaret Rose couldn't get the hang of it. It was pleasant to be popular with the grown-ups, but, oh, what she would have given to possess Margaret Rose's courage, to dare not to care when Miss Mingay rapped your erring fingers with her pencil, when the headmistress scolded you for inattention or picking your nose in class, when prim maiden ladies leaned over their boxprivet hedges and threatened to report you to your parents for giving cheek.

Years later, the meteorological office would contradict her memory of that summer. Sunshine: average, it said; rainfall: average. She remembered only the early-morning mist covering the marshes so that it seemed you were looking out over a series of lakes, the blue sky a dome over the horizon, the lawns in the park turning into hay, the pavements scorching your bare feet, the sun hanging, copper-coloured and reluctant to sink, evening stone surfaces retaining the day's heat, the dazzle of twilight flowers in suburban gardens, and the faltering sounds of unwilling piano practice drifting through open windows. Margaret Rose never practised upon the piano. 'We could go on the sands,' she said. It was early yet. Their music lesson was first on Miss Mingay's list, while they were still sleepy-eyed, stumble-fingered.

'My mum won't allow me to. Anyway, I've got to get my Aunt Dolly's meat.'

'I'll come.'

The child pondered. Was Margaret Rose's company preferable to being alone? She called Margaret Rose 'friend' because she was unaware of the word that might have described their relationship more accurately. They attended the same school, they lived in the same neighbourhood, therefore it was accepted that they should spend their free time together. It was, however, an unequal relationship: sun and satellite, king and courtier, one who led, and one who followed, however reluctantly.

'I'm coming anyway,' Margaret Rose said. And the matter was settled. Just as she felt sorry for Ronnie, in spite of his repulsiveness, so she felt vaguely sorry for Margaret Rose and was afraid, despite much evidence to the contrary, that Margaret Rose might possess feelings that could be hurt.

Aunt Dolly had two parcels: topside of beef and a sheep's heart. The child held this second parcel at arm's length. Aunt Mu was quite content with a bit of roast beef or neck-end of mutton stew, but Aunt Dolly was passionate for all the disgusting, *human* parts of the beast: heart, kidneys, brains, sweetbreads.

'I thought you'd run away with a black man.' She unwrapped the meat and sniffed at it. 'I expect you dawdled.'

Aunt Mu was out, having her new corsets fitted. All the time in the world and she had to choose a Saturday morning! The kitchen was full of steam. Aunt Dolly mangled ferociously. It was martyrdom pure and simple. The washing could well have waited until Monday.

'On your feet all day and every day just so that we can keep our heads above water and then come home and do the washing – no consideration – I wish *I* was a lady of leisure – if there's one thing I can't abide it's laziness – my lady there doesn't know what work is – Mr Woodham said to me only the other week Dolly you're a marvel I don't know how you do it.'

She possed at the clothes in the dolly-tub. Her hair was bound up in a turban scarf, her feet encased in large tartan carpet-slippers; you could see the shape of her bunions – in the winter she had savage chilblains, and spent every evening anointing them with Snowfire. Her eyes were very little and bright, and there were patches of deep colour on her cheekbones. Sometimes she was worse than others. Her mother said that it was Dolly's time of life, but her father said that she must have waved goodbye to that when Adam was a lad.

She transferred a heap of scalding washing from the washboiler to the sink with the aid of a jointed stick. Her arms were long and muscled like a man's. You would never believe that it was the same Aunt Dolly who wore a black tailored suit and a white pin-tucked blouse during the week to be a manageress at Wood-ham's Drapery. She had eight employees under her, and was responsible only to Mr Woodham. Her father said that Aunt Dolly and Mr Woodham were 'like that' and interlocked his little fingers. They partnered one another at the whist drives, and on Sundays they took flowers to the cemetery and laid them on their respective family graves. But, her father said, there was nothing 'like that' between them. A different 'like that'. Mr Woodham was a bachelor. And Aunt Dolly was one of life's natural-born unmarried ladies.

Margaret Rose wrote with her finger on the steamed-up kitchen window. What she wrote must have been either rude or scurrilous because she rubbed it out again immediately. She nudged and whispered, 'Let's go. It's boring.' Her manners were very rudimentary. She knew that all her dimpling and eyelash-fluttering cut no ice with Aunt Dolly. The child hung on, waiting to see whether the customary sixpence would be forth-coming. Aunt Dolly scrubbed fiercely at a Peter Pan collar and the straps of a big, complicated brassière. She ran the edge of the green soap along them and scattered them with soap flakes as though attempting to wash away the sins of the world. Various other female undergarments simmered in the boiler together with the dolly blue. The child gazed, fascinated. 'Oh, do get from under my feet,' Aunt Dolly said. 'Doesn't your mother have any errands for you to run? You're spoiled to death, the lot of you, these days. When I was your age I was helping to bring up the family. I had no spare time to be getting under people's feet. Of course people think better of you if you never do a hand's turn – you can slave your guts out and what thanks do you get – there'll be an alteration in this house or I'll know why – if there's one thing I can't abide it's laziness – Mr Woodham said to me only the other week Dolly you're a marvel I don't know how you do it . . .'

They slipped out unnoticed. 'She's potty,' Margaret Rose said. 'Only potty people talk to themselves. They'll send the yellow van for her and put her in a padded cell in the loony-bin.'

The child considered these remarks to be extremely ill-advised in view of the dubious mental stability of Margaret Rose's own immediate relations. She decided to show off. 'My dad says she's frustrated.'

'What does frustrated mean?'

'Don't you know what frustrated means?'

'No. And I bet you don't know either.'

She had an idea of the literal meaning of the word, but didn't intend to chance her arm in case she was wrong. It reminded her of when she was small, when she'd learned to read before she could understand the meaning of certain vital words. Her mother's library books. About people called Lady Eleonora and A Gentleman of Substance, about roses and moonlight and disgrace. 'The Lady Eleonora, perplexed, opened her reticule.' Perplexed? Reticule? She asked her mother. Her mother took the books away from her, said, 'Fresh air,' and sent her into the garden.

27

'What does it mean, then? You don't know.'

'Of course I do. We're not all as ignorant as you.'

This repetitive and monotonous wrangling continued until they reached the child's home. 'Let's go on the sands,' Margaret Rose said again. 'Ask your mum. She'll let you. It's so hot nobody could catch cold. My mum says that's why you're always ill, you're wrapped up in cotton wool. My mum says that if you took off all those clothes and ran around a bit you'd be a lot healthier.'

This from one who, a few days ago, had been shrieking in agony, at death's door, from one whose mother had been talking in whispers about mastoids and brain tumours. There were so many obvious retorts that the child was spoiled for choice. It was always the same. Margaret Rose could insult and disparage to her heart's content and some natural delicacy prevented one from paying her back in the same coin.

'*Ask* her,' Margaret Rose said. 'Won't mummy let baby out on her own? Is she afraid baby will fall in the sea and drown?'

The child opened the back door and went through the scullery into the kitchen. Voicing a request to go down to the beach unaccompanied was a waste of breath. One summer afternoon when she was five her father had taken her to the sea-bathing lake. He intended to teach her to swim but the sun was hot, and he was tired, and after a while he fell asleep with his hat down over his eyes. She'd wandered off in the company of a bigger boy. He walked sure-footed along the narrow parapet that bordered the bathing lake. She followed – entranced by his bright golden hair, his scarlet bathing costume – lost her footing, and fell into the water. The water at that end was barely three feet deep, but she was barely three feet high. She went down and came up and went down and came up. The water down there was jade green. She was astonished, not having expected death so early on in her life. It seemed a long time before a man pulled her out and awakened her father. She was wearing only her knickers. Her father tried to dry them out before they went home, but her mother got to know about it and gave him hell for weeks afterwards. As a result of this, trips to the beach, either with her father or unaccompanied, were strictly taboo.

Her mother was opening the lunch-time post. There was the gas bill and a postcard from Cousin Marjorie at Bridlington and a letter with black edging.

'Can I go on the sands with Margaret Rose after lunch?' She waited. The tone in which she'd made the request invited a negative response.

Her mother looked up and said, 'All right, I suppose so, as long as you stay down this end, you keep well away from that bathing lake, and you're back for four o'clock. I dare say Margaret Rose has got her head screwed on the right way.' She didn't seem to be paying much attention; she kept glancing down at the letter. 'I might as well tell you,' she said. 'The Major has passed on. The funeral is on Tuesday. I expect we'll have to go. To show respect.' She tapped the edge of the letter against its envelope, stared unseeingly through the window. 'I don't mind telling you I begrudge the expense. I got rid of my black for mother years ago. I wonder if Dolly's costume would fit me? I could get a hat from the Co-op with my divi . . .'

They kept well away from the bathing lake, and the funfair, and the pier, and the man who made pictures in the sand with coloured bottle-tops; away from the day-trippers with their red faces and pallid bodies and embarrassing lack of inhibition, away from the Punch and Judy man and the scabrous donkeys and the sandcastle competitions and the mingled odours of sweating humanity and shellfish and candy-floss and Guinness. In the Marine Gardens Pavilion Uncle Arthur's Kiddies Party was in full swing: a stunted eleven-year-old with auburn sausage curls sang like Gracie Fields and won a bar of Dairy Milk Chocolate and two tickets for her parents to see Uncle Arthur's Evening Follies. Factory girls screamed at the top of the ferris-wheel and exposed their shiny-stockinged knees. The miniature railway clanged past the miniature golf-course behind whose miniature slopes acts of lust were often committed at dusk. Sweaty pennies cascaded into the metal cups of slot-machines and middle-aged matrons eased their feet out of their peeptoed sandals. Lost children collected together at the Lost Children's Kiosk, and a girl from Oldham who thought she looked like Rita Hayworth was voted Miss Rose of England 1952 by a partisan jury. An aeroplane on a pleasure flight scratched a white line against the sky.

All these goings-on were invisible and scarcely audible at the other end of the beach, that part where sand degenerated into marsh grass, where high tide turned the marshland into a series of islands, where you could dip your jam-jar into a pool and garner a harvest of minute and unidentifiable fish flickering through murky liquid, or gather fistfuls of marsh daisies and purple vetch which invariably wilted before you got them home, or collect shiny black mussel-shells which you intended to stick on to a trinket box you were making for your mother but you never got round to it and after a week your mother threw them out because they were beginning to stink.

'Aren't you *lucky*!' said the second cousins in Halifax and Huddersfield and Doncaster when she visited their grey houses in their grey towns, 'Living by the sea.' She supposed she was. Wealthy people moved to the seaside for the health-giving properties of the ozone. She had seen rich ruined old faces taking tea on the verandahs of The Grand and The Majestic. At the end of the Promenade there was the remains of what had been a Bath-chair rank, where, before the war, dilapidated dowagers could hire equally dilapidated – but impoverished – male pensioners to push them along the sea-wall. Perhaps, if she'd lived in Huddersfield or Doncaster, she'd never have made it to the magic age of ten.

Margaret Rose took off her shoes and her frock and anchored them to the ground with a piece of driftwood. She was nearly eleven, and had the very beginning of chests.

'You must be roasting,' she said, digging her toes in the ribbed sand. 'How can you bear it?'

She was roasting. She longed to take off her dress, but that would mean exposing the shameful liberty bodice and the vest that had sleeves in it. Margaret Rose would never let her forget it, nor the fact of the just perceptible difference in their development. She, the child, wouldn't have chests for years and years after everybody else, she knew it.

She compromised by removing her sandals and tucking her dress into her knickers. Recent healed grazes and scratches showed pink against the brown of her legs. Margaret Rose's torso was uniformly tanned, but that was perhaps her natural colouring. Her father said she looked like a gypsy. Her father said had Mrs Spencer been playing away?

They ambled down to the headland, collecting gulls' feathers and buttercups, stopping to pick fragments of broken shell from between their toes. Her mother would have a fit if she knew. She was fanatical about picking things up from places: wooden floors, swimming-baths, lavatory seats; one should remain shod upon the first, never sit down upon the last.

But perhaps her mother was still gazing abstractedly at the black-bordered letter. While Margaret Rose prattled on about her new bike, her new shoes, how she was entered for a beauty competition, how she was to dance a solo in the ballet class, how her father had shot fifty-three Germans during the war – Margaret Rose's lies were always transparent, but this last begged a ridiculous degree of gullibility; Mr Spencer, being too old for army service, had worked in a munitions factory and done a spot of firewatching, and everybody knew it – while Margaret Rose weaved truth and half-truth and fantasy into an intricate tapestry, the child pondered upon the Major's death.

It had been on the cards, of course, as her father had said. He had been living on borrowed time. She was neither shocked nor upset nor particularly moved. Nevertheless, what a waste it seemed: to get born, to go through wars – he'd told her: duckboards in the trenches and rats as big as dogs and running two Germans through at once with his bayonet and the man next to him having his head blown clean off his body and tots of rum and mademoiselle from Armentières and the Boches shouting Merry Christmas across No Man's Land and singing '*Stille Nacht, heilige Nacht*', and the man hanging on the barbed wire, his guts spilling out, screaming – to survive all that, just to die.

No more *Hiawatha*, no more silver threepenny bits, no more dry trembling kisses – no more Major. He had gone to be with Jesus. She couldn't really believe that, no matter how hard she tried. Heaven was too vast and difficult a concept. It was much easier, when you were acquainted with Blind Pew and Captain Hook and Mrs Spencer, to visualize Hell.

Chapter Four

'THAT'S THE WAY,' Aunt Muriel said encouragingly. 'You've got the hang of it.'

The child, her tongue between her teeth, executed the last piped-icing rose with a flourish, stepped back from the tray of cakes to admire her handiwork. The cakes were to be part of the post-funeral tea. Funerals were famous for making you hungry.

'We've done a good afternoon's work,' Aunt Mu said, gathering up utensils, handing over the bowl to be scraped out – she'd left a generous quantity inside it. 'I think we can be proud of ourselves.'

The child scraped. Her contribution had extended no further than piping roses on the raspberry buns, but Aunt Mu made you feel valuable, made it seem as though she couldn't have managed without you, taught you, with gentleness and patience, to master the accomplishments that Aunt Dolly – and even your mother – assumed were beyond your capabilities.

So many different varieties of grown-up: her mother, sharp, irritable, impatient; Aunt Dolly, all repudiating angles, nose and elbows, always looking out for the bad things; and Aunt Mu, lap and comfort; Aunt Mu, who washed your hair so that the soap never got into your eyes and the comb never hit a tangle, who accepted your clumsy assistance in her kitchen without protest, who played Chinese Chequers and let you win, for whom you felt love in a way that made you feel disloyal towards your mother.

Chalk and cheese were Aunt Dolly and Aunt Muriel: the spinster and the widow of the spinster's brother; sisters-in-law, held together throughout the incompatible years because of economic necessity and because irritating habits and annoying foibles yield, if nothing else, the comfort of predictability.

Aunt Dolly came in from business while they were spreading out the feast in the dining-room. She sat down in the plush armchair and massaged the blue knot of varicose veins below her knee. 'Expecting royalty, are we?' she said. 'Or is this a new branch of Joe Lyons?' She was sharp and sarcastic on account of never having been married. When she went to the bathroom you could hear her muttering, '. . . money to burn . . . Lady Bountiful . . . who *earns* it, that's what I'd like to know,' all the way up the stairs.

'Why do you put up with her? Why do you let her trample all over you? She used to try it with me, until she found that she'd picked the wrong one. You should assert yourself.' Such sentiments the child had heard her mother express after one of Aunt Dolly's more spectacular bouts of megalomania. But Aunt Mu had merely smiled and shrugged, as if to imply that there were worse fates than being Aunt Dolly's doormat.

'A good spread,' Aunt Mu had called it. But they didn't seem to be hungry after all. They pushed sliced ham and cucumber and artistic radishes around their plates. Her mother was wearing one of Aunt Dolly's dark business suits. It was very tight around the bottom and across the chest. Her hat, from the Co-op, was rather more successful: black, certainly, but with a hint of coquetry, a wisp of Wicked Lady veiling. Her cheeks were flushed and her brown eyes were bright. 'No, no,'

34

she said impatiently to further offers of food. She could hardly wait until the meal was finished, the table cleared; she was bursting to impart some news or other, you could tell. And anxious to be rid of her daughter. 'Why don't you call for Margaret Rose after you've eaten?' she said.

'I can't. She's gone to the hairdresser for a permanent wave,' the child said disgustedly.

'Well, take a ball into the garden, then.'

'You take care where you're bouncing balls in this garden,' Aunt Dolly said automatically, covering a plate of left-over bread and butter with a damp cloth. No sense in waste. It would do for tomorrow.

'I want to draw a picture.'

Her mother clicked her tongue against her teeth in vexation. Children came into the world carrying contrariness on their chromosomes. Or so it always seemed whenever you wished to exclude them from conversations.

Her father had to be off. It was his British Legion night. He left rather earlier than was necessary. The company of too many pernickety women with eyes that never missed a trick daunted him. He'd have a pint in the Saracen's Head, where nothing more than a mild degree of bonhomie was expected of him.

They were glad to be rid of him. They pulled chairs into a group around the hearth. Because of the heat, the grate was filled with a fluted paper fan and concealed by a tapestry fire screen. Aunt Dolly took off her shoes and rested her tired, calloused feet on the coolness of the brass fender. She opened the door of the oven that was situated next to the grate and took out a packet of Craven-A and a cigarette lighter that had been made out of the wreckage of a German bomber by the boarder they'd had during the war. She allowed herself one cigarette every evening. She smoked very elegantly, her head thrown back, the smoke issuing from her nostrils, like a film star. As she smoked, she rubbed absently at a mark on the black-leading. Every other house in the street had had its vast range ripped out and replaced by a beige-tiled fireplace. Aunt Dolly though that such profligacy for the sake of being modern was little short of criminal.

The child took her drawing-pad and her HB Venus pencil to the corner of the room. She was going to draw a horse, one much better than her last effort. She had observed a horse's anatomy more closely since then. She would draw very quietly, not even breathing hard, and eventually they would forget her presence. Or, like her father, speak low and think that way she couldn't hear them.

'I thought I was going to melt,' her mother said. 'Not a patch of shade anywhere. It was an ugly cemetery, Dolly. New, you know. No trees. A little chapel like a Nissen hut. And one of those parsons that never knows when to stop.'

'Was there a bun-fight, a tea, afterwards?' Aunt Dolly asked, inhaling greedily, making the most of her one cigarette. She was anxious to know whether they'd provided a second, unnecessary meal.

'Oh, no. Just a glass of sherry at the house of the woman next door. Not like the Major's. She let us have a look in. What a pig-sty! Good stuff it had been, once. You could have written your name in the dust. And the kitchen! This thick! Still, I suppose being on his own a widower. And this lady next door – Mrs Macheter – she said he wouldn't have anyone in to clean. Didn't like anyone touching his things. Not that there was much to touch – A few bits of tarnished silver and some books, his military stuff. Anyway . . .' She turned her head to look at the child. The child was absorbed, not listening to a word they were saying. 'Anyway, you'll never guess who turned up for the funeral . . .'

There was a pause while they each reflected that it *was* unlikely that they would guess. 'Poor old soul,' Aunt Mu said irrelevantly. The other two turned their heads and looked at her. Whatever sentiment there might have been had ceased with the interment.

'Mumble, mumble, mumble,' her mother said, 'his son!'

'Didn't know he had a son,' Aunt Dolly said, unmoved by this stirring piece of information, flicking ash into a tiny china pin-tray.

'He *didn't*,' her mother said. 'I mean not with his – mumble mumble – wife. He always told us that his wife – his dear wife, he used to call her – couldn't have children.' The child peered out of the sides of her eyes and saw Aunt Mu flush up. 'No,' her mother said. 'Not his wife. You know what I mean.' In case they didn't, she mouthed the words 'Wrong side of the blanket' twice, at each of them in turn.

'Dirty old devil,' said Aunt Dolly. *Her* face was flushed now. 'How old was he – this son?'

'Late twenties, early thirties.'

'And the Major was what – eighty-two?' Aunt Dolly said. 'Dirty old devil! And you'd had no idea before?'

'Not a clue,' her mother said. 'Nobody had. "I'm his little secret," this chap – Charlie, his name is – said, as bold as brass. "But I reckon he's past being embarrassed by now, don't you?"'

'The mother, then,' Aunt Mu said hesitantly. She seemed much more embarrassed than Aunt Dolly, even though she had been a married lady and Aunt Dolly had not.

'She died five years ago,' her mother said. 'This – Charlie, he said that it had to be kept quiet because of

37

the Major's wife and then, after she snuffed it – passed on, I mean – the Major was too old and set in his ways to be bothered with a new family. His mother had gone right off the Major by then, anyway, he said. He wasn't a bit bashful about it. We didn't know where to look, Jack and me and Mrs Macheter.'

Aunt Dolly stubbed out her cigarette. 'I can't see why he turned up at all,' she said, 'unless, of course, he's hoping to gain.'

Hoping to Gain. It sounded like one of the rules of a board game; Monopoly: Go to Jail, Do not Pass Go, Hoping to Gain.

'I don't know about that,' her mother said. 'There's nobody else for it as far as I can tell. But I don't think there'll be all that much to gain at any event. The house was rented, they say, and he only had his army pension. Anyhow, this – Charlie, was off with the solicitor as soon as the funeral was over. There wasn't a proper will-reading or anything like that, but we were told he's left Veronica fifty pounds.' This last was spoken so quietly that the child almost missed it.

Fifty pounds. She was rich. And unsurprised. It was only fitting.

Their three heads were close together, nodding, like the Chinaman, like the metronome on Miss Mingay's piano. Aunt Dolly shifted her stockinged feet from place to place on the fender, and little winces of pain crossed her face. Aunt Mu's needles clicked; the wool, oatmeal flecked with brown – a sensible colour that wouldn't show the dirt – sped through her fingers. Her mother pushed the hair away from her forehead, tapped her fingernails on the arm of the chair, seemed in a state of stimulation. Little lights danced in her brown eyes. Such small excitements were sufficient these days; life seemed so grey.

Chapter Five

MARGARET ROSE'S HAIR was cut short and curled into tight ridges all over her head. Because of her dark complexion and pronounced features, this made her look faintly negroid.

'Doesn't it suit her? Doesn't she look a picture?' Mrs Spencer said, gazing through the dirty kitchen window into the back garden, where Margaret Rose was perched on the fence eating plums and spitting the stones into next door's herbaceous border.

The child thought that such protestations of maternal pride were obscene, and said nothing. Personally she thought that Margaret Rose looked a devil. Ronnie sat in the corner reading *The Rainbow*. Or, to be more precise, looking at the pictures in *The Rainbow*. On the kitchen table were the remains of breakfast, Margaret Rose's red tapshoes, a hat-box full of buff envelopes which contained bills, and a half-completed letter which Mrs Spencer was in the process of writing to her sister Gwen in Weston-super-Mare. The child wondered what Mrs Spencer *did* all day long. Write letters? Worry about bills and how to pay them? Sit and dream about Margaret Rose's golden future?

She opened the window, called, 'Your friend is here,' in a trilling voice. She never said anything normally. Margaret Rose pretended not to hear; it was her latest affectation. 'She's in a world of her own,' Mrs Spencer said fondly. She turned and looked at Ronnie. The benign expression vanished from her face like chalk rubbed off a blackboard. He was poking into his ear with his little finger and then inspecting his finds. His face was all wrong, as though it had been put together hurriedly with no thought for symmetry. 'Only a mother could love him,' as her mother would say about unattractive persons. But apparently Ronnie's mother didn't love *him*. As the holidays progressed, the child was beginning to understand why her mother felt sorry for him.

Tears came into her mother's eyes when she talked about the evacuees during the war: ladies had brought them round from door to door as though they were turbanned pedlars presenting merchandise. Slum children from Liverpool, they were, hard-faced, wary-eyed. Gradually selections were made. The group dwindled until it was composed of the very ugly, the bed-wetters and those who looked as though they might be verminous. No one wanted *them*. Ronnie seemed like a latter-day evacuee.

Mrs Spencer shook her head and sighed. You could tell that the summer holidays were going to seem an eternity.

At last Margaret Rose deigned to descend from the fence. She sauntered down the garden path, leaned against the outside lavatory, picking blistered paint from its door with her thumbnail. She kept shaking her head from side to side to draw attention to her hair. The child was determined not to comment upon it.

Ronnie came out to the coal-shed with a bucket in his hand. Under cover of his coal-shovelling, he presented a mime for the child's benefit, a mime of hatred of Margaret Rose, her primped hair, her red shoes, her big greedy features. He concluded this display by

40

running a finger across his throat and spitting into the slack. Margaret Rose was not entirely unaware of this mute antipathy. She said very loudly, looking in the opposite direction, 'He's a bastard.' She never spoke of him by name.

'What's a bastard?' She'd read the word – in the big history book that she consulted in the school library; it said William the Conqueror, bastard – but she didn't know its meaning.

'Don't you know what a bastard is?' Margaret Rose said, sneering, getting her own back for frustrated.

'No. And I bet you don't know either.'

'It means a very bad person.' Margaret Rose said, 'worse than a bugger.'

Her father said bugger often. She had never heard him say bastard.

'He'll be going back soon,' Margaret Rose said, loudly again. 'And next time they'll never let him out. He's dirty and sullen and disobedient.' She was parroting her mother. Left to herself she would have formed her own opinion of Ronnie, and his dirtiness, sullenness or disobedience wouldn't have entered into it.

'Let's get away from here,' she said. 'He really nauseates me.' Nauseates was very definitely a Mrs Spencer word.

He followed them at a distance. That summer it was quite usual for them to turn round and catch sight of him darting into a gateway or, if there was no convenient gateway, standing stock-still with his head down until they moved off. He lowered their tone. They lost a good deal of caste. Burlington Court girls were not generally followed at a distance by ugly, slummy, thirteen-year-old boys, unless it was for the purposes of persecution. But there was nothing they could do about it.

'It's so-o bo-oring,' Margaret Rose moaned, tearing chunks of grass out of the recreation ground. Like the child's mother, Margaret Rose demanded constant stimulation: a permanent wave, an evening at the cinema, a day in Blackpool. Reading, drawing, practising the piano were tedious occupations, smacking of school, of compulsory education. She longed to be grown up. Or, at least, fourteen years old. 'Let's go for a bike ride,' she said. She had ridden the new bicycle home from the shop two days ago. It was coloured a metallic purple, it had a three-speed gear and a dynamo and the very latest downward-sloping handlebars. She had pedalled around the neighbourhood until it was dark and Mrs Spencer had sent her husband and Ronnie out as a search party.

'*I* can't. I've got a puncture.'

'Mend it.'

'I don't know how. My dad's doing it tonight.'

'I bet I could do it.'

'Come and try then.'

She wouldn't be able to do it. Her eternal confidence in her talents was unfounded. She was just the same when it came to spelling tests at school. 'Easy,' she'd say, and then stand up and spell 'gorgeous': gorjess.

They took the bicycle into the back garden and turned it upside down. Margaret Rose knew that you required a bowl of soapy water and a rubber patch. Beyond that, her knowledge was sketchy. After half an hour she decided that the tyre was irreparable. 'Must be more than a puncture,' she said, spinning the wheels. She had lost interest in the idea of a bicycle ride anyway. There wasn't anywhere to go that they hadn't been twenty times before.

The child's mother came out into the garden. She'd washed her hair and put lipstick and powder on her face. She said, 'I'm going to the shops. I've left the insurance man's money on the sideboard. Will you pay him when he comes? I *think* it's his day.'

42

They abandoned the bicycle. There was three and fourpence worth of silver and copper in a neat little pile on the sideboard. Margaret Rose eyed it. The child put it in her pocket. Just to be on the safe side. Margaret Rose had once stolen three packets of chewing gum from the corner shop and a Dinky toy from the counter at Woolworths. The child could understand stealing because of deprivation; what she couldn't understand was stealing for the sake of stealing. And Margaret Rose certainly wasn't deprived, not when she could have a new bicycle and a permanent wave and red leather shoes all in one week. No one knew how the Spencers did it. Mr Spencer had no settled and ordered niche in life. Last Christmas he had been a clerk in a shipping office, at Easter he had sold tickets for the miniature railway, this month he was selling vacuum cleaners. Her mother needed a new vacuum cleaner but refused to buy from a firm that had the foolhardiness to employ Mr Spencer.

Margaret Rose bashed out 'Chopsticks' on the upright piano. The keys were loose and yellowed, suited only to the most delicate fingering. 'Don't *bang*,' the child said. 'You're not exactly Paderewski, are you?' That was what her father said whenever she did her practice: 'Make way for Paderooski.'

Someone knocked at the front door. She took the money out of her pocket and the insurance book out of the sideboard drawer and went to answer it. A tall young man with black hair wearing a dark suit was leaning against the porch. A new insurance agent. She held the book and the money towards him.

'Very kind of you, Princess,' the man said. 'What am I supposed to do with it?'

'Sign the book.'

'Autographs a pleasure,' the young man said. 'Oh, I get you, you think I'm the insurance man. No. That isn't me. Is your mum in?'

She didn't know whether to say yes or no. She'd heard all about the awful men who preyed on children alone in the house. 'Margaret Rose is here,' she said.

'Is that your mum?'

'No.'

'Your mum is Mrs Bell, isn't she?' the man said, sighing a bit as if it was just his luck to encounter an idiot child.

'Yes,' she said reluctantly.

'And you're Veronica.'

'How do you know?' she said, blushing. It wasn't a nice feeling to know that someone you didn't know knew you.

'Not a lot Charlie doesn't know,' the young man said. And just at that moment, as her eyes were out like chapel hat-pegs, her mother came through the front gate.

'Mrs Bell,' the young man said and made the gesture of taking off his hat, though he wasn't wearing a hat. 'Oh,' her mother said, and blushed too. 'Mr . . .?' Either she couldn't remember his name, or had never been told it, or wasn't sure whether or not it was the same as the Major's.

'Charlie,' the young man said. 'You remember me, don't you? We met under sad circumstances.' But he was smiling as he said it.

'Yes, of course,' her mother said. 'Do come in, won't you?' She preceded him into the hall, put down her shopping bag, picked it up again, fiddled with her scarf. She seemed very flustered.

'You did say, drop in if you're ever in the district,' the young man said. 'And, well, I was and I did. I hope it's not inconvenient.'

'Oh no,' her mother said. 'No. Not at all.' Protesting too much. She had indeed said, 'Do call on us if you're ever in the district,' but she certainly hadn't expected her offer to be taken up with quite such alacrity.

Margaret Rose swivelled round on the piano stool, inspected the stranger from head to toe with unabashed curiosity. Most adults shifted and fidgeted under such

44

fierce scrutiny. The young man stared her out. It was Margaret Rose's eyes that dropped first; she flicked at the sheet music which was spread across her knees.

'Don't move a minute,' the young man said. 'I'm trying to think who it is you remind me of.' He put his head on one side and surveyed her. 'Who is it now?' he said.

Topsy, the child thought savagely, Little Black Sambo, a Hottentot.

'I know,' he said suddenly. 'Betty Grable!'

Margaret Rose giggled. And well she might. He's mad, the child told herself. Margaret Rose in no way resembled Betty Grable. Betty Grable was *blonde*.

'Definitely,' he said. 'The spitting image.'

Her mother came back with the tea. 'I don't know if you'd prefer a drink?' she said worriedly.

'This is fine,' he said, helping himself to three spoons of sugar and two custard creams. 'Just the ticket.' He looked round the room approvingly, looked at Margaret Rose who was dimpling away like fury, looked briefly at her mother. The child stared at her feet because she knew his gaze must soon come to rest upon her.

It did. 'I believe you're a rich lady now,' he said. Margaret Rose's ears pricked up at that. For answer the child shifted her feet on the carpet. The money had been deposited in the Burnley Building Society. She had a pass-book with her name on the front of it, but she was forbidden to touch it; it was appreciating for her as she got older.

'Is it just the day you're here for, Mr . . .?' her mother asked. She always got the order of her words mixed up when she was nervous. Her tea cooled, untasted.

'Charlie,' he said. 'Like I told you. "Mister" makes me feel a hundred and two. No, I'm staying here for a bit. Treating myself. Sold all the bits and bats, brass gongs and firing-pieces and whatnot, and told myself, Charlie, you need a holiday. Buck you up a bit. In view of the circs.'

He snapped a custard cream between his teeth. His teeth were white and square and strong, but his face was very pale. It looked like hers did after the pneumonia, or when she'd had the shadow on her lung: pale, the skin almost transparent and stretched taut across the bone. You could tell that he was greatly in need of a big dose of ozone.

'I'm staying at the Marlborough,' he said. 'Just dropped in to dump my gear and came on over here. Anyone know anything about it?'

No one did. It was a private hotel – or a guest house, depending upon how posh you wanted to be – situated in a seemingly endless row of almost identical private hotels or guest houses. Sometimes, at night, you looked through the windows into the lighted front rooms and saw almost identical groups of holidaymakers eating their tray suppers.

'Oh well,' he said, rubbing the crumbs off his hands with a very clean handkerchief. 'It will suffice, as they say. Better a cottage where love is, etcetera and so on. Or something.'

She was trying to place his accent, to fit him into some sort of category, but it was difficult. His voice made such rapid swoops between different kinds of accents: mock Cockney, RAF officer class, mock Scouse, BBC posh, and ordinary flat Lancashire. His appearance afforded no clues either: his hair was short and neat, his shoes polished, his suit so dark and self-effacing that you couldn't tell whether it was Savile Row or the fifty-bob tailor's.

Her mother was more direct. 'Where is it you come from?' She couldn't yet bring herself to call him Charlie.

46

'Stationed last down in the Smoke,' he said.

Her mother looked blank. 'London,' he explained.

'Are you in the army?'

'No. Just a figure of speech. I mean to say that was Charlie's last fixed abode, place of business. I move around quite a bit. I sell things.'

'What sort of things?' her mother said eagerly. Salesmen were always useful to know; they could get you a bit knocked off.

'Vacuum cleaners,' he said, shifting in the armchair.

'*Do* you?' her mother said, all animation. 'How coincidental. I'm looking out for a new vacuum.' She suddenly looked wary. 'You don't, by any chance, work for the same company as Mr Spencer, Margaret Rose's father, do you?'

'What's that, Sunflower?' he asked.

'The Northwest Carpet Cleaning Company,' Margaret Rose chanted, drumming her fingers on the closed lid of the piano. The conversation was becoming boring. She tried to think of ways of steering him back to the subject of her resemblance to Betty Grable.

'No,' he said. 'Not that one. They're our greatest rivals.'

'You must meet Mr Spencer,' her mother said. 'I expect you'd have a lot to talk about. Though Mr Spencer has only been with his firm for a short while.'

And before that stood in a queue at the Labour Exchange to collect his dole. He had been seen.

'Yes. Well. Maybe,' Charlie said. 'Actually, I could be moving out of vacuum cleaners. Not much scope, you see. I need scope.' He stretched his legs out in front of him as if to emphasize this need. 'One good thing,' he said, 'with the old man's few bob, it gives me a chance to take my time, look around. How's the job situation here?'

'Well,' her mother said, trying to look as if she was *au fait* with the economics of local employment. 'Well. I suppose it all depends on what you can do.'

47

'Mostly anything,' Charlie said. 'Versatile, very versatile, that's me. You've got to be, in this world. Like my old lady used to say: "Keep one jump ahead, Charlie; don't dig yourself a rut or else you'll feel feet on your face before you know it."'

He smiled widely, as though remembering some private joke. He had one of the nicest smiles that she'd ever seen: his lips opening to just the right width, his teeth well-shaped and all fitting correctly into the space thus created. In no way did he resemble the Major his father. It was impossible to imagine that the Major might have been a good-looking man in his youth; he seemed to have been old for such a very long time.

He put his tea-cup on the sideboard. 'Better be making tracks,' he said. 'Leave you good people to your domestic whatsit. Just wanted to pay my respects.'

Margaret Rose, who had been musing visibly on ways to retain his company, said: 'You could see my new bike if you want.'

He looked at his watch. 'Where is it?'

'It's at home. In the shed.'

'Perhaps some other time, Sunflower. Charlie has a lot to do just now. Give us a bit of time to get settled in, eh?'

This tactic was known as Humouring Margaret Rose. Funny how stupid childish people like Margaret Rose had to be humoured. Nobody ever came straight out with it and said no. Except Aunt Dolly.

Her mother was folding a lace paper doily into small and smaller sections. 'Perhaps you would care to come round for supper?' she said. 'You could meet Jack then.' Like Margaret Rose's mental processes, her mother's were very close to the surface. It was obvious that running through her mind were the thoughts: Is it presumptuous? Can I prevail upon Muriel to make one of her steak and kidney pies and warm it up in the oven? Really, it's tea, but I can't call it that, and dinner sounds too grand – but supper sounds late. If I'd paused for thought I could just have said 'a meal'.

She stood, shredding the edge of the doily, expecting some polite excuse. She was taken aback when Charlie said promptly, 'Much obliged. What time would you like me to report?'

There were little twinges of mingled excitement and dread in the pit of the child's stomach. Her parents entertained rarely, basically because her mother knew so few people whom she considered to be worth entertaining. Every so often her father's relatives from Halifax or Huddersfield or Doncaster would descend and then her mother would provide tea and shop cakes with a faint pained expression on her face because most of the relatives were a bit common. Her second cousins were rowdy and unselfconscious, real children. She never knew what to say to them and was further cut off by the language barrier: they spoke broad and almost incomprehensible Yorkshire; she spoke Burlington Court Lancashire. Their parents stared at her and said, 'Isn't she quiet! Isn't she oldfashioned! Isn't she a bookworm! I wish our Billy/Carol/Susan was like that,' wishing nothing of the sort.

Chapter Six

'WHAT MOB WERE you in then, Charlie?' asked her father.

And Charlie, as expected, told them that he had been in the RAF. 'The Raff'. Bomber Command. Raining presents down over Cologne and Dresden, leaflets first and then high explosive. 'The Pathfinder, they called me. Used to set fire to every haystack from here to there. Till my ears went. Then it was North Africa.'

Her father listened, entranced: Cairo, Mersa Matruh, the Sinai, fellahin and bints and Kwoyyes ketir, and one foot in the Nile, and it was – and so we say farewell to this land of sunshine and showers, pellagra and bilharzia and Ethiopian clap – (speak it low for fear of the child hearing; the child in the corner, labouring over her definitive study of The Horse). Her mother had gone to make the coffee; she knew that coffee was much more refined than tea.

'Came through it without a scratch,' Charlie said. 'Only me and one or two more out of the original lot. Went on an OCTU whatsit, only the trigonometry stumped me. Couldn't get the hang of the trig.'

Her father leaned across the table, drinking it in. Oh so very different from the Stores in Dorset, where the only particle of excitement had been when they were sent to defend the coast with broom-handles and guns minus ammo.

'You must have found it a bit different, back in Civvy Street.'

Her father offered Charlie a Senior Service, but Charlie preferred his own: Du Maurier out of a scarlet box. Pansy fags for such a dashing young fellow. The sort you could imagine having been decorated, but was too modest to tell you so. You saw them everywhere, the bright brave young men who'd come to nothing in the real world. He, Jack, had donned his demob suit with relief; in the Stores they had called him Mutt and Jeff, Cloth-Ears, had spoken to him through the trumpet shapes of their hands.

Her mother poured coffee into little china cups. She'd had to wash those cups that afternoon; they'd lain so long unused on the top shelf of the china cabinet that they were filmed with dust.

'Charlie,' she said, 'is looking for a change of occupation. Something with scope.'

'Ever done anything in the engineering line?' her father said.

'Not a lot. Selling's my field.'

And you could imagine him, swinging a case of samples, producing that smile for the benefit of lady shopkeepers, using his hands a lot to emphasize the quality of his wares.

'I'll put out some feelers,' her father said, leaning back in his chair, draining his coffee cup at one go. Her mother's upper lip was curled. Put out some feelers! You'd have thought he was Chairman of the Council, President of the Chamber of Trade, instead of a menial at an engineering factory who'd been passed over twice for promotion.

'Shouldn't think you'd have much difficulty,' her father said. 'You're very – personable.' He was proud

51

of the word; he repeated it in his head. The exact word. He was a nice fellow. The poor bugger couldn't help being a by-blow. Anyway, he wasn't a real illegitimate. The major had, after all, registered his paternity. Not the same as having one side of the birth certificate blank.

'How's your hotel?' her mother said. And her father said, 'How's your digs?' at exactly the same moment.

'Been in a lot worse barracks.' Charlie leaned over towards her mother, his cigarette at an angle in his mouth, Humphrey Bogart style. 'Couple next door to me. This afternoon. Battling. Going at it hammer and tongs. One of them threw something. Something heavy. It hit my wall. Damn near came through it. I was out of there fast, like a mole on a motorbike. Saw them afterwards. You'd have thought butter wouldn't melt. They were paying the bill. Old Mother Riley had given 'em the heave-ho. He was a right little runt and she was one of these touch-me-not-me-name's-temptation numbers. Couldn't they go it, though. Phew!' He removed his cigarette at the critical moment before it burned his lip.

'You get all sorts in private hotels,' her mother said. She had nearly said, 'guest houses,' but corrected herself in time. 'I had a friend who used to help out in one during the season. The things that went on! And always the people you'd least expect. All human life is there, my friend used to say.'

'My friend' was Carrie Mortimer who had told her mother that a certain guest who was three sheets to the wind had been excused in a dressing-table drawer.

'There were two old dears moving in as I came out,' Charlie said. 'I only hope *they* don't start flinging their false teeth around in the middle of the night.'

'Let's go into the sitting-room,' her mother said. 'Bring your drawing, Veronica. She's very talented, you know,' she said to Charlie. 'I don't know where she gets it from. I couldn't draw a straight line when I was at school.'

The child gathered up her drawing materials. Her mother was behaving in a silly fashion: talking to her in that put-on, distant voice like Aunt Dolly in the shop, saying she couldn't draw as though it was something to be proud of.

'You *can* draw, can't you, Princess?' Charlie lifted the picture from her lap, held it at arm's length, assessing its merits, genuine surprise in his voice, as though he was used to doting mothers over-estimating their children's capabilities, as though he'd expected her mother's judgement to be about as accurate as his comparison of Margaret Rose with Betty Grable.

'That what you're going to be?' he asked. 'An artist? In a garret?'

She took her drawing back from him, made a few alterations to it, was still not entirely satisfied. She always got ten out of ten at school, where neatness combined with sufficient verisimilitude was the sole criterion. 'I'm not going to be anything in a garret,' she said. Not a garret. Nor a cellar. Nor a semi-detached villa.

'I haven't decided what I shall be yet,' she said, her head bent, her index finger grey with graphite. The end of her pencil was chewed. 'If you chew your pencils like that,' her mother said, 'you won't need to decide. You'll be dead of lead poisoning.'

'Still,' Charlie said, 'still, you've a bit of time yet, haven't you?' His face altered. He stared straight through the artistic display of gypsophila that her mother had created in the willow pattern jug and bit the skin at the edge of his thumbnail. 'I never wanted to be anything,' he said. 'Not that I can remember. I was a lazy little devil. Too much playing hookey was my downfall. The School Board man round to my old lady saying if Charlie didn't behave himself he'd be away with the bad lads.'

'That's what happened to Ronnie Spencer,' she said.

'Who's Ronnie Spencer?'

'Margaret Rose's half-brother.'

'Tough luck on Ronnie Spencer,' Charlie said. Her mother was making adult faces at him as much as to say: 'The child has it all wrong. There's more to it than that.'

Her father poured bottled beer into glasses. 'Will you have a cigar, Charlie?' he said, opening the box that he'd won in a raffle at the British Legion's Christmas Dinner.

'Never use them, thanks,' Charlie said. 'Not one of my expensive tastes. Got all the others though.'

Her mother smiled at him. She had expensive tastes herself. She had been born for orchids and furs and limousines like the heroines in her library books, and ended up over a porcelain sink in a semi-detached with the coal bill behind the clock on the mantelpiece.

It was pleasant to meet a kindred soul, someone who didn't say: 'Count your blessings' or 'It could be worse' or 'God's good' or, most aggravating of all, like Dolly, 'You and your big ideas.' Getting plain modern furniture on the HP was Big Ideas. So was sending the child to a private school. And taking a taxi home from the Odeon in town after you'd seen Ava Gardner leading the kind of life that you knew should rightfully have been yours.

While her father talked to Charlie about politics – her father was a Labour man (being a Labour man meant hating the bosses, but being entirely unsympathetic towards the Commies who infiltrated the firm and were automatically made shop stewards); Charlie was a Non-committal man – the child studied their visitor. She felt the need to fix him, to pin him as they did the butterflies under glass in the Natural History Museum, but there were too many contradictions implicit in his appearance and his behaviour. She sensed that there was something about him that signified not belonging – to a street or a town or relatives or a particular job – that his face would have fitted equally well into the setting of a society ball – one of those depicted in the yellowed magazines in the dentist's waiting-room – or behind a barrow in the street market.

'I can hear your brain ticking,' he said. He brought his fist to his forehead in a parody of famous statuary. 'You'll wear it out. Little and often, that's the ticket.'

'It's her bedtime, anyway,' her mother said. 'Come on now, Veronica.'

She was being Veronica'd to death tonight. Normally her mother used her name only when she was calling her downstairs or talking about her to someone else.

'Good night,' she said with dignity. It was most galling to be treated as a child and sent to bed just when the evening was gaining momentum.

'Good night, Princess. Sleep tight.' He treated her to his smile. She was reluctant to leave. The room came into focus with him inside it; he animated the space around him, describing arcs with a restless foot, tapping his cigarette against the side of the ashtray that her father wasn't allowed to use because it was too pretty to be a receptacle for dirty cigarette ash. She couldn't even listen on the stairs, because voices from the front room were inaudible on the stairs. She propped her drawing on the mantelpiece and admired it, until the darkness blurred its outlines, until she heard the voices at the front door. It was very late. She heard her father's deep-toned laugh. She heard Charlie say, 'Cheerio then,' several times, and then the groan and

55

click of the door being closed. She heard him whistling 'Annie Laurie' as he went up the street. He was a very nifty whistler, interspersing the melody with imaginative trills. She pictured him executing a duet with a lamp post like Gene Kelly, leaping three feet into the air and bounding up the steps of the Marlborough two at a time, blowing a kiss to Old Mother Riley. She slept, dreamlessly.

> 'Bloodstains on the pillow,
> Bloodstains on the knife,
> Doctor Buck Ruxton
> You murdered your wife.'

This was the fifth rendering in less than twenty minutes. After each one Margaret Rose glanced sideways to see what effect it was having. Even on a blue, sunny, salty morning such as this the doggerel insinuated its awful message. Margaret Rose had obviously never had a dream in her life, otherwise she would not dare to stock her subconscious so recklessly with fearsome images. Perhaps she didn't have a subconscious.

They were passing the big house on the Promenade, the erstwhile home of another doctor of similar homicidal tendency. Doctor Carpenter had drowned *two* wives in the upstairs bathroom. Since when the house had been unoccupied except for the war years when the ATS had been billeted there. It was now the custom for rough local boys to enter by means of prising away the boarding across the windows, and ensconce themselves until darkness fell, when they would shriek and wail and frighten the living daylights out of unsuspecting passers-by.

Margaret Rose embarked upon her quatrain yet again. 'Shut up. Please,' the child said.

'Why? Are you scared?'

'No. It's just morbid.' Morbid excused a lot of cowardice.

'. . . you murdered your wife,' sang Margaret Rose defiantly, at full throttle. It was revenge for not having been present at supper the night before. 'They say somebody spent the night there,' she said, indicating the derelict house, 'and his hair turned quite white. Shall we buy some liquorice?'

'The ATS ladies,' the child said, 'their hair didn't turn white, did it?'

'Oh you know everything, don't you? Miss Know-all.'

The liquorice shop was situated in the Parade, a street which branched off the Promenade. Parallel to the Promenade, running behind it, was the boarding-house street, Charlie's street. She would find some pretext to walk along it, even though they had walked into town by way of the sea-wall and their feet ached and they were about to spend their bus fare home on liquorice.

Queues for café lunches stretched along the pavements. Wilting waitresses performed miracles of agility between crowded tables, bearing plates of cod and chips, shepherd's pie, prunes and custard, multi-coloured ice-cream. Those not queuing for lunch were queuing at the oyster stalls or the novelty shops, or bringing their pints of old and mild outside the public houses. The shop windows were crammed with striped beach balls, virulently coloured sticks of rock, vulgar postcards, inflatable toy animals, objects that no one in his right mind could possibly desire.

The liquorice root juice stained their mouths. When Charlie, who was issuing from Yates's Wine Lodge, bumped into them, the first comment he made was, 'Hello, you two – tombstone teeth.'

Another few seconds and they would have been on

the other side of the road, making for the boarding-house street. Her mother talked a lot about fate, but she made it seem a purely malignant force.

He put one hand on each of their heads and bent down to talk to them. He smelt, juicily, of some kind of winy drink.

'I thought you were at the Marlborough,' the child said, to demonstrate to Margaret Rose that she was conversant with his domestic arrangements.

'Not at lunch-time, Princess. Just been out for some medicine. Now I'm about to start foraging for some chuck. It looks like it'll be afternoon tea judging by these queues.'

'You should go into Market Lane,' Margaret Rose said, chewing ferociously. 'There's cafés there, but the trippers don't find 'em.'

She directed him, accurately. She always rose to the occasion in such situations; the child herself would have been unable to think of any alternative.

'I'll chance my luck there, then,' he said. 'Have you eaten yet? Would you care to join me?'

'Yes,' Margaret Rose said with alacrity; she was mad about cafés: the lace tablecloths, the carafes of water, the little flowers in silver containers, the waitresses who had to put up with your bad behaviour.

'We can't,' the child said. Regret squeezed her stomach. 'We have to be home for lunch.'

'And we have to walk because we've spent our bus fare,' Margaret Rose said.

Was there no end to her effrontery? The child turned away. 'Hold your horses,' Charlie said, jingling the change in his pockets. He handed them each a sixpence and told them not to spend it all at once.

The child was unable to speak. Margaret Rose's gratitude was effusive enough for both of them.

He disappeared into a throng of floral frocks: young

girls, arms linked, who turned to watch his progress and, egged on by one another, called, 'Hello, gorge-ous.' He made a sudden pouncing movement, and they scattered, shrieking. Terribly common behaviour, her mother would have called it; she'd have thought so herself, if he hadn't been involved in it.

'We can get the bus now.' Margaret Rose admired her sixpence. 'You *are* gormless, aren't you? You're the one who's supposed to know him. If it was up to you, we'd be walking back.'

'It's very rude to ask people for money. It's worse than rude.'

'Why? If he knew we had no bus fare he'd have given it us. And how could he have known if we didn't tell him?'

There was a kind of behaviour, the child realized, that had nothing to do with Burlington Court or Sunday School or any pre-conceived code. It was instinctive – to people like Margaret Rose. The rules didn't concern those sort of people. In any situation, they acted to gain advantage. And they were always successful! Margaret Rose couldn't do her lessons, so she copied the answers. If the conductor hadn't reached her seat by the time the bus reached her stop, she'd alight without paying her fare. She had stolen chewing-gum and a Dinky toy so blatantly and con-fidently, certain that she wouldn't be apprehended. And she wasn't. Stealing was wrong. Cheating was wrong. But what prevented the child from indulging in these activities was not the knowledge that they were wrong, but the fear of being found out, the fear of people thinking badly of her.

'You saw Charlie?' her mother said. They were eating liver and mashed potato. The child detested liver, despite the fact that she knew it was bursting with goodness and would make her grow, upwards and outwards. The taste of the liquorice lingered in her mouth. She cut up the liver into smaller and smaller pieces in the hope that its size would seem to diminish.

'You saw Charlie,' her mother said again. She was in the habit of repeating herself because of her father's bad hearing.

'He gave us sixpence. Two sixpences. Margaret Rose and me.'

'That was nice of him.' Her mother noticed her plate. 'Finish your liver.' Though she hadn't finished *hers*. She got up from the table, opened the cabinet door, rooted at the back of the cupboard, brought out an oblong tin cash box. Any spare housekeeping money was saved in this cash box towards the splendid summer holiday they were all going to have one day. Usually they spent a few days in Halifax or Huddersfield or Doncaster. One year they'd had runabout tickets on the railway; she remembered the Great Orme at Llandudno, Wordsworth's Cottage at Grasmere and the disappointingly unatmospheric parsonage where Charlotte Brontë had written *Jane Eyre*.

There were nine pound notes and some silver in the box. Her mother stood looking at them for a long time. She chewed the skin on the inside of her mouth; she gave herself ulcers that way. At last she said, 'You could do with a new frock. You've outgrown everything you've got.'

This was not true, but the idea seemed to stiffen her mother's resolve. She crammed eight of the pound notes and the silver into her purse.

The ostensible purpose of the expedition was to buy the child a new dress. This process was usually an ordeal; the child shrank, in silk, in net, in organdie, under the patronizing or too-friendly gaze of salesladies who usually said, 'She does look bonny in that one. It fills her out a bit.' They lied. Bonny was Margaret Rose.

Today, things were different. In Bennington's the assistant brought out a plain frock, its only adornment a band of smocking across the yoke. Its colour was a deep muted pink, the shade of wilting Dorothy Perkins roses. It was not a child's colour and it suited her; it was quite perfect. Her mother said, 'That's fine,' and got out her purse. Her mind was not on the matter in hand. The child had the feeling that however unbecoming the dress, her mother would have said, 'That's fine,' and got out her purse.

She made for the exit, but her mother said, 'Don't be in so much of a hurry. I want to have a look upstairs.' Upstairs was Ladies' Gowns. And looking became trying on. And where her mother had been so easily satisfied in the Children's, she was super-critical one floor up. The saleslady here gave you the impression that she was not accustomed to serving anyone of an inferior rank to a duchess; and her mother was usually nervous of snooty shop-assistants. Today, however, she gave as good as she got. The child sat on a gilt chair, her feet dangling, and yawned as her mother paraded in front of a mirror in flowered print and ruched satin and tailored linen. In an adjacent cubicle a woman was trying on petticoats. She had an enormous bottom, and her thighs bulged over the tops of her stockings. Did growing up *have* to include the encroachment of obscene fat? She could imagine *that* woman bouncing.

'I'm glad you're suited, madam,' the saleslady said with a big wide false smile. Her mother swung the carrier that contained the floral print.

Next door to Bennington's was a Freeman, Hardy and Willis. In the window there was a pair of sandals the same colour as the frock. Her mother paused a minute and then went in and bought them. In Boots she bought her usual packet of whatever-they-were she usually bought and then went over to the cosmetic counter where she added a Creme Puff, a little bottle of Evening in Paris and a lipstick called Sugar Plum to her purchases. 'I need some stockings,' she said.

'Why don't you go to Woodham's?' the child said. 'Aunt Dolly will let you have them cost.'

'It's too far,' her mother said, and then proceeded to walk much further in the opposite direction to Pearson's where, Aunt Dolly said, the shopgirls were dopey and didn't know a collar-stud from an elastic stocking.

'I'm exhausted,' her mother said, wiping a hand across her forehead. Her cheeks were pink, and the powder had caked in the creases around her eyes. 'Let's have an ice.'

They sat in an ice-cream parlour, their shopping on the floor beside them, eating banana splits. The child gazed at the revolving orange crush dispenser, trying to figure out what had come over her mother. Spending like a man with no arms, as her father would say, spending lustfully – the eight pounds odd must have melted ages ago, dipping into the housekeeping, avoiding Woodham's because Aunt Dolly would say, 'What's all this in aid of?' eating banana splits when you never knew whether or not those dirty ice-cream servers ever washed their hands. It was disconcerting: to see her cautious mother throwing caution to the winds. Just when you thought you'd got people weighed up, the child pondered, they upped and did something completely out of character. But not her mother. Never before.

Chapter Seven

'HE'S GETTING TO be a fixture, that young man,' Aunt Dolly said.

There had been a couple of evenings at the cinema, a night or two at the British Legion, a hot-pot supper and social at the Assembly Rooms: the three of them. Being neighbourly, her mother called it – she who had never before felt the need.

'Tongues will start to wag,' Aunt Dolly said. And her mother had gone quite red and replied, 'Keep your evil thoughts to yourself.'

What the child couldn't understand was why her mother ran Charlie down to her father, and yet defended him to anybody else.

Margaret Rose hung about the house continually. Anyone who was so free with sixpences was worth cultivating. She was absent though, having her teeth filled, the day he said, 'When are you going to take me on the town?'

She looked over the top of *The Talisman*, suspiciously. Adults were always making fatuous half-promises, issuing spurious invitations; one grew accustomed to it. However he didn't have the silly teasing expression on his face that usually accompanied such offers.

'The local amenities,' he said. 'You know, big

dippers and candy-floss and sand up your jumper, that sort of thing.'

He sat quite close to her, but made no attempt to touch her. She thought of Mr Spencer and his bottom-patting and bow-tweaking, the Major's arm-squeezings and papery kisses.

'It's very expensive,' she said. She had eight and threepence-halfpenny in a blue cardboard egg with a slit in the top, but that was supposed to be for the League of Pity.

He smiled. 'I think I can run to it,' he said. 'What about tomorrow? As long as your mother has no objections.'

Her mother nodded happy acquiescence. Anyone else making such an application would have been subjected to an in-depth character assessment.

'Bring your pal,' Charlie said. 'That forward little piece, Whatsername.'

'Her name's Margaret Rose.' And I hope she dies before tomorrow.

But her constitution was excellent. She wore red shorts and a gingham blouse and carried a red plastic purse containing five separate shillings. There was a way of opening the Spencers' electricity meter so that they could reclaim the shillings with which they'd fed it; there was panic at the end of every quarter when the electric man came to collect.

This purse was displayed prominently, but never opened. It was Charlie's treat. He made that plain when they arrived to meet him at the Marlborough. The landlady had ushered them into the glass verandah which was tacked on to the front of the hotel. Her name was Mrs Grainger and she suffered from asthma. Charlie said she had a face like a distressed bulldog. They sat on two white-slatted garden chairs which left red ridges on the backs of their thighs. Little kids carrying buckets and spades wandered in and out, emptied sand from their sandals, stared, inspected their legs for imaginary jelly-fish stings. She and Margaret Rose ignored them as one always ignored holiday children who had no business to be littering the sands and crowding the funfair and rending the balmy summer air with their ill-bred racket.

Charlie wore an open-necked shirt and a pair of white flannels. He looked as though he was about to open the bowling. She was a bit ashamed for him at first, until she realized that such clothes were eminently suitable for the day's activities. By now his hands and face had acquired a faint tan, but the skin that showed in the V of his shirt was still pallid. Something that he was intent on remedying. 'Have you brought your costumes?' he said. He had. In a towel that had Marlborough embroidered across its hem.

'Under my knickers.' Margaret Rose demonstrated.

'What about you, Princess?'

'I can't swim.'

Usually she pretended that she could, but today, when she would obviously be called upon to perform, it was impossible.

'We'll have to do something about that.' He hailed Mrs Grainger and they confabulated earnestly and then she wobbled upstairs and reappeared with two more Marlborough towels and a small woollen bathing costume.

'Left by one of our guests,' she explained, 'and never claimed. It *has* been laundered. Needless to say,' she said, 'I expect these articles to be returned in the same condition.' She looked closely at the child as though searching for grime, nits, other evidence of personal negligence.

'You're a marvel, Myra,' Charlie said. 'I'll guard them with my life.'

She hid behind a sand dune to put on the costume. It was baggy and shapeless, and she had a horrid premonition that when it got wet it would sag irretrievably at the front.

Margaret Rose had wanted the bathing lake, but he said, 'The crummy bathing lake when we've got the sea at our feet! Tide's in. It's easier to swim in the sea, Princess,' he said, when she emerged on trembling legs from behind the sand dune.

'Anybody can *swim*,' Margaret Rose said scornfully, wading out to the point where the sand shelved suddenly. Someone had thrown her into a pool when she was small, and she had swum; it was as simple as that. 'And why do you call her Princess? That should be me. With my name.'

'She looks like a princess,' he said, lifting her on to his shoulders. There was black hair and a scattering of moles on his pale, broad back.

'What do I look like?' Margaret Rose leaned her sly face sideways out of the waves.

'I told you. Betty Grable,' he shouted, treading water.

That pleased her. She moved through the surface of the water executing a faultlessly clean breast-stroke. Betty Grable was better than a princess. More glamorous.

'Hold on tight,' he said, lowering himself into the sea. He swam slowly but powerfully. She felt like the boy on the back of the dolphin. 'Just to get you used to the water,' he said. And she had to admit that the sea, moving and grey-coloured, was far less daunting than the glassy green surface of the bathing lake, where limbs beneath the water were magnified into great pale monstrosities of flesh, where every sound bounced back ten-fold from the tiled sides, where golden-haired boys in scarlet trunks could lead you to your doom.

His black hair was sleek. That on his chest and shoulders floated like seaweed. They retreated to the shallows. He stood up and shook himself. She slid down the bones of his spine.

'Try by yourself now,' he said. 'Don't be afraid. Look at her.' He indicated Margaret Rose, who was putting on a positive cabaret act of aquatic acrobatics for his benefit. 'If the sea can hold her up, it can certainly do the same for you.'

He demonstrated breathing tactics to her. He made her run into the waves to overcome that awful shuddering gradual feeling. He supported her, under her stomach, her chin, had her floating on her back. She trusted him implicitly, knew that his hand would always be there, and, unlike Mr Spencer's, there for just as long as it was needed. She put her head under the water and opened her eyes; down there was not dirty and gritty as one would suppose, but fawn and clean with bone-white fragments of shell embedded in its surface. 'You're playing a blinder,' he said. 'We'll have you in the Olympics yet, no danger.' And when, three-quarters of an hour later, she performed two strokes unaided, he fell about with admiration. 'Didn't I tell you?' he said. 'Trust Charlie. And, on that note of triumph, I think we'd better call it a day.' He cupped his hands and called through them, 'Hey, you, Esther Williams, get yourself back on shore, will you?'

Margaret Rose came in with the waves, swimming like a porpoise. She made her exit from the water by way of a somersault. 'You don't need teaching much, do you?' he said, looking at her hard, his hands on his hips.

'I can swim like a fish,' she said truthfully. She shone at all activities which required physical coordination. 'Come on, dozy,' she said, 'and get changed. Or you'll be po-o-orly.'

She hopped across the beach, demolishing some little kid's sandcastle *en route*. The little kid opened his

67

mouth to protest and then closed it again when he saw the fierce expression on her face, and started digging, resignedly, in a fresh spot.

Charlie had retired to the concrete Gents to change out of his wet trunks. They watched him padding through the spiky dune grass, circumnavigating the huge cylindrical stones that had been placed on the shore during the war to deter the Germans from doing something or other. They were positioned at six foot intervals. Margaret Rose could jump the spaces between, and proceeded to do so. She hadn't dried herself properly; there was a damp patch on her bottom for all the world to see. The child noticed, with satisfaction, that immersion in sea-water had frizzed her permanent wave.

Parents sat propped against the sea-wall watching their offspring, admiring Margaret Rose's agility, eating tuna-fish sandwiches. In the distance donkeys plodded along, back and forth, carrying their burdens: embryonic horsemen, and wailing cowards, who had to be held on by the donkey man. Lifeguards warned off reckless wanderers from the quicksand area around the pier. Scenes so familiar that she had ceased to see them. She looked afresh, as if through a newcomer's eyes, Charlie's eyes. It was beautiful, she supposed, in the manner of landscapes that one was supposed to admire: lush valleys, mountain ranges, patchwork fields. It left her unmoved. The odd, the strange, the squalid, attracted her: the mysterious, forgotten alley-ways that lay behind main thoroughfares, the row of abandoned pale-washed villas beside the headland where moonlight bleached their silhouettes, Doctor Carpenter's house, windowless, blind.

'You're always thinking, aren't you?' He had reappeared from behind a sandhill, drying his hair on the Marlborough towel. 'You should be like your little pal. I'll bet she doesn't strain her brain.'

'I was thinking,' she said, 'Of how, if you come back here in a hundred year's time, the scenery'll probably be the same, but all the people'll be different, but the same too, in a way. Just as if people didn't matter. Even the donkeys.'

He lit a cigarette. The match burned nearly down to his fingers before he tossed it away. 'That's life,' he said. 'The show must go on.'

'It's sad.' She dug her toe into the sand, deeper and deeper, to where it was moist and brown and the little crabs lived.

He looked at her sideways. 'You're deep, aren't you? You shouldn't look so hard for the sadnesses. Stop on the surface, Princess; it's safer there. Anyway,' he said, 'there's one way, isn't there, you won't vanish? You keep drawing those pictures and they'll hang up in museums for ever and people won't be able to forget.'

'They might decay. Or the lines would fade. Or people wouldn't like them. Eventually.' It came upon her that nothing remained, not even Grandma's weeping cherubim, nothing except the earth and the sky and the sea. Did other people possess this knowledge and manage to live with it? She felt alone and terrified. The sea lapped mockingly, secure in its immortality. People were more important than the sea. Surely? If only she could really believe Miss Tibbs.

'You know what I think?' Charlie said. 'I think, all things considered, it's pretty fantastic that we're standing here together now. What about that? It'll always have happened. No matter what.'

'I thought,' said Margaret Rose frigidly, 'I *thought* you were taking us for lunch.'

Chapter Eight

THE POSHEST PLACE, with a grandiose lack of advertisement, called itself simply, 'The Tea Rooms'; there was thick carpet on the floor and wood panelling on the walls and bulls'-eye glass in the bow windows, and you didn't just sit yourself down at any old vacant table, you waited for a waitress who wore a hat that reminded you of Florence Nightingale at Scutari to usher you to your appointed seat.

There were a lot of French words scattered about the menu. 'Crème Marie-Louise,' Margaret Rose read out in an accent that made your toes curl. 'What's that?'

'It's bean soup,' Charlie said, 'bean soup. *Been soup.*'

It took a while for the penny to drop, but when it did Margaret Rose showed them up dreadfully, spluttering and giggling and having to be revived with sips of water.

The waitress who served them was young and trim and rather pretty, and doodled on the edge of her pad while she waited for them to order. '*Sole bonne femme,*' the child said. It was the one dish she could be sure of not mispronouncing. 'Egg and beans and chips,' Margaret Rose said, discounting the menu entirely. 'And peaches and cream.'

'We *might* be able to do an egg with French fried,' the waitress said. 'I'd have to ask.'

'That's right, sweetheart, you go and ask,' Charlie said, not a bit put out by Margaret Rose's uncouth behaviour. He removed an artificial anemone from a vase and handed it to her. 'Here you are, Betty Grable,'
he said. And changed her name to Dorothy Lamour when she stuck it in her hair.

The child gazed at her table-napkin, her face crimson. The lunch part of the day was what she had most looked forward to. Being associated with such inelegant goings-on was spoiling it for her, minute by minute.

They were just starting into their Been soup when Margaret Rose looked round, said, 'Oh no,' and made a noise like vomiting. They followed her gaze. On the other side of the window, flattened against the glass, was an unmistakable set of features. Margaret Rose shook her fist. Her answer was the distorted image of a tongue being stuck out so far that it almost severed itself from its roots.

'Friend of yours?' Charlie asked.

Margaret Rose drank soup, silently, disdainfully.

'It's her half-brother,' the child explained. The Face at the Window that showed no sign of removing itself.

'The famous Ronnie?'

The child nodded. If they'd had any sense they'd have known that he'd show up sooner or later.

'I never thought,' Charlie said. 'I suppose I should have invited him along.' And, to their immense chagrin, he wiped his mouth with his napkin, got to his feet, went outside and reappeared with Ronnie in his wake.

The waitress was summoned, another spindle-backed chair was pulled up to the table, another place set. The child put down her spoon, all appetite gone. People were staring. And no wonder. Ronnie was very, very dirty. Not surprising, when she reflected that he'd worn the same clothes since arriving at the Spencers. His black pumps had a hole in the toe where the canvas had parted from rubber, the hem of his sleeveless woollen slipover was frayed and ravelled to a depth of three inches, the front of his shirt bore the traces of previous meals.

'What are you going to have, Ronnie?' Charlie handed him the menu. He looked a bit taken aback, as though he'd just noticed how very unprepossessing Ronnie was at close quarters.

'He can't read,' Margaret Rose said, her eyes on the ceiling. She had removed the anemone from her hair and was demolishing it savagely.

'Oh,' Charlie said. 'Never mind, Colonel, we all have that difficulty at some time or another. How does soup followed by egg and chips sound?'

Ronnie nodded, sat on his hands. If only he could eat like that, the child thought, then we would be spared the sight of the sores and the dirt.

'At home,' Margaret Rose said, 'he eats in the kitchen.'

'Is that so?' Charlie said. The waitress leaned around Ronnie very gingerly and placed the soup in front of him. Ronnie disengaged a hand and picked up his dessert spoon. 'Hold hard, old man, let's get your eating-irons organized,' Charlie said, handing him the soup spoon. 'Do you know, in the North African Desert, I ate everything with a spoon? Wasn't worth the bother of a knife and fork, you see. They used to bang everything into the same tin: first course, second course. Mince and spuds and rice pudding. Ate 'em all together. Ruined me taste-buds, did that war.'

Ronnie stared, open-mouthed. Charlie guided his hand to the soup, just as you would guide the hand of a baby.

'How revolting,' the child said and then blushed in case they should think she was referring to Ronnie.

'Oh, it was revolting,' Charlie said. 'So were we – almost. If I hadn't got to Hitler when I did, there'd have very likely been a riot.'

Margaret Rose was kicking Ronnie under the table; you could tell by the way his soup-hand kept jerking. 'What were you doing following us?' she said. 'You've been told not to do it.'

'Don't get so het up,' Charlie said. 'It's a free country. Maybe he's so overcome with your charms that he can't help himself. Isn't that right, Colonel?'

She had not thought Ronnie capable of blushing, but blush he did, from neck to forehead. She had not thought that his suffused countenance could look any uglier, but it did.

Margaret Rose had pulled her chair to the furthest corner of the table, so that she was obliged to eat her meal at an angle. The child followed suit, but less drastically. Outriders to the central couple, they watched and listened as Ronnie bolted his chips and Charlie rattled on about the North African Desert and how he'd gazed upwards at the sky of the southern hemisphere and dreamed of toasted cheese. Just like Ben Gunn.

Ronnie cleared his plate – and the remains of the child's food, too, which Charlie transferred, saying, 'You don't mind, do you, Princess? Looks like we've got a bottomless pit here.'

It was behaviour more suitable for the cafeterias and snack bars which lined the sea front; the Florence Nightingale woman looked outraged, their own waitress couldn't suppress a snigger. 'I expect you usually get a better class of person in here,' Charlie said to her. 'Not a crowd of scruffs like us.' She fiddled with her note pad which was chained to her waist, at a loss for a reply. She didn't look straight at him, but darted little glances from under her eyelids. After he'd paid the bill he stood talking to her for what seemed an eternity while the child and Margaret Rose contemplated the pattern on the carpet and Ronnie searched with his tongue for morsels of food that had adhered to the side of his mouth.

'Is everybody replete?' He rejoined them, rubbing his hands together, a satisfied look on his face. Nobody except the child understood the meaning of the word replete. 'An elegant sufficiency?' For answer, Ronnie made no attempt to smother a belch. All through the afternoon he was subject to flatulence. At Burlington Court that was the worst crime you could commit. That, and not pulling the chain after use.

The fairground music, the racket of whirling mechanisms, the shuddering collision of the dodgem cars, affected her like a punch in the stomach. She trailed behind them, slightly breathless, tiny hairs bristling on her bare arms and legs. The second cousins from Huddersfield and Doncaster were avid for the crash and the roar and the odour of jostling humanity in the funfair. She was obliged to accompany them and, because she was ashamed of betraying her fear, she rode with them on the ferris wheel and the flying boats. Afterwards, her mouth rigid with the effort of not screaming, she'd run behind the amusement arcades and vomit until her throat ached.

Margaret Rose made straight for the Big Dipper. You could see the passengers on its current run, tiny figures way above the ground, their mouths open in soundless shrieks as the carriages teetered on the brink of a vertical descent. Even the second cousins baulked at the Big Dipper. Once, a youth had stood up on the topmost gradient and lost his balance and the carriage had rolled down to the ground with his left arm wedged in its front bumper. The rest of him was quickly covered with a macintosh.

'*Come* on,' Margaret Rose shouted, pushing at the turnstile – the point of no return – which led to the realization of one of your worst nightmares, that most dreaded of situations: to be caught up in some terrifying activity and to know that you could not change your mind, go back, to know that what lay ahead would last for several lifetimes.

She lifted one lead-heavy foot from the ground. Terror beckoned her forward, insidiously. Her mouth would not form the word 'no'; she dare not let him see what a coward she was. And then an ally appeared at her shoulder, unexpectedly – she would never have dreamed! 'I'm not going on *that*,' Ronnie said. A series of little farts issued from him; they sounded like rain on a corrugated iron roof.

Margaret Rose leapt down the steps, a miniature Fury. She came up close to him, closer than she normally did. 'Nobody's asking you,' she said. 'Nobody asked you to come. So just go home you great baby, pee-the-bed, and don't interfere with other people.' She looked at Charlie. 'He's soft. He wets himself. Are we getting on?'

'You wouldn't get me on that,' Charlie said, 'not for a gold clock as big as a banjo. Me and the Colonel here are going on the bobby-horses, aren't we? Nice and gentle. Come on, organ-bum. Do you like the bobby-horses?'

Ronnie nodded. 'And the helter-skelter. And the dodgems.'

Margaret Rose remained where she was, her face a thundercloud, debating whether or not to open her purse and ride defiantly alone. Alone, though, you rattled about in the carriage, tilted perilously from side to side minus the buffer of another body. The man probably wouldn't let her on by herself, anyway. She raced after them and flung herself on to a piebald horse

75

called Florabelle just as the roundabout was beginning to gain momentum.

The bobby-horses held no terrors. You gripped with your knees and felt the barley-sugar pole slipping up and down between your fingers, riding buoyantly to the sound of some of the Major's Strauss music. Coming round the corners of the helter-skelter on a rough hairy mat, between Charlie's knees, was a purely pleasurable experience too. Even sitting as passenger in a dodgem car with his arm tight around you was bearable; no one managed to hit Charlie: the wheel spun through his hands and, incredibly, seemingly inevitable collisions were avoided at the last second. Margaret Rose occupied a dodgem car solo and spent most of the time chasing Ronnie around the circuit and ramming him viciously.

As with the swimming, she realized, it was simply a matter of having someone that you could trust, who had confidence in you until you had enough confidence in yourself.

There were coaches parked ten deep in the car park. Their occupants emerged, clutching plastic macs and sandwiches and Box Brownies. They shrieked with mirth, made clumsy dancing steps, frisked like ponies let out into fields after winter confinement. They wore talleyman clothes: clean, shiny, shoddily made. They were determined to enjoy themselves at all costs. 'We'd better join hands,' Charlie said, 'or we might get separated.' They walked thus, four-abreast, forcing their way through the crowds to the perimeter of the funfair where the amusement arcades and the shooting galleries were situated. Charlie threw darts and tennis balls, fired guns, rolled pennies, all with a deadly accuracy. He said it was the fruits of a mis-spent youth, and called the stall-holders 'squire' or 'missis'. Ronnie shot down three moving ducks and was awarded a plaster Skye terrier with a tartan bow around his neck. He fondled it as though it was his most precious possession. It was perhaps his only possession; she had seen inside his hold-all when he came to the Spencers; it contained two pairs of pyjamas, two pairs of drawers, two vests, three shirts, a pair of short trousers, a pullover and a striped tie. Nothing else, not a book or a ball or a bag of marbles.

Charlie was laden with various sorts of shoddy merchandise: dolls and teddy bears and ashtrays and tin key rings and plastic jewellery. Margaret Rose claimed most of them. She had no taste whatever. They would go very well on the Spencers' sideboard next to the jugs that said Scarborough and so on, and the tankard that played a tune.

The Esplanade was ankle-deep in crisp bags and trodden ice-cream wafers. A huddle of old people out of the charabancs sat under a glass verandah. The women pulled their skirts up to their knees, crossed their hands over the handbags in their laps. The men chewed on their pipe stems and looked out across the sands to the distant tide-line. One of the charabancs had come from the Mental Defectives Home. The teachers, or warders, or whatever they were, demonstrated how you made sand-pies, how you built a castle, how you slid down a sand dune. They were enormously enthusiastic. They looked as daft, if not dafter, than their charges, who preferred to poke among the litter. Some of them had huge heads, some had deformed limbs. One little boy in leg irons weed unselfconsciously against a sandhill. 'Now Jimmy', the teacher said, 'we know we don't do that, don't we? We ask for the toilet.' Two small moon-faced fat girls giggled endlessly. One child of indeterminate sex, with slobber on its chin, raised its head to the skies and howled.

'That's the kind of school Ronnie goes to,' Margaret Rose said, making grotesque imitative faces at an infant imbecile.

Ronnie glowered. 'It isn't,' the child said.

'It is. It's the Silly School.'

'It *isn't*. Is it, Ronnie?'

Ronnie clenched his fists inside his pockets.

'The Silly School,' said Margaret Rose, 'where they can't read and write, where they pee the bed.'

'Bugger you,' Ronnie said. 'Bugger you.'

'Sticks and stones may break my bones but words will never hurt me. He's a bastard, my mum said so, and all bastards go to the Silly School.'

'So was William the Conqueror,' the child said. It was the only retort she could think of. But, as she was saying it, Charlie took hold of Margaret Rose's shoulders and shook her very hard. 'Less of that, young lady,' he said, 'or I'll wash your mouth out with soap. And if that's what your mum says, she ought to know better.'

Margaret Rose stood stock-still. All the breath had been knocked out of her. Her mouth was wide-open. No one had ever laid a finger on her before. 'Not one more word,' Charlie said, 'or I'll kick you up the pants. Understood? Now, let's go and grab some tea.'

Margaret Rose took over Ronnie's rôle, following them at a distance. In the snack bar she ate a biscuit and drank a strawberry milk-shake in silence. She looked daggers, at Ronnie, at Charlie, at the child because the child, as usual, was in adult favour. It'll only make it worse, the child thought, much worse. Margaret Rose will go home and tell her mother and her mother'll belt Ronnie and make him stop in the coal-shed. The long-term consequences of Charlie's short-term attempt at justice were best not thought about.

Charlie put his arms behind his head and flexed his shoulders.

'It's been a great day,' he said, blowing out plumes of smoke. 'I've never enjoyed meself so much with me clothes on.'

He hadn't had his clothes on. Not in the sea, at any rate. 'Will you finish teaching me to swim?' she asked anxiously.

'Nothing surer. Can't leave you floundering at two strokes, can we?' He tapped Ronnie on the shoulder. 'What about you, Colonel, can you swim?'

Ronnie shook his head. Margaret Rose opened her mouth and then closed it again.

'Well then, we'll have some coaching sessions. You and the Colonel. Living by the sea and neither of you can swim! I don't know.'

'Did you live by the sea?' she asked. 'When you were little? Is that how you learned to swim?'

'For a bit. Blackpool. But we moved round a lot, the old lady and me. One step ahead of the rent man. Oswaldtwistle, Budleigh Salterton, Chipping Sodbury.'

She laughed, sure that he was inventing the place names.

'*Will* you learn me to swim?' Ronnie said, through two striped straws and a mouthful of milk-shake. There was obviously a three-minute time-lag between hearing and comprehension.

'What's that, Colonel?'

'He says will you teach him to swim,' the child interpreted. Teach him to talk too, while you're at it.

'You present yourself at ten a.m. sharp on the beach by the Gents tomorrow morning and I'll teach you to swim.'

'I'll call for you,' the child was about to say, and then thought better of it. The milk of human kindness had begun to flow in his direction, but not to the extent that she could bear to be seen in his company without the insurance of another person.

79

'Got that? Ten o'clock?'

Ronnie nodded.

'*If* he's allowed,' Margaret Rose said to her milk-shake glass.

'Shall I come and square it with your mum?'

'She's not my mum,' Ronnie said indignantly and with surprising distinctness.

'His mum's in Manchester,' the child explained. 'Mrs Spencer's his step-mother.' Or something.

'Your step-mum, then. Make sure she knows you've not been pinched by the gypsies.'

The child supposed that if Mrs Spencer knew any gypsies she'd pay them to relieve her of Ronnie.

'Is she in now? Grab your tackle and we'll go and ask her permission.'

This was real excitement. It was St George and the Dragon, modern dress. All the way in the open-topped bus her insides were rising and falling more violently than they had done at the fairground.

Mrs Spencer opened the door to them. She had on the kimono that she wore for her 'rest and relaxation'; sometimes she wore it to do eurhythmics in the front room. Engaged thus, she looked an utter fool. But a sinister fool.

'This youngster,' Charlie said, 'wants to learn to swim. and I've offered to teach him. Is that all right by you?'

Thank heavens, at least, he hadn't called her missis.

'I don't know about that.' She gave him a long cool look from head to toe. 'It's very good of you to give Margaret Rose a day out, but I'm not sure that I can spare *him*. I'll have to ask Mr Spencer.'

Margaret Rose followed her mother into the house. The door was closed behind them.

'A lady with all the social graces,' Charlie said, leaning against the scalloped porch. Ronnie trod deliberately on a patch of marigolds. The child's ear was level with the letter-box. The letter-box was rusted and wouldn't shut properly. She could hear voices raised in altercation and then feet shuffling to the front door. The feet, in carpet slippers, belonged to Mr Spencer.

'Come in, come in,' he said, ushering them into the morbid sitting-room. The apocalyptic horsemen gazed down upon them vengefully. 'The wife,' he said to Charlie, 'you know . . . the ladies . . . sometimes . . . not at their best . . . their very best . . . difficult . . . must forgive . . . make allowances. What!'

Mr Spencer never looked properly dressed. Always he seemed to be minus one or two articles of clothing. Today it was his collar, his tie and his shoes. Shouldn't he have been out selling vacuum cleaners? Margaret Rose entered the room, picked up the musical tankard, wound it and lifted the lid. 'Drink! Drink!' it played, and through it and despite it Charlie said, 'Your lad wants to learn to swim. Do you have any objection?'

Mr Spencer folded the fingers of his left hand over his right thumb. His hands were never still: patting, tweaking, poking. '*Wonderful* idea,' he said. 'Great opportunity. Most kind. Not a bad lad. A bit lacking in the upper storey, perhaps. Very sad. The circumstances. Most kind. Tomorrow morning, the wife said? You must say thank you very much, Ronnie, to the gentleman.' Ronnie made noises in his throat. 'You're the gentleman, I believe, who's in the same line as myself. Latterly. Myself, that is.'

The tankard ran out of steam. Margaret Rose drummed her feet loudly against the rungs of her chair.

'Myself latterly, too,' Charlie said, looking Mr Spencer right in his wandering eye. They gave you the impression of two boxers sizing each other up. And

81

you knew that Charlie would win hands down on wiliness.

'Perhaps I can offer you . . .' Mr Spencer said, going to a cupboard where, as everyone knew, there was stored a solitary bottle of Empire port.

'Sorry, squire. Can't stay. Got a heavy date. Some other time.'

'Of course, of course,' Mr Spencer said. His eyes were like those of the Mona Lisa, which were said to follow you all round the room.

'Daddy,' said Margaret Rose. 'I've got a pain.'

He rushed over to her. 'Where, my precious?'

'What a set-up,' Charlie said, as they closed the gate behind them. 'What a crowd of creeps!'

That summed up the Spencers most accurately: a crowd of creeps.

'That old pensioned-off Casanova,' Charlie said, 'and Tokyo Rose in her boudoir gown. They'd give you the willies.' He looked down at her. 'Shouldn't talk out of school, should I? Still, I daresay you're discreet, aren't you, Princess? Like the three wise monkeys.'

They reached the corner of the street. His bus was approaching the stop. 'Thank you so much for a very enjoyable day,' she said, winding one leg around the other, partly because of shyness, partly because she needed the lavatory.

He gave her a quick, light tap on the top of her head. 'You know something, Princess?' he said. 'I could fall in love with you, no bother at all. You stick around for another few years,' and boarded the moving bus at a flying leap.

There were odd occasions when life exceeded all expectations, when the threat of the boys under the railway arch and the nightmare crew dwindled to nothing, because happiness made you all-powerful, invulnerable. She skimmed the homeward pavements, each leap seeming to take her as high as Nijinsky. 'I needn't ask if *you* enjoyed yourself, her mother said. 'As long as you haven't caught cold . . .'

She decided to keep quiet about the swimming – until the following morning, at any rate. No sense in inviting a lament to the tune of health hazards and what could be picked up from other people's bathing costumes. 'I thought he might have brought you back,' her mother said, her head bent; she was basting the meat inside the oven.

'He had to rush. He's got a date.'

Her mother looked up. Her face was flushed from the heat of the stove. 'Has he?' she said, in a tone that made you think she was pleased that Charlie was broadening his social horizons.

Chapter Nine

'I DON'T KNOW what's come over your mother,' Aunt Dolly said, 'allowing you to rove around all over the place with this character. At one time she wouldn't let you over the threshold without a written guarantee. Still, I suppose she knows best.'

She supposed nothing of the sort; you could tell. The whole of her face was drawn together towards her pursed lips. She slammed the change drawer shut, handed over a threepenny bit and the packet of knicker elastic.

Miss Praxted, an amiable lady with white hair like cotton-wool, rearranged a drawer of support-stockings and handed the child a glacier mint. She looked at Aunt Dolly and looked at the child and lowered one eyelid.

Trade was slack, so Aunt Dolly had the juniors polishing the brass strips that edged the counters. Molly, the senior saleslady, was perched atop a pair of stepladders fastening complicated undergarments on to a pink plaster torso. As she battled with various hooks and eyes and buttons she sang, 'One in the dear dead days beyond recall.' Her voice had an edge of wistfulness, as though the words held some deep private meaning for her.

'I can swim eight strokes now.' She lingered in the shop, sucking her glacier mint, looking at her reflection in the tilted full-length mirror, hoping that Ronnie would grow tired of hovering in the doorway, and make for home, alone.

Miss Praxted clapped her hands together rapturously. 'You'll be able to jump in and save me,' she said. 'I swim like a brick.'

The child agreed politely, wondering how or when an occasion demanding such heroism could possibly arise. Aunt Dolly said Miss Praxted was only ten pence to the shilling.

'*I* should want to know more about that young man's credentials,' Aunt Dolly said to the air. The white bow under her chin had been starched to knife-edge sharpness. She looked like a judge about to place the black cap on his head. 'You might as well take this with you.' She brought a parcel from under the counter. 'Have you come up on the pools at your house, or what?'

'What is it?' The child tried to edge up a corner of the brown paper, but it was securely tied with one of Aunt Dolly's finger-proof knots.

'Mind your business,' Aunt Dolly said. And Miss Praxted said, at the same time, 'It's ever such a pretty blouse. Your mother noticed it in the window, but we didn't have it in her size so we've had to order it.'

'So you'd better frame yourself and get it home,' Aunt Dolly said, glaring at Miss Praxted, 'in case she wants to wear it tonight.'

'She's not going anywhere tonight, is she?'

'*I* wouldn't know, would I? I'm not party to your mother's social arrangements. Are you going to dawdle around here all day?'

The child came through the shop doorway and turned sharp left, pretending that she hadn't noticed the stocky figure to her right. The figure pounded after her. 'You're going the wrong way,' it said.

'I prefer to go this way.'

'OK,' it said, falling into step beside her. She resigned herself, inclined her head to look at him. His damp hair stood up in spikes. His natural colouring had been revealed as much fairer than you'd have thought. He smelt pungent but pleasant. Charlie had bought a bar of Wright's Coal Tar soap and sent Ronnie into the water with it and instructions to lather himself thoroughly. There were problems with baths at the Spencers on account of the immersion heater just eating money. Margaret Rose was bathed once a day, her parents once a week; Ronnie was supposed to ablute at the cold-water tap in the kitchen.

'Did you get into awful bother on Friday? Did Margaret Rose tell on you? What did Mrs Spencer do?'

'She had her nerves,' Ronnie said.

'She didn't belt you?'

'No. She just had her nerves.'

Mrs Spencer's nerves manifested themselves in various ways, from lying on the bed with a damp cloth on her forehead to full-blown hysteria. Full-blown hysteria was the best. It was riveting. Mrs Spencer would hold both hands to her head and gasp and shriek and inform all those within earshot that she couldn't stand it a moment longer, that nobody knew what she had to put up with, that she didn't know what she'd done to deserve it. Mr Spencer would take her hands between his own and call her 'my love'.

'Don't you hate Mrs Spencer?'

'Yes,' he said. 'She'll go to Hell when she dies.' His eyes were bright, he was relishing the idea of Mrs Spencer frying eternally.

The idea was comforting, but it was a long time to wait for retribution. And, anyway, who could be sure? Miss Tibbs wouldn't be drawn out, preferred to talk about Heaven where, it seemed, they were all destined to die of boredom.

'How long do you think it will be before you can swim?'

'Don't know,' he said. 'P'raps I won't. Ever.'

'You will. Charlie said you will. You just have to relax and let yourself go,' she said smugly.

Ronnie, so far, was unable to do this. His fists were bunched, his legs were taut and rigid. And yet, her mother said, it was bladder relaxation that caused him to wet the bed. It was a disgrace, her mother said – not Ronnie wetting the bed, but the fact that Mrs Spencer didn't always change the sheets afterwards. 'No wonder that child smells,' her mother said, 'sleeping in the same sheets night after night. Really, that woman isn't fit to look after the cat.' Once her mother had gone up to the box-room where Ronnie slept, bundled up the bedding and hauled it home, where she scrubbed at it on the washboard. After it was dried and ironed – although some of the yellow patches were ineradicable – she'd taken it back to the Spencers', together with the child's old rubber cot sheet, and said to Mrs Spencer, 'I think your mattress has had it, but you might as well use this. Didn't it occur to you before?' Mrs Spencer had shaken her head like an unstuffed rag doll. No, it hadn't occurred to her; she had more than enough to worry about as it was.

'I have to get some hair shampoo,' the child said, turning towards a chemist's shop. 'You can go home, if you like.'

'It's OK.' He stood in the entrance, glaring at the Kodak girl, while she made her purchases: a tube of Gordon Moore's toothpaste and a sachet of Richard Hudnut shampoo; and plotted their route homeward, through unfamiliar streets where she would be unlikely to be recognized, making a semicircular detour so that they would reach the Spencers' house first. Charlie had waved them goodbye, said he had fish to fry, and

87

Ronnie had attached himself to her. Margaret Rose would have said, 'Get away, snotnose.' But the child was not Margaret Rose, and her subtle dissuasions were lost on him. It was most annoying to be obliged to walk half a mile out of one's way for the sake of anonymity. He trudged on imperturbably, new to the neighbourhood, most probably unaware that there was a quicker way home. The prospect of making such a diversion, morning after morning, encouraged her determination to learn to swim, quickly. But if she learned to swim, quickly, there would *be* no more mornings.

'What do you want to do when you're grown up?' she asked Ronnie. It was impossible to imagine a future for him, though she presumed that a Farm School fitted one for farming.

'I'm going to be one of them men that drives the roundabouts in the Kiddies Playground.'

'Not the Big Dipper?' she asked wickedly. He didn't reply.

She thought it was as well to have modest ambitions if one's capabilities were also modest. 'You'll be leaving school next year, so you'll be able to start. Will you go back to live with your mother?' She supposed that there must be Kiddies Playgrounds in Manchester.

'Not likely. I don't know.'

'Is she worse than Mrs Spencer?' But no living soul could be worse than Mrs Spencer.

'No,' he said vehemently. 'But me mam's not fit, you see.'

'What's the matter with her?'

'Eh?'

'What illness has she got?'

'She's not got an illness. She's just not fit.'

Ah. Light dawned. Like Mrs Spencer, not fit to look after the cat. 'Not a fit *person*?'

'Yeah.'

'You could go in the Y.M.C.A.' And play snooker and table-tennis and present yourself for morning prayers; she had seen them in town: earnest, gangling young men in windcheaters.

'Yeah.'

Her mother was beating the carpet-runners which were hung over the clothes-line. The cane carpet-beater went to and fro, and clouds of grey dust rose into the blue morning. 'If I don't get a new vacuum soon,' her mother said, 'I shall go spare.'

She was like a cat on hot bricks lately, forever carpet-beating, polishing, thwacking dust and cobwebs out of corners with a stiff broom, applying herself to the housework with an almost religious fervour.

'Have you dried yourself thoroughly? You didn't stop in the water too long, did you? You know what the doctors said, don't you? You haven't left off your liberty bodice?'

'Yes. No,' the child said. 'Yes. No.' She held the parcel forward. 'Aunt Dolly sent this for you.'

Her mother put down the beater and cradled the parcel in her arms, but made no attempt to open it. She chewed the rouge off her lips; she wore make-up all the time nowadays, even when she was going at the housework as though it were some kind of penance. 'What did your Aunt Dolly have to say for herself?'

The child had learned the art of diplomacy at a very early age. One did not repeat Aunt Dolly's acid comments unless one wished for bloodshed. 'Nothing much. Are you going out tonight?'

Her mother unplaited the cane on the handle of the beater. 'Where would I be going?'

'I don't know. I thought you might be going to the Social again with Dad and Charlie.'

'Did you? You know what thought did?' She applied herself to the carpet once again. She beat it so fiercely that dark stains appeared on the cloth under her armpits, despite the Odorono that she used every morning.

After a time, she said, 'What's he up to today, then?'

The child misunderstood. 'He went back to the Spencers.' For his meal. Mrs Spencer's got her nerves again. Can I see your blouse?'

Her mother paused, beating arm suspended. 'He's gone to the Spencers'? I thought that you said there was some trouble with Mrs Spencer the other day?'

'He's got to go back there though, hasn't he? With his mother not being fit. He looks a lot cleaner, anyway. Charlie made him soap himself in the sea.' She looked at her mother's face. 'Oh. You mean what's Charlie up to?' She considered. 'He said he had fish to fry. He said he had to see his uncle.'

'His uncle?' her mother said, her brow creased with lines of mystification. 'I've never heard him mention any uncle.'

That was what he'd said. They'd come off the beach and walked down the Parade. Charlie had said, 'Hang about. I won't be a sec.' and gone inside a place with blank windows that said 'Sydney Barnes – Turf Accountant' on the door. She supposed vaguely that a turf accountant was a man who had something to do with measuring up acres of land. A few minutes later Charlie had reappeared, tearing up a piece of pink paper. 'Still running,' he'd said. And when she'd asked him if he was coming back for a cup of tea, he'd replied, 'Sorry, Princess. Got other fish to fry. Got to go and see Uncle,' and waved them goodbye.

'I suppose we'd better eat,' her mother said, closing the wardrobe door upon the blouse. Her mood of super-efficiency was evaporating fast. In the kitchen, she put two eggs into a pan of water, turned the timer upside down and watched the sand trickle to its base.

Energy seemed to have drained out of her, as the sand was draining from the glass.

'Got one to spare? I'm that ravenous I could eat my way through a flock mattress.'

Blocking the sunlight in the doorway, replacing the sunlight, the perfect antidote to the fly-buzzing boredom of summer afternoons, he stretched a tentative arm inside the kitchen door as though extending a flag of truce. 'Oh *you*,' her mother said, turning her back and rattling through the cutlery drawer.

'Can I come in?'

'Of course you can. Don't be so silly.'

'Eggs à la Nancy,' he said, sitting himself down at the kitchen table. 'Just the ticket. I like 'em just when they start to go hard.'

Her mother managed to do everything with her back turned. The child was acquainted with this tactic: one kept one's head averted until the blush had subsided.

'This one's coming on a treat,' he said. 'Has she told you? There'll be no holding her in a day or two. She'll be swimming the Channel. How about you, Nancy? Can I tempt you into your bikini?'

'That'll be the day. I think I'm a bit long in the tooth for that, don't you?'

She had given him no choice of reply. What else could be say but, 'Long in the tooth? You? Don't you ever look in the mirror?'

The child attempted an objective assessment of her mother's appearance. She had dark curly hair and a round face and dark blue eyes. She wasn't fat and she wasn't thin and her teeth were nice and white and even. Sometimes lorry drivers whistled at her. Aunt Mu and the Major said that she, the child, was pretty and that she resembled her mother. Therefore, she supposed that her mother must be pretty too. But handsome was as handsome did, Aunt Dolly said; it was better to be good than pretty. Aunt Dolly was good. Good people were awful.

At Burlington Court they said that you should receive compliments gracefully and modestly. Her mother said, 'Get away with you,' and thrust his eggs in front of him with a singular lack of grace. He sawed thick slices off the loaf and helped himself to butter. Her mother stood with the teapot spout poised above his cup. 'I like it hot and sweet,' he said, 'Like my women.' This, the child supposed, was what Aunt Dolly meant when she talked of feet under the table.

Her mother sat down next to him. She slid her wedding ring up and down her finger, to the knuckle and back again. Above their heads swung the fly-paper, clotted with corpses. Two of the survivors copulated frantically on the window sill. 'I never knew that you had an uncle in this area,' her mother said accusingly. 'You said that you didn't know a soul around here.'

He leaned back in his chair, undid the top button of his trousers. 'What uncle? Haven't got an uncle. Haven't got a relative in the world.'

'You said that you were going to see your uncle,' the child reminded him hesitantly. Perhaps this was something that should not have been repeated.

'Oh! *That* uncle,' he said, smiling. 'Everybody's uncle, gentleman with the three balls, if you'll pardon my French.' He pulled back his shirt-cuff to expose the pale place on his wrist where his watch had rested. 'The old so-and-so,' he said. 'Tight as a nun's. That watch was worth a bit. Still, it'll keep the wolf from the door for a few days. Then it's back to the cold cruel world of employment for Charlie.'

'Are you spent up?' her mother asked, disbelievingly.

'Skint. Boracic.'

'What about the stuff you inherited? You said that you sold it. You said that it'd keep you going.'

'There was this horse, you see,' Charlie said, dislodging particles of food from between his teeth with the sharpened matchstick that he kept for this purpose.

'It lost,' her mother said.

'Oh no. It won. So did the rest. Charlie's hit his lucky streak, I thought. No sense in going against the omens. I was doing fine. Till yesterday. It hasn't passed the post yet and it's got all my winnings on its back.' He transferred the matchstick from his teeth to his nails. He had one or two habits that, in anyone else, she would have found most unprepossessing.

'Have you started looking around for a job?'

'Don't talk so drastic,' he replied, lighting a cigarette. 'Don't give me the jitters. As a matter of fact, all my hopes are pinned on a little beauty in the three o'clock at Sandown. Know what it's called?' They shook their heads. Gambling was a sinful habit, except for half a crown each way on the Grand National. 'It's called Nancy's Fancy,' he said. 'See what faith I have in you. It's twenty to one, and if it comes up Charlie's in clover.'

'How much have you put on?'

'A fiver.'

'Five pounds!'

'It's only small-time these days,' Charlie said apologetically. 'I remember once on Tattersall's . . .' His eyes grew cloudy with reminiscence.

Five pounds squandered on a horse! What you couldn't do with five pounds.

'Are you paid up at that boarding-house?' her mother asked him. With this new financial intimacy between them, all talk of private hotels had gone by the board.

'Oh yes,' he said easily. 'No danger there. Myra'll be good for a bit of credit, I reckon. She's not a bad old stick, Myra.' He seemed disinclined to pursue the subject. He turned to the child. 'How's your pal, since this morning?' 'Ragtime Cowboy Joe, the Colonel? Did he get his ear chewed off again?'

'Not really. Mrs Spencer has got her nerves.'

'I'll bet she has. What exactly is the situation there?' he asked her mother. 'Where does the lad fit into the picture?'

Her mother pleated the tablecloth, debated within herself. At last she said, 'It's a similar case to your own. Except that the mother won't accept her responsibilities. Or isn't capable. I don't know.'

'So the poor little sod's packed off to the Farm School and offloaded on his dad now and again? I'll bet that mangy-faced cow gives him a life of it.'

Their heads went together. 'Disgraceful,' she heard her mother say. 'It's a crying shame. The NSPCC. But you know what you get for poking your nose in where it's not wanted. Besides, I can see her point of view. Not the easiest of children. I can't say I'd take kindly to *my* husband bringing home his . . .' At this point she produced the mother and father of a blush, bright crimson.

'Little mistake,' Charlie supplied for her. 'Don't get het up. It doesn't bother *me*. Got past bothering long ago. *My* old lady wasn't exactly one of your Yiddisher mommas if it comes to that. No.' He studied his filed matchstick reflectively. 'I cramped her style a good bit. You don't get many offers with a kid hanging on to your skirts.'

'No,' her mother said, beginning to clear away the pots. 'I suppose not.'

'Not unless, of course, you look like Nancy. Your mum's a smasher, isn't she, Princess?'

The child was embarrassed, and made no comment.

'Just like you'll be one day. Are you going to lead me to your wireless? Is it in good nick? It won't fade out on us, will it, at the crucial moment?'

'We've just had new accumulators.' Her father had carried them home the previous day. Her mother was all for a radiogram off the electric, but her father said why get rid of an instrument that was in perfect working order? There were certain areas in which her father was obtuse, one of them being the desire for change where no change was necessary.

They sat, as her father usually sat, with their ears pressed up close to the front of the set. Crackles of interference punctuated the commentator's assessment. Nancy's Fancy was an outsider. It was a two-horse race according to the commentator: Black Prince or Pride of Erin. The child sat very still, fixed her eyes on the tuning knob. She knew that an enormous and concentrated effort of will was needed, that the merits of the contenders had nothing to do with the outcome of the race. Fate could turn a twenty-to-one outsider into a winner. Charlie took little quick puffs at his cigarette. 'Get on, get on,' he instructed the smooth-voiced commentator. 'Don't prolong the agony.' The start was delayed because of a recalcitrant horse that didn't like the idea of starting stalls. And then the bell sounded and there was the noise of hooves pounding for a position. 'I can't,' Charlie said, getting up and going into the kitchen. 'I can't. Tell me when it's over.'

It was over in less than a minute. The child opened her eyes. Her hands were wet and trembling. She had expended more nervous energy than the horse itself. The expressionless white oval of Charlie's face appeared in the small space between the door and the jamb. A face you would see in the dock, on a scaffold, stifling the infinitesimal hope that insisted on springing eternal.

'You can breathe again,' her mother said. 'We did it.'

And nobody could have argued the fact that it had been a joint effort, that the three of them had managed somehow to pour life and strength and determination

95

into a third-rate nag driven by an apprentice so wet behind the ears that he thought he could go on to conquer the world.

Chapter Ten

MARGARET ROSE HAD a boyfriend, a suitor. She described him in precise detail from the colour of his hair to the size of his shoes. She described his single-minded devotion, the notes she had received, the replies she had tendered, the intimate nature of their relationship. Saliva rushed into the child's mouth as she listened to the descriptions. That they were untrue did nothing to diminish the nausea. The mythical anatomy of the mythical boyfriend that Margaret Rose dwelt upon so salaciously seemed real enough. Another phase of dirty talk. 'Do you know and do you know?' Margaret Rose said, and the child shivered, wanted to stop her ears against the unsought-after, undesired knowledge. 'And, as well . . .' Margaret Rose said. Something terrible happened to girls when they were twelve, something that lasted the rest of their lives. Every month, Margaret Rose said. 'It'll happen to you, too.'

Oh no. Perhaps, as in the case of the boyfriend, this was also fantasy. But one could never be sure. 'Men and women . . .' Margaret Rose said, and the child walked away from her voice into a future of pain and blood and some sort of physical activity that sounded like a major operation without anaesthetic.

Mrs Spencer was in the sitting room turning the pages of photograph albums. She did this quite often, as though to reassure herself that her past had indeed existed. 'When I was a young girl,' Mrs Spencer said, indicating an unfocused sepia blur of cloche hats and drooping dresses. The child looked over her shoulder, kept her distance, recoiling from Mrs Spencer's female-ness, such as it was. 'At Clacton,' Mrs Spencer said. 'Jubilee Day. Victory celebrations. My dear sister Gwen.' Some of the photographs had captions beneath them: 'Myself and Brother Reginald at the piano,' 'Reginald and Uncle Wilf in Uniform – Eh what!' 'Mother and Daddy on the putting green at St Ives – Watch the Birdie!' The photographs of Mr Spencer in soup and fish with a number on his back were jumbled together, loose, at the back of the album.

Mrs Spencer smelt of Dettol. This was not a reassuring odour of germ-free cleanliness, rather it reminded one of hospital corridors and scalpels and hands scrubbed raw for action. 'Where's Margaret Rose?' she said, shutting the album with a sigh. Her past seemed to afford her more pleasure than her present.

'In the garden.'

'Why aren't you with her?'

Because I am escaping from her. Although you are no refuge, at least she can't be rude in your presence. 'I felt a bit sick,' she said.

'Don't start to be sick here.' Mrs Spencer got up rapidly, scattering loose photographs on to the rag rug. 'I wouldn't know what to do with you.'

You'd lie me down and dose me with milk of magnesia and bring a bowl. 'It's going off now,' she said.

'Then you'd better keep very still and quiet.' Mrs Spencer spread an old tablecloth over the end of the sofa, just in case. Mr Spencer wasn't very much use in the house, but in his absence any crisis assumed gigantic proportions. What a tiresome sickly child it was anyway. Mrs Spencer blamed the parents. For molly-coddling, for an old head on young shoulders, for a still and silent presence that was an irritation in itself.

The child was quite happy to keep very still and quiet. A good book would have been a bonus, but the Spencers' was not a bookish household. On the shelves beside the fireplace, together with the souvenir jugs and plaster vases, were *The Complete Home Doctor*, the Bible and some second-hand copies of the *Reader's Digest*. She selected one of the last and read about Captain Scott and his gallant band of men and the mysterious member who appeared and disappeared and could never be accounted for. Despite the intriguing nature of the article, she couldn't concentrate. Grievance lay uppermost in her mind. Her parents and Charlie had gone to the races. After the races they were doing a show in Liverpool, followed by dinner. Subsequently Charlie would drive them back in a car he'd hired for the purpose. Then they would collect the child, half-asleep, from the Spencers' sitting-room. They would bring a breath of cool outside air in with them. Their eyes would be bright, and their cheeks flushed with excitement and drink. They would talk, interrupting each other. They would hum snatches of the tunes they'd heard, say they'd never tasted such good food since they didn't know when. Their pleasure would be exclusive, incommunicable, feeding the child's resentment until the day inevitably ended in tears.

'It's all right for some,' Mrs Spencer said. This statement was accompanied by a tremulous sigh. She had said it several times during the course of the morning: sitting with her elbows on the breakfast table, surveying a litter of toast crusts and blobs of marmalade, standing at the sink peeling the potatoes for lunch. Whenever she said it, more lines appeared in her already lined face, her lips turned inwards upon themselves. 'Off jaunting,' she called it, what her parents and Charlie were doing. 'Off jaunting' was something that belonged now in her past, in the photograph albums.

The child put away the noble death of Captain Scott and took up *The Complete Home Doctor*. She flicked past curvature of the spine and phthisis and exophthalmic goitre to the section that looked likely to confirm or disprove Margaret Rose's dirty information. Graafian follicles there were, and fallopian tubes and spermatozoa and pictures that resembled cross-sections of frogspawn. She had just reached 'Imprudent behaviour at the time of the menses' when a hand reached over the back of the sofa and removed the book from her grasp. 'I don't think that's *really* very suitable for a child your age.'

'What's everyone doing cooped up indoors on a day like this?' Margaret Rose entered the room; brown, she was, plump, a perfect physical specimen.

'Hallo, my precious.' Her mother rumpled the tight black curls, stroked the bare brown arms, pressed kisses upon the ruddy cheeks. Mrs Spencer looked at her child and found no fault. The child's mother looked at hers and saw every flaw and deficiency, and loved despite these great obstacles to loving. Or so it seemed to the child.

'I'm bored,' said Margaret Rose. 'She won't play outside.'

'She feels sick, pet.'

'That's just in her mind,' said Margaret Rose. 'What she needs is fresh air and exercise.'

Her mother didn't contradict her. They both looked at the child contemptuously. The child said, 'We could do a jigsaw. Or play Ludo.' Margaret Rose's jigsaws were childishly simple; any board game more complex than Ludo was beyond her, but Margaret Rose in the house was safer than Margaret Rose outside it.

She fetched the board and the counters from her toy box. There weren't enough counters; they had to extemporize with buttons, and it was relatively easy for Margaret Rose to claim the wrong button if it happened to be in a winning position. The child forced herself to lose consecutive games. The alternative was Margaret Rose whining and sulking and calling upon her mother for support. It was much harder to play badly than to play well, despite the disputed buttons. And, anyway, only a moron wouldn't realize that she was being allowed to win. 'My game,' said Margaret Rose, so triumphantly smug that the child longed to break the Ludo board over her head.

'Two little maids from school,' Mr Spencer said, laying a cold and fleshy hand upon each of their heads. He had entered the room soundlessly. The child jumped a foot. Margaret Rose didn't flicker so much as an eyelash. 'Two little maids all a-merry. How's Dolly Daydream today, how's the Brain of Britain?'

'Very well, thank you,' she said gravely, concentrating fiercely on the shaking of a dice in an egg-cup. Mr Spencer's awful facetiousness could only be countered by a determined solemnity.

'Ah, youth!' Mr Spencer said. 'Gather ye rosebuds. Golden lads and girls all must like chimney sweepers come to dust.' He was prone to this kind of seemingly irrelevant quoting into the air around his head.

'Well?' Mrs Spencer said. She was wearing her kimono. She had been lying down with her feet higher than her head. She looked like a character out of his beloved *Mikado*, come to exact some sort of ultimate vengeance. 'Well?' she said.

Mr Spencer shook his head and spread his arms wide.

'No?'

He shook his head again.

Mrs Spencer sat down on the end of the sofa. Her lips disappeared. All the light reflected in her eyes was drawn inwards to be extinguished in the tiny black pupils. She tapped the ends of her long fingernails on the top of the occasional table. A draught rustled the paper and the soot and the old hair-combings in the grate. 'Why not?' she said.

'They wanted a younger man.'

'Did you *go*?'

'Of course I went.'

'How much longer?' Mrs Spencer said. 'I've just about reached the end of my tether, I can tell you.' The fingernail-tapping increased in tempo to an erratic rhythm. The child moved her counter three squares, and stole a glance. There was tension in every line of Mrs Spencer's body, despite her rest and relaxation. A foot on the lino joined the fingernails in the same staccato tattoo. Perhaps Mrs Spencer was going to have her nerves. She hoped so.

'I can't do more than try, can I?' Mr Spencer said. He looked at his wife with little furtive glances from under his eyelids.

'Try!' she said. 'Try! Where does that leave me? My parents said I'd rue the day. They said make your bed and you'll lie in it. And they were right. What did I do to deserve it, though? Tell me. Tell me!'

No one told her. Mr Spencer scratched himself in several places. Margaret Rose said, 'You're cheating. That's my counter.' The child gazed at the board so fervently that all the squares mingled with one another.

'I wish I was dead,' Mrs Spencer said. No one answered that, either.

It was all to do with Mr Spencer's employment. Or lack of it. He no longer sold vacuum cleaners. He no longer did anything, except go for interviews where interviewers took one look at him and said they wanted a younger man.

'Sometimes,' Mrs Spencer said, 'I ask myself why I simply don't pack up and go. Why I simply don't buy a train ticket to Weston-super-Mare and leave it all behind me. I can't hold my head up.'

The child looked round curiously to see whether Mrs Spencer had suddenly suffered a misplaced vertebra or a curvature of the spine, then realized that she was speaking metaphorically. Holding your head up must, indeed, be difficult when you lived in a state of perpetual anxiety, when you bought your child a pair of red leather shoes because Margaret Rose, being Margaret Rose, had to have them, and all the time you knew your credit at the butcher's and the grocer's was running out fast, when you raided the electricity meter and knew that the electricity man on his bicycle was approaching the front gate, when you had to endure your child's friend delivering notes from your child's headmistress to say that the fees were overdue. Holding your head up was well-nigh impossible when the prospect of council schools and the NAB loomed on the horizon. If you lived in a shack beside the canal you accepted such things as natural and proper; if you lived in Jubilee Villas you did not.

And all the while Margaret Rose captured enemy counters and Mr Spencer twisted the fingers of his left hand with those of his right and made animal-like noises at the back of his nose. He moistened his lips and opened his mouth to speak. She expected him to say, 'Something will turn up,' but he said instead, 'Where's the boy got to today? I haven't clapped eyes on him since breakfast.'

'*I* don't know. You don't expect me to be responsible for him, do you?'

'Don't expect you to be responsible for anything,' he muttered.

The Spencers' rows differed from her parents' rows in that Mr Spencer seemed afraid of provoking his wife too much. The child supposed the reason was that, whereas her mother concluded her rows with silent sulks, Mrs Spencer concluded *hers* with raging hysteria.

'We should keep an eye on him more,' Mr Spencer said, nobly claiming a share of the responsibility. 'Never know what he gets up to. Mischief. Get lost. You never know.'

'Good riddance to bad rubbish,' Margaret Rose said. 'I hope he falls in the canal and gets drowned.'

The child gasped. The Spencers didn't react one way or the other. Miss Tibbs in Sunday School would have fainted clean away. The child had often wished death by drowning on various people: Mrs Spencer, even Margaret Rose herself, but only in her innermost heart. To speak the words aloud was a different kind of wickedness, inviting retribution. How would Margaret Rose feel if Ronnie really did drown?

'Will we have our tea?' Mr Spencer said diffidently. He was weighing the possible provocative or offensive content of every sentence before he uttered it. 'If I can find the boy I'll send him for a tin of salmon.' He rose to his feet, walked heavily into the kitchen. 'Boy!' he called. 'Boy!' as if to a dog or a black slave. Mrs Spencer sat motionless. The patterned kimono that she wore was not very clean. Her wedding ring hung slackly on her finger. If she wasn't careful it would fall off and roll along the floor and through a crack in the boards. Her mouth was screwed up and her eyes ringed like a nocturnal animal's, but it seemed that nerves of only the mildest order were on the cards.

'You're hopeless, aren't you.' said Margaret Rose. It was not a question. 'You may be very clever at school but you're not much cop otherwise, are you? I'm fed up, anyway. I'm hungry. Aren't we *having* any tea?' She got up from the table and faced her mother. Her attitude said, 'You may be having your nerves, but I'm hungry, and we all know which is the more important, don't we?' The child packed away board, counters and buttons into their box. From the kitchen came sounds indicating that the boy had been located. The room, the house, pressed in upon her: the claustrophobic sad sepia wallpaper, the mustard dado, the tinkling jug and squat ornaments, the steel engraving of the Four Horsemen, Mrs Spencer in her soiled kimono with dirt between her toes, came closer and closer, stifling her with their dust and gloom and sadness. She went into the kitchen. Even Mr Spencer and his hands and the Rodine and the sink smelling of yesterday's cauliflower were preferable.

Mr Spencer searched the perimeter of the salmon tin for the key that opened it. 'Little fingers,' he said, 'are needed. The right tools for the job.' She took the tin to the doorway, away from him, pretending that she needed the light. Ronnie sat in his usual place on the padded fender beside the empty grate. Mr Spencer moved around the table with a fistful of cutlery that had mostly been acquired from hotels, cafés and London-Midland Railways, and a pile of plates that didn't match one another. Salmon was a luxury, she thought, as she wound out a strip from the waist of the tin. Bread and jam would have been more appropriate for their financial circumstances. 'It's a hard old world, Veronica,' Mr Spencer said, filling from the Saxa tin the salt half of a cruet that was shaped like a pair of fishes. 'Want the advice of a complete failure?'

She decanted the salmon into a green glass dish, licked her fingers, folded her arms across her chest and awaited something to the tune of 'Annual income twenty pounds . . .'

105

'Never take on – um – responsibilities unless you're really sure. Never be persuaded. Stand firm. What!'

If he meant by responsibilities marriage and children, then he was wasting his breath, preaching to the converted. The idea was distasteful, alien, entirely inappropriate.

'Grief,' he said. 'And sorrow. And the innocent shall suffer.'

Nevertheless, he bucked up amazingly during tea. He recited *The Wreck of The Hesperus* most movingly, he played *Goodbye Dolly Gray* and *You are My Sunshine* on his mouth-organ, he said that Ronnie should have a career in the navy, at sea. He said the Farm School was all very well, but it was the navy that made a man of you. He said that, present commitments permitting, he was going to see about it immediately. For an encore he played *Bobbing Up and Down Like This*, and they all had to bob up and down like that, even Mrs Spencer, who thought that mouth-organs and popular tunes were very low-class indeed.

Mrs Spencer's contribution to the general festive air was a series of parlour games that she remembered from her own genteel childhood: Up Jenkins, Simon Says, Mrs McGinty's Dead. 'Simon says "Put your hands on your head." Put your hands on your head.' And up went Margaret Rose's hands and Ronnie's, and Mr Spencer's, though he was pretending not to understand the rules. In the kitchen the tabby cat sprang and landed softly and solidly on the table, lowered its head to the glass dish that contained the pink and silver remains of the salmon and began to gorge. In the sitting-room, because the child so monotonously won all the games that demanded skill or memory, they played forfeits where chance was the sole criterion. The knife spun in the middle of the lino. 'Around and around it goes,' Mr Spencer said, 'and where it stops nobody knows.' Ronnie was the first victim. In a hoarse, breathy voice he sang, 'Ah poor bird, take thy flight, for a mother's sorrows, on this sad night.' The actual words, as one knew from school, were, 'far above the sorrows of this sad night,' but Ronnie's misheard version seemed entirely appropriate for Ronnie. Margaret Rose embarked upon the nine times table, but couldn't get further than nine sevens, and so lost her hair-ribbon. The child recited the first few stanzas of *Hiawatha* and remembered the Major. Mr Spencer tried to palm them off with: 'It was the schooner Hesperus that sailed the wintry sea . . .' and when they protested, played *Cruising Down the River* on his mouth-organ instead. Mrs Spencer insisted on calling it a harmonica. The child thought with dread that *she* might sing, but she contented herself with *Home Thoughts from Abroad*.

A full bright moon illuminated the interior of the room, shining steadily on the lustre jugs and the revolving knife and the words and lances and banners of the Four Horsemen. Mr Spencer had risen to switch on the light, but Mrs Spencer had said why waste electricity, in the present circumstances particularly, and they all thought of little clocks and dials whirling around at a tremendous rate devouring precious kilowatts. In the moonlight's glow Mrs Spencer's face was all bone. 'Alas, poor Yorick!' Mr Spencer said, and stretched out an arm and there was Mrs Spencer's face, a ready-made illustration to the monologue.

'Tell us a ghost story,' Margaret Rose implored her father. For this was where his real talents lay. He was not a born vacuum cleaner salesman or a ticket-collector or a shipping clerk. If there had been some sort of opening as a raconteur of macabre tales, Mr Spencer could have taken on the world. The child's mouth went dry. To listen to Mr Spencer in the moonlight telling the story of the man who woke in the dark and stretched out a hand for the matches to light a candle – and felt the matches being placed in his hand, was to invite the company of a legion of nightmare figures. Yet, though she knew the inevitable consequences, some perverse part of her nature wished to be terrified. In the *Illustrated Junior Encyclopaedia*, under 'S', there was a full-colour, full-page plate of a monstrously hairy South American bird-eating spider. To look at it, she knew, resulted in the spider-dream where serried ranks of them marched up the bedcover towards her face. And yet she looked, always, mesmerized by its repulsiveness.

The lard-white face of Mr Spencer swam up out of the gloom and saved her. 'I'm going to make us all a big frothy mug of cocoa.' Exhibitionistic story-telling was hard to resist, but Mrs Spencer must be placated. That was the reason he had made the tea and was now offering to make the cocoa.

'We haven't much milk,' Mrs Spencer said sadly. 'There's a tin of condensed in the safe. You'll have to use that.'

'There's not much left,' Margaret Rose said quickly, forestalling accusation. She was a condensed milk addict. 'Somebody's been at it.' This last accompanied by a direct look into the furthest corner, where Ronnie was taking advantage of the darkness to dislodge bogies from his nose and secrete them down the side of his chair.

'We'll manage,' Mr Spencer said airily. 'Never say die. *Nil desperandum*.'

His repertoire of Shakespearian quotes and foreign phrases was constant, never increased. You knew he would say, 'Out, damned spot!' and, 'Alas, poor Yorick! *Nil desperandum*' and '*Voulez-vous promenader avec moi, joli mademoiselle*?'

He improvised with the cocoa. Improvisation was the thing. She blew the skin to one side and sipped at it. It was

108

hot and wet and relatively tasteless. Apparently the Spencers were low on cocoa too. The hands moved round the face of the tin alarm clock: ten forty-five, eleven o'clock. They should have been in bed hours ago, and they knew it. In the corner, Ronnie's chin hit his chest and woke him up. What if her parents never came back? What if they had had an accident? She could imagine Charlie driving nonchalantly and fast and going smack-bang into a concrete lamp-standard. It wasn't fair. Parents had no business to go off jaunting and leave their children worrying themselves sick. A little tear ran down her cheek and into her cocoa. A second made to follow it but she sniffed it up her nose. The clock hand moved off the hour and she knew then how unlikely it was that they would ever return. Through the tears which could no longer be contained nor sniffed up, she peered at Ronnie with more fondness and a new respect. How had he survived?

When they came, it was suddenly and loudly and they laughed too much and petted her too fervently. Her relief was so great that, all pride abandoned, she said, 'I thought you weren't coming back.' How could you be so silly?' her mother said. 'As if. It's that imagination of yours. You brood on things and work yourself up into a state.' Which was all very well but, nevertheless, they deserved punishment for their thoughtlessness, and if there *was* a Heaven and if there *was* a God in it, they'd get it,

Chapter Eleven

IT WAS COOL and green and dim in the shade of the rhododendrons. Pigeons with mauve breasts and rose-coloured necks pecked at the thin impoverished earth between the roots. Caged guinea pigs – square at both ends, you couldn't tell one from t'other – scurried in and around heaps of sleeping rabbits, who flapped their ears languidly. Canaries and budgerigars and parakeets preened themselves. The peacock glared through his wire grille, the boundary of his meagre territory, and suddenly, without warning, fanned his tail. A hundred iridescent eyes appeared as he screamed, and little children with bread in their hands gasped and scattered. The cob and the pen led their dingy offspring down the lake, a royal progress. They were beautiful and dangerous: a boy had had his arm broken by one swipe from a flared wing.

The rhododendrons seemed too perfect to be entirely the work of nature. She touched the blooms; their heliotrope papery translucence reminded her of the artificial flowers that Aunt Muriel fashioned from crêpe paper and twigs. 'That comic!' she heard her mother saying to Charlie. 'I haven't laughed like that for a long time . . .'

She was reminiscing about their night out: the variety show they'd seen; the ten shillings she'd won on a grey called Mary's Cavalier, the Dublin Bay prawns they'd eaten, and the *Bombe Surprise*. 'A real blow-out,' her father had called it.

Behind the rose garden, alone on its plateau, stood the fernery, a brick building with windows made of thick opaque green glass and doors scrawled with the messages of generations of scrawlers. They entered, and followed in single file the narrow path that led between the high banks of greenery. Artificial water-falls splashed into grottoes. Copper coins glinted under the surface of the water; goldfish behind stones flicked their vermilion tails. Palm-trees pressed up against the glass roof. She kept to the centre of the path, imagining huge and gruesome tropical insects ensconced in the greenery, waiting to drop from sticky-spun filaments. Fly-eating plants gaped their evil jaws; if you were to touch them with a fingertip, the obscene fronds that fringed their mouths would undulate, caress, grasp.

A trailing fern brushed Charlie's face, which had a pale green cast to it. All their faces did. He recoiled, shuddered fastidiously. 'Give you the creeps,' he said. 'It's like the east coast of West Africa.'

This was fantasy land, like Eldorado and Atlantis, or Fornication, which, Margaret Rose had informed her, was the place you waited while it was decided whether you were fitted for Heaven or Hell.

'I like it,' her mother said. It was dim and secret and away from the press of ugly humanity. The sound of water trickling and splashing gently soothed one's nerves. That was the difference between her mother and Charlie, and the difference between her mother and her father, the child perceived. *They* liked crowds and camaraderie, laughter and jostle. *She* needed to be apart, a member of an exclusive group – or couple – which found its enjoyment in unexpected places. Her mother lingered, trailed her hand in a pool until her wrist ached with the cold. 'What will we do?' she said.

Charlie struck a match, his hand cupped round the flame. He lit his cigarette, took a quick puff and held it behind his back. 'Play it by ear,' he said.

'What does that mean?'

'Means what it says. Can't have everything cut and dried. You say, "What will we do?" and expect an answer. Can't give it to you.'

The child could. She took an aniseed ball out of her mouth, wiped it, and put it in her pocket for later. 'You said the Local History Museum,' she said.

'So we did. So we did. You're like the Memory Man, Princess.' He lifted her up until their faces were level. She could see the light blue of his eyes that shaded to a rim of grey around the iris, the little flecks of bloodshot in the white, the slightly enlarged pores around his nose and the tiny little black hairs that were going to poke through as bristles nestling in his chin. 'You're a queer little cove, aren't you?' he said. 'Were you the same, Nancy, when you were a kid?'

'I don't remember,' she said, pushing the hair away from her forehead with an unconscious irritable gesture. It was so long ago, down all the years of roasting meat and washing up and paying the insurance man, boiling steam-kettles and pouring Lucozade and listening to *Friday Night is Music Night* with a pile of mending on her lap. 'At least,' she said, 'I remember being lonely a lot, and bored. You wouldn't understand that.'

'Wouldn't I?' he lowered the child to the ground. 'Bored perhaps not. But lonely, certainly. All those different schools. Couldn't get the hang of the system. By the time I did it was time to move on. All the little cracks: 'Where's your dad?' She wore a wedding ring and called herself Mrs, but they weren't fooled. You learn to build a damn great wall around yourself in those circumstances, if you're going to survive.'

'She must have had a hard life.' Her mother stripped a spray of fern until its skeleton lay in the palm of her hand. If the park keeper saw her she'd get into bother.

'Sometimes hard, sometimes easy. Too easy. Cars they had, and gold watches. Used to chuck me under the chin and call me sonny. "Run out and play, sonny. Here's a tanner." Bought her a radio, one of them. And once we had fifty tins of corned beef. She believed every word they told her. She was a fool.'

'We are fools,' her mother said, 'women.'

He laid his hand on the child's shoulder. 'I'm not much good, you know,' he said.

'Perhaps I do know,' she replied. 'It doesn't make me any less of a fool. More so in fact.'

'She had these wild dreams. Next week it would all come right. We'd be in clover. The right feller round the corner, and then it would be clothes and gins and expensive restaurants for ever more. Always next week. Sometimes, when she was down, she'd say, "If I wasn't lumbered with you . . ." Next week never came. She died waiting for it.' He grimaced, puffed at his cigarette. 'Make your heart bleed, wouldn't it?' he said.

'It closes at five-thirty,' the child said. 'the Local History Museum.'

'We're on our way,' Charlie said, grabbing a hand each and running them through the wet and overhanging clumps of vegetation towards the exit.

One spoke quietly inside the Local History Museum. Little children leaning too far over the glass cases or sliding along the shiny floor had their hands or their legs slapped. A woman in a blue overall sat in a cubicle surrounded by picture postcards and took their sixpences. They were her only patrons. It took bad weather to induce people to abandon the outdoor pursuits in the park. In the Victorian Room a life-size model of a lady in a bustle and a befeathered hat dispensed tea, perpetually, in tiny china cups. 'Here's my head,' Charlie said, 'my bum's following.' He could be awfully rude sometimes. Once, on the beach, he had said that a female fellow-bather had a bottom like an Eccles cake.

She inspected the escritoire surmounted with aspidistras, the andirons that were fashioned in the form of dogs' heads, stood on tiptoe to admire the samplers that had been embroidered by Harriet Wilkins aged twelve, ran an illegal finger over the saffron keys of an ancient harmonium. The interior of the room was not so very different from the interior of the aunts' house. 'I'll sing thee songs of Araby,' Charlie read from the sheet music propped on a piano. 'I would too. If I thought you'd listen.'

Her mother scratched at a spot on her wrist. The more she scratched, the more inflamed the skin eruption became. 'How many more have heard them?' she said.

'A good few, I dare say.'

'I dare say.'

'Does it matter?'

'I don't know,' her mother said. She ought to be made to wear cotton mittens like Margery Parker at school who suffered from weeping eczema. 'I don't know much.'

Faded accounts of lifeboat disasters, under glass, confronted them in the next room. *The Silver Bell, The Sandiego, The Pyramus*, lost with all hands. Ancient lifeboatmen with beards down their chests, looking like Michelin Men in their curious life-jackets, stared stolidly at the camera. Thomas Tyler had died, and his brother William, their sons George and Thomas,

Daniel and Percy. Their names lived for ever more. *The New Amsterdam*, put out of Bremen on the fourteenth of September, 1885, ran aground and left two survivors: the ship's boy and a monkey.

'There are so many difficulties,' her mother said, 'not the least of which . . .'

'There's a very old saying, where there's a will . . .'

'I know. Maybe I haven't the guts. And where would it get me?'

'Nowhere, probably.'

'Do you have to be so honest?' she said, her eyes fixed on the lifebelt that had brought Jan Jenkyns and the monkey – whose name was Perlita – to shore.

'I don't *have* to be.'

The botanical drawings were exquisite. The child pressed her face against the glass that covered them, sighed at the chasm which lay between her own proficiency and that of Miss Beatrice Crowe who had executed these drawings in 1902. They were technically so accurate, yet so imaginatively beautiful that they made her throat ache. One day, perhaps, with application and perseverance . . . One day, certainly, if it killed her.

They climbed the slippery stairs. Shells, bird's eggs and model soldiers lay to their left. She turned that way, leaving the worst, most fascinating room until the last. Huge scallop shells and conches and cowries from the Indian ocean boasted their brilliant colouration above the humble native cockles and mussels. If you could lift up the glass and put one of them to your ear, you would hear the beat of a different, bluer, foam-flecked sea. The model soldiers were thrice-padlocked. They were extremely valuable and, before this precaution had been taken, a boy had been stopped at the door and made to turn out his pockets, which proved to contain two battalions.

'You're leaving the decision to me,' her mother said.
'I'm not in a position.'

The Light Brigade charged, eternally, into the valley of death. There weren't six hundred of them, though.

The child and Margaret Rose had once tried to blow birds' eggs. Their attempts had been unsuccessful. Maybe you needed a special tool, not just a pin, a steady hand and plenty of breath as it told you in *The Child's Book of Indoor Pastimes*. Robins' eggs were the prettiest. She had often tried for that particular shade of blue, mixing the colours in her Reeves paint-box; she had never quite captured it. One day she would be old enough to go to the Art School, where there would be all the colours in the world. It was Mecca, that big brick municipal building in which men with beards and girls in peasant skirts carried portfolios and T-squares and licked their handkerchiefs to remove smudges of paint from their faces.

'You've got friends, haven't you?' Charlie said.

'There's Carrie Mortimer,' her mother said. 'We were at school together.'

'Would she be reliable?'

'I don't know. Perhaps. She was always fast – at school.'

Sunlight shafted through the tall narrow windows, danced in a pattern on the child's forearm. After the Art School, she would go to a hot country, Spain or Italy, where the sun intensified all the colours, where the sea was ultramarine, the sky cobalt and the rocks cast Tyrrhenian purple shadows.

They retraced their steps to the top of the stairs and then turned right. The exhibits started off innocuously enough: sweet little examples of the taxidermist's art: jenny wrens and robin redbreasts and song-thrushes, their beaks open wide, delivering soundless rhapsodies. Dab-chicks and mallards with glossy blue-green heads

116

lay in beds of rushes; a family of partridge (*perdix perdix*) raised their cherry-coloured faces to observe their near relation, a cock pheasant whose many-hued markings were exactly symmetrical. The coot, with his startling white patch, had a cock-eyed look; the lapwings teetered on a rocky ledge, their quiffs raised like question marks. A solitary sandpiper, true to its name, stood aloof from a gaggle of little terns. 'Great tits,' Charlie said, and her mother flushed up and the child knew that that was somehow rude.

The next case contained birds that were pretty to look at, prettier than their names, masked shrike, great grey shrike, shag, twite, implied. It wasn't until you reached the middle of the room that the horror began, building up progressively from the mischievous magpie and the jackdaw, to the raven, dead black, omen of doom, and the carrion crow whose name tied in with pestilence and death.

'There's nowhere to go, anyway,' her mother said. She had resumed her fidgeting, picking away at the gnat-bite or whatever it was on her wrist.

'We'd find somewhere.'

'I'm scared.'

'Of finding a way? Of being found out?'

'Of you. I'm not very . . . I'm cold.'

How on earth could her mother be cold? It was hot and stuffy inside the museum with the smell of melting wax polish and warm brown varnish in your nostrils.

'How many people have you told that?' Charlie said.

'How can you say that? Nobody. Except . . .'

'Well, then.'

Cygnus cygnus, the whooper swan, and the mute swan, *Cygnus olor*, a sad name, she thought, but it was one of the same that had risen from the lake and broken the boy's arm. It occupied a case to itself; even in death it looked arrogant, supercilious and certain of its power.

'I suppose men like you laugh at a woman of no experience,' her mother said. 'The young girls without a mark on their faces, as free as the air – till they get caught – that's what you need.'

Charlie tapped his finger against the glass as though hoping to arouse two perky, but dead, chaffinches (*fringilla coelebs*). 'What I want and what I need are two different things.'

The long show-case, stretching from the centre of the room to the door, was the *pièce de résistance*. 'Birds of Prey' was lettered in Gothic script above it. The kite, the hawk, the peregrine falcon. You stood at a distance. So lifelike were they that it seemed they might flap their wings and burst through to freedom, shattering glass into a thousand fragments, landing on your shoulder, rending your flesh with the talons that held down their victims: the mice, the hedgehogs, the little birds. Mock blood had been painted on to the ravaged, inert bodies. The predators' tiny glass eyes gleamed, their curved beaks tore at fur and flesh. They reminded her of Mrs Spencer; their cruelty was unrelieved, total. Though, of course, it wasn't cruelty; it was simply the manifestation of their natures: kill, or die.

'I wasn't alive,' her mother said. 'I was like a robot. I'd got so used to not enjoying myself.'

'But you did once? Surely?'

'When I was a girl. Me and Carrie Mortimer, going down the Prom, our arms linked, trying to click. We were as mad as hatters. What we weren't going to do! Makes you laugh. She's married to a real pig, Carrie. Drinks. She was ever so good-looking once. People used to turn their heads. Now she looks fifty. Why aren't *you* married by now, anyway?'

'Never much appealed to me. 'Course, I'd never had

any example of happy married life. Most of the married men I'd come across were buying my old lady gins or tins of corned beef. They used to tell her their wives were cold, not interested any more.'

'There's no true feeling, is there?' her mother said. 'Everyone's out for what he can get.'

'That's true.'

'Can you wonder I'm afraid of getting hurt – more?'

'I may be a lot of things,' he said, 'but I'm not cruel.'

'You don't have to be. The result'd be the same.'

Last of all were the owls. Watching, waiting. The ones that featured in so many of Mr Spencer's ghost stories. Barn owls, long-eared owls, tawny owls, all with similar, horribly human faces above their bird bodies. They knew everything, you could tell. One of them, (*stryx flammea*), was depicted in mid-swoop. A mesmerized vole offered up its life. It hadn't a chance. Dog eat dog, as her mother said.

It was a relief to move from bloodied beaks and claws to the gentle otter, the bristly badger (*meles meles*). Except that the badger's irregular, needle-like teeth seemed quite capable of inflicting the same atrocities as the predatory birds. You could stroke an otter, though, or a sleek fox, or a dog. They'd had a pup once, when she was small, but it caught distemper and got fits and had to be put down. She'd hidden at the back of the garden, behind the compost heap, and wept until she was almost dehydrated. Pip, he'd been called, and you could tell from his face when they took him away that he knew he'd been betrayed. Her mother had said it was best not to get attached to anything, then you couldn't be hurt.

The woman in the blue overall stood in the centre of the hallway and rang a brass hand-bell. She rang it with unnecessary vigour, considering that they were the only people in the place. 'Man the lifeboats,' Charlie said, 'women and children first. Did you know, in the Titanic, they went down singing *Abide With Me* to the tune of *Alexander's Ragtime Band*? Or the other way round.'

They blinked in the sunlight, even though it was filtered through thick green foliage. The swans returned down the centre of the lake, never veering from their straight course. Rowers had to manoeuvre their boats to the sides. A small crop-headed child held an earnest, one-sided conversation with an unresponsive Belgian Hare rabbit. The peacock turned his back and sulked and kept his tail tightly furled.

They ate on the terrace of the café. Charlie bought her a rubber ball. It had multicoloured streaks running through the grey rubber; it smelled new and inviting. After she'd eaten her bun and drunk her tea she practised bouncing it on the side wall of the fernery. It bounced satisfyingly high. She overheard snatches of conversation every time she ran back to the table to catch it: 'I didn't bargain for it . . . Aren't you glad, though? . . . Our Dolly's got a nose like radar . . . You'd think me cheap . . . I wish I could go back fourteen years . . . Nancy . . . Make the decisions for me . . . Please.'

The blue shadows mounted in the corners of the park. Children had their unwilling arms thrust into woollen garments; parents began the disheartening task of packing rainhats and cricket bats and half-eaten sandwiches into hold-alls; the working population arrived, in ones and twos, disengaged their dogs from leashes, watched to see that they relieved themselves before they got home; a solitary bandsman, arrived early, essayed a few experimental blasts through his trombone. The parents and children dragged their tired and dusty feet past the drinking fountains, the Garden For the Blind, the bowling green, towards the exits,

leaving the park for music lovers and old-age pensioners and courting couples.

'I have to get the dinner,' her mother said, brushing
crumbs from her floral print, touching her mouth with
her little finger to check if any had lingered there.

He piled up pennies into a column on the table,
flicked at them with his finger and sent them crashing.
'Will we?' he said. 'Nancy?

'Don't ask,' she replied, 'when you know already,'
and walked off very briskly, leaving them both behind.

Chapter Twelve

'COULD WE FIND a porter? Could we heck,' Aunt Dolly said. 'I said to her, perhaps Jack will be here to meet us. You never know, pigs might fly.'

Jack looked into the middle-distance while a little silence passed over the gathering, like the Angel of the Lord.

'"What a home-coming," I said. I said to the ticket-collector, "If this is the way that you run your station, then I'm not surprised that everybody goes to Blackpool." "Don't make a fuss, Dolly," *she* says. That's just the trouble: nobody does make a fuss.'

She – Aunt Muriel – raised her eyes to heaven and continued her inspection of the rosebushes. The annual two-week holiday in Colwyn Bay was over and the garden – according to Dolly – resembled the Burmese jungle. An offensive was necessary. And an offensive always generated an evil humour. It was ever thus.

'Well,' said her mother, 'you enjoyed yourselves. That's the main thing.' How was it that some people needed so little, and called it enjoyment?

'We had a lovely time,' Aunt Mu said, calling the child's attention to a perfect blossom. 'All the familiar faces. And except for a few days you couldn't quarrel with the weather.'

'Damned heat,' Aunt Dolly said, adjusting the dress-preservers under her armpits. Dresses looked incongruous on Aunt Dolly; she was built for business suits. 'We're really in for it. When this lot breaks, it'll break, make no mistake about it.' She attacked an innocent sprig of privet with a lunge of the shears. 'And what about you? What have you lot been up to during this last fortnight?'

Nobody answered her. Nobody had been up to anything. Her mother rolled a sixpence along the garden seat, caught it just as it fell off the edge, rolled it, caught it again. It was maddening.

'Still consorting with that Whatshisname, I expect. Well, I suppose if you don't care about people talking, that's up to you. But talk they will, believe me.'

'Talk about what? What are you on about?' The views Dolly held were pre-war, pre-First World war. Antiquated, she was.

'Don't act so gormless, Jack Bell.'

'Are you trying to imply . . .?'

'I'm implying nothing.'

'Well, then.' He tapped the side of his nose. 'Just keep that out. And we'll all be a lot happier.'

She snapped the shears shut. 'I only speak my mind,' she said. 'The difference is, I say it to your face.' She collected fork and trowel, carried them down to the garden shed. Frail weeds in the herbaceous border cowered at her coming. She hummed a tune as she uprooted them. She was not mightily offended. Being insulted was an occupational hazard when one poked one's nose into other people's business.

'Lobelia,' Aunt Mu said. 'Alyssum. Gypsophila. White rock. Primulas and candytuft.' She and the child moved along the opposite border. The child admired the plants as her aunt named them. They were planted at regular distances from one another, flowered neatly, looked as though they had been stuck into the earth rather than grown from it. The child preferred wildness and luxuriance; rose-smothered hedges, huge violent silken poppies, bramble and briar, even the sinister convolvulus that strangled everything before it in its onward march. The aunts' garden resembled a child's drawing: two rectangles of green bisected by a straight grey path and bordered with regular blobs of primary-coloured flowers. 'She likes everything tidy,' Aunt Mu said wistfully, as though she too would have liked to fling handfuls of seeds into the air to bloom wherever they landed. 'She works hard.'

It was true. Pushing the heavy mower, creosoting the fences, digging the plot for the runner beans – they were men's jobs. Aunt Dolly could do them, though. 'I'll not be defeated,' she said, with a sidelong look at Jack, a man, useless article.

Her mother sat on the white wrought-iron garden seat that was there for ornamentation rather than for sitting on. She was not interested in horticulture. Gardens were settings, merely. She would sometimes look at stately home gardens in glossy magazines and say, 'Why can't ours look like that?' preferring not to realize that such seductive landscapes were the result of toil and sweat.

'This heat!' she said, yawning and fanning herself with a copy of the *Watchtower* that a forceful Jehovah's Witness had sold to Aunt Mu. 'It's too good to last.' Good things never lasted; that was the nature of life. Even though, for a month, they had sweated gently during successive breathless evenings and, in the dark blue dusks, Aunt Dolly had watered her verdant grass. This was against the law; everyone else's lawns were scorched yellow.

Aunt Mu brewed a pot of tea and they drank it outside. A song-thrush came to land on the lawn and rhapsodized for a second or two before Aunt Dolly sent it on its travels with a wave of her arm. They conversed in murmurs, intermingled with the murmurs that issued from next door's pigeon-loft. 'That cooing,' Aunt Dolly said, 'will eventually drive me insane. One day I'll go in there and I'll wring those wretched birds' necks.' She might do it, too. Once she had drowned a litter of kittens in the dolly-tub because of a neighbour's squeamishness. The child had glimpsed these unfortunates: new-born, veiled still, going mutely to their doom. She had seen the mother cat, bereft, distraught, mewing. She realized then that Aunt Dolly, just like Mrs Spencer, could be ruthless, that her hand could not be stayed once her mind was made up. Vacillation had no place in her scheme of things. She was certain, direct, unstoppable.

As once her mother had been. But no longer. Lately, she couldn't be certain of her mother's next move, whether she would leave the dishes in the sink and rush out to buy herself a new frock, or put one of the heavy 78 records on the old wind-up gramophone and sit listening to it for hours on end, the washing and the ironing and the cleaning waiting in silent reproach. The records were mostly of gentlemen with foreign accents and a lot of breath singing about sparkling eyes and gardenias. They were very old, the records – and the gentlemen too, she supposed – and sometimes the needle stuck in a groove and had to be lifted on to the next one. 'I'm only a strolling vagabond – abond – abond – abond.' This drove her mother to distraction. 'Everything antiquated, done for, past it,' she said, giving the instruments a vicious bang, and bruising her knuckles.

'And your holidays – will you be going to the relations?' asked Aunt Mu, passing a plate of scones.

'I expect so,' her father replied. 'Not much in the kitty for anything else.'

125

'There wouldn't be, would there?' her mother said. 'Not until you shape yourself and get promoted.'

'Maybe a few less frocks and fripperies and we might have managed a proper holiday.'

Aunt Dolly sat forward eagerly. Nothing like a good row. To relieve the monotony, the anticlimax of the first day back after a holiday.

Attempting to remedy her blunder, Aunt Mu compounded it; opened her mouth and put her foot into it again: 'Still,' she said, 'it's as well to know what you're going to. You don't run the risk of unpleasant surprises.'

'No,' her mother said. 'No, there's no danger of being taken by surprise. It's routine, my life. You could set your clock by it. In the spring I spring-clean, at Christmas I cook a turkey, and every summer I go for two weeks to the relatives in Doncaster, or Huddersfield or Halifax.'

'You're badly done to, you are,' Aunt Dolly said. She gathered mucus in her nose and dissipated it in a tremendous sniff. She had no patience with moaners, particularly those who had nothing to moan about.

Her mother rounded on her elder sister just as she used to do when she was a child and before she realized the futility of the battle. 'Am I never supposed to complain? Is that your exclusive prerogative? What's so marvellous about my life?'

'You've got a good husband, a nice home and a child,' Aunt Dolly said straight off, pat. Aunt Muriel nodded; it was true. 'You go to watch too many daft films,' Aunt Dolly said, 'filling your head with tommyrot. Life's not like that. Except perhaps for a few film stars. It's time you grew up, my girl.'

'We're really getting the home truths today, aren't we?' her mother said. 'Why do you always make me feel guilty? As though I shouldn't expect the same things as other people.'

'Which other people?' Aunt Dolly said. She knew, though: the people who lived in the huge houses by the park, the houses where lights shone until the early hours in the windows behind velvet curtains and sleek cars rolled up the driveways and ladies in fur coats drank sherry at six; the people who led luxurious and exciting lives. 'You've always been spoiled, that I do know.' So spoiled that she could never bear to be crossed. 'You'll regret it all your life,' Mother had said when she'd announced her intention of marrying Jack. Mother had begged, pleaded and threatened, and the more she'd begged, pleaded and threatened, the more determined to spite her Nancy had become.

'Don't let's fall out,' Aunt Mu said unhappily. She passed round the plate of scones again, as though food could neutralize anger. 'Those two sisters of mine,' Herbert had often said, and shaken his head. He had been a peaceable man, Herbert, quite unlike the rest of his family.

'Oh don't stop her,' her mother said. 'Let her get it off her chest. Not that it comes as any surprise, what she thinks of me.'

'You were always treated like Lady Muck,' Aunt Dolly said, 'and it gave you silly ideas. You can't deny it, can you?'

'Not if *you* say so.'

'I just think it's time you learned some sense. You're old enough now.'

'Pack it in, will you?' her father said. If there were faults to be found, *he'd* find them. 'You're too fond of minding other people's business, Dolly. Stirring up trouble.'

'Oh yes?' Aunt Dolly said. 'Oh yes?' The battle shifted its ground. 'If you don't mind being taken for a fool, that's your look-out. Far be it from me . . .'

'What the hell are you talking about?' her father said. He'd missed many of the salient points of the altercation.

127

He'd once tried a hearing-aid on the National Health, but had derived no benefit from it.

'I'm talking about those that have eyes to see and see not.'

When Aunt Dolly became belligerent she always sounded faintly biblical.

'You're never happy, are you?' her mother said, 'unless you're making somebody else miserable? No wonder you never found a man to marry you. A dog's life, he'd have had.'

'Being married isn't the be-all and end-all, you know. And maybe I was more particular than some I could mention. I'm quite happy as I am.'

'Of course,' her mother said, nodding over to Aunt Mu, 'of course. You've got *her* to act as your victim. She may stand for it, but I'm damn sure that I shan't.'

'Who could you mention?' her father asked Aunt Dolly. Like Ronnie Spencer, he tended to be a few sentences behind the rest of the company.

It was turning into a free-for-all. Aunt Mu stroked the child's hair, rhythmically, thought back to the time when she and Herbert had had their house in Laurel Crescent with everything just so and never a wrong word.

'I could mention a great deal if I had a mind to,' Aunt Dolly said. She adopted her enigmatic look, which she'd perfected a treat.

'Well you'd better get mentioning, then, hadn't you?' her father said. 'Do you mean that she could have picked better than me? Certainly she could. We all know that. But she didn't. So let's not hear any more about it, you evil-minded bitch.'

'Let's go into the house,' Aunt Mu said, 'and see if the pot plants are doing all right. Did you water them as I told you?' She was powerless to avert full-scale warfare; the important thing was that the child should

128

be removed before something was said that everybody would regret.

'I did water them,' the child said. 'I knew she'd play Hamlet with you for forgetting to remind me, if I didn't.'

They inspected the African violets and the cinerarias and the Busy Lizzies. Aunt Mu touched her on the shoulder, hesitantly. She said, 'You know, Veronica, people say a lot of things they don't mean, in the heat of the moment.' Her face was kind and dear, and sometimes you wanted to lose yourself in her bosom, but there was loyalty at stake, and, besides, was comfort all that you wanted? The child looked away, resolutely. Please God, let her not say any more, she prayed. Please God, don't let her think that I'm old enough now for some sort of an explanation. Let her just carry on as she always has done, as though nothing untoward is happening.

'We're going now.' Her mother stood on the back doorstep. She rubbed at her eyes with a screwed-up handkerchief. Her cheeks were blotched with red patches and the thin wrinkled skin around her eyes was puffy. 'How do you stick it?' she said to Aunt Mu. 'Day in, day out?'

'I've got used to her. We all have our funny ways. She's concerned for you.'

Her mother ignored the last comment. 'Funny ways!' she said. It was no use talking to Muriel, who always behaved with impartiality, saw good in everyone.

'She talks to me as though I was a child,' she said when they were on their way home.

'You should ignore her. She likes getting people worked up. Haven't you realized that by now?'

They had reached a wary kind of truce, her mother and father. They had joined forces against the convenient common enemy, Aunt Dolly.

'I am a married woman with a child,' her mother said, as if to convince herself. 'I do as I like.'

But when she came upstairs to tuck the child into bed, she hugged her very close and covered her face with kisses. Somewhere there lay a desperate need for reassurance: I *am* a grown-up woman and a good mother. Tell me that I am.

The child lay still and endured this histrionic display of maternal affection. There was no way in the world that she could give her mother the reassurance that she needed.

Sometimes, and for no apparent reason, Margaret Rose withdrew the precious gift of her company. She and the child would confront one another on the threshold of the Spencers' back door and she'd say, in the manner of Miss Otis's butler, 'I'm not playing with you today.'

'Why not?'

'Don't want to. Goodbye.' And the door would be closed in her face.

Today was such a day. The hot, still afternoon stretched before her. Another ridge of high pressure built up over the Atlantic. At Woodham's, Aunt Dolly sat down in the office and struggled her feet out of her shoes and then came out and tore a strip off Praxted for doing the very same thing, but in full view of the customers. In the Marine Gardens, Mr Spencer lowered himself into a vacant deckchair and kept a wary eye out for the ticket-collector while he listened to 'Your hundred favourite tunes' as rendered by the resident orchestra. At four o'clock he would report to the manager of a firm of armature winders on the outskirts of town and take part in another fruitless interview.

Her mother was on tiptoe in front of the mirror. She was painting her face: vanishing cream, Vaseline, creme puff, and Sugar Plum lipstick. She spat into a small flat

130

box of black stuff, rubbed a little brush into it and applied it to her eyelashes. Her hand was trembling and she smudged black into the wrong places. 'Damn,' she said, and spat on her handkerchief. 'What are you doing here? I thought you were going to the Spencers'.'

'She won't play with me.'

'Oh God,' her mother said, pausing with the brush halfway to her eyelid. She was using a great deal of bad language lately. 'It's every time that I want to go somewhere, something crops up.'

'Where do you want to go?'

'I want to go to Carrie Mortimer's. I do like a *little* time to myself. If it isn't a crime.' She slammed the flat box and the creme puff and the lipstick on to the mantelpiece.

The child's silence said: 'What's stopping you? Why are you taking it out on me? I can't be held responsible for Margaret Rose's whims and fancies.'

'You'd better go round to your Aunt Muriel's,' her mother said. 'I don't want to leave you here by yourself. I'd never hear the last of it.' Terrible things could happen to children left alone in the house. They could set fire to themselves with matches, cut themselves open with carving knives, overturn paraffin heaters, open the door to staring-eyed maniacs. 'I'll drop you off on the way.' She undid the buttons on her frock, shrugged it off her shoulders, shook it to the ground and stepped out of it, undid her suspenders and pulled off her stockings. Laid on the back of an armchair were a fresh pair of stockings, a pink rayon petticoat with lace on the bodice, a flowered cotton skirt cut on the bias, a very white cardigan knitted last winter by Aunt Mu, and the new blouse. 'Don't *watch* me,' her mother said as she donned these garments. She was all fingers and thumbs. She tore a piece of

131

skin from her hand on a recalcitrant zip and had to run for the Elastoplast before blood was spilt on her finery.

'Where does Carrie Mortimer *live*?' the child asked, fingering the blouse buttons. Carrie Mortimer was merely a name from her mother's girlhood.

'The other side of the recreation ground.' Her mother slipped off her ordinary workaday petticoat. She wore a brassière that made her chests look more pointed than they actually were. There were little clusters of blue veins at the top of her thighs and the skin around her midriff was very white and slightly pitted like the rind of a grapefruit.

The other side of the recreation ground embraced a good quarter of the town, included the middle-class, Japanese-cherry-blossom-lined crescents and avenues, the grey stone terraced railwaymen's houses and the canal shacks. 'Does she live by the canal?' She had always thought of Carrie Mortimer with her ruined good looks and her husband who drank as being a slum-dweller.

'No, of course she doesn't. Whatever gave you *that* idea? Now, are you ready? Are you *clean*? Tell your Aunt Muriel that I'll be back for tea.'

She rose on tiptoe again to the mirror to adjust her hat. Her hair had been disciplined into obedience with big steel curlers. She sighed. What she saw did not entirely correspond with what he expected to see, which was an eighteen-year-old face, a complexion that was enhanced by cosmetics rather than concealed by them.

The child smelled washing, heard the old groaning mangle as Aunt Mu turned its rollers over pillow-slips and towels and anti-macassars. Aunt Mu would let her iron handkerchiefs and play with the starch. She enjoyed that. But not this afternoon. The heat made one restless. Her customary sense of obedience forsook

her, and she turned from the gate. She would collect
her mended bicycle from the shed at home, ride it into
town, and buy a forbidden and therefore delicious
ice-cream from the cart of the old Italian who looked
as though he never washed anything, least of all his
hands.

Her bicycle was propped against a defunct oil stove
and a gate-legged table that her father had bought for
ten bob from a chap at work and that her mother had
said was riddled with woodworm, and trust him to be
taken in. She edged into the shed gingerly, for fear of
spiders and disgusting forms of insect life. There was
one small cross-barred window at the front, but at the
back it was very dark. She heard a scratching noise
and backed away to the door. Mice were only slightly
less terrifying than insects. The scratching was followed by a sound that was, unmistakably, that of a
human being, sniffing up nasal mucus. And she knew
then, as her legs turned to water, her body was
overwhelmed by the paralysis of utter resignation, that
it had happened at last, as she knew it must someday:
he had arrived, the composite character of her nightmares: the man who lay in wait for little girls, with a
pocketful of sweets and a mind that was twisted.
During the few seconds that elapsed between seeing
the blurred white face and recognizing it, she offered
herself up to her long-suspected destiny. Margaret
Rose would have screamed and run. The child stood
and waited. To fight, to resist the inevitable, was not
in her nature.

'You mad raving idiot!' Her heart resumed its
beating, at a terrific rate. 'You loony! You frightened
me to death.'

The face, pale and scrofulous, belonged to Ronnie
Spencer. He gawped at her. 'What on earth are you
doing at the back of our shed?'

133

'Hiding. Waiting till the coast's clear.' He stood up and climbed over the mildewed sacks. She stepped back in case he had woodlice about his person.

'Who are you hiding from?'

'Her.' He jerked his head in the general direction of Jubilee Villas. As he came closer to the light she saw that a proportion of the area of the right side of his face was swollen and discoloured. Deep purple. Tyrrhenian purple.

'Did she hit you?'

He nodded.

'Why?'

'She got her hair off. That pig said I'd mucked up her bike.'

That pig was Margaret Rose.

'Said I'd bust the dynamo. I'd never rotten touched it. I wouldn't touch her rotten bike.'

'What did she hit you with?' she inspected his cheek. His right eye had receded into the puffed flesh.

'She'd been ironing. She chucked it at us.'

The child gasped. 'Was it hot?'

'No.'

Still, you could *kill* someone doing that. A much worse state of affairs than a beating with Mr Spencer's leather belt.

'I'm off now, anyway,' he said.

'Off back to the Spencers'?'

'No,' he said. 'Off back to me mam.'

'But your mother's not fit. You *said*.'

'She might be. Now. Any road up, I'm not staying there. Will you lend us some money?'

'I haven't *got* any money. Except in the Building Society. And they won't let me draw it out. They have to have my parents' signatures. Haven't you got any pocket money?'

He looked at her as though he didn't know the meaning of the words.

134

They were stymied. And then she remembered. 'Wait there a minute.'

The blue League of Pity box, egg-shaped, lay on the mantelpiece in her bedroom. You took a knife, slid it into the slot, poked around until you located a coin and then, with your tongue between your teeth, you guided it out. It took twenty-five minutes until the last halpenny of the eight shillings and threepence-halfpenny tinkled on to the rest of the money in a heap on her bed.

Ronnie didn't comment on the length of time she'd been away. She had thought often that for him time passed at a different, personal rate. 'How much is it to Manchester?' she said. 'How much is the train fare?'

'Don't know.'

He was quite hopeless. 'It won't be more than eight and threepence-halfpenny, will it?' she said, handing him the money. He trickled the coins through his fingers. 'Shouldn't think so,' he said. 'Why didn't you ask Charlie for the money?' Charlie would surely have been the obvious person to borrow from.

'I went round to the boarding house, but he wasn't there.'

'But he said that he was going to get some kip this afternoon.' A good kip, he'd said, with the Do Not Disturb notice hung on the doorknob. 'Shift me hangover,' he'd said, pulling at the mauve skin under his eyelids. 'Never take up boozing, Princess. Take my tip.'

'Well, he wasn't. *She* said he'd gone out in that hired car.'

'Will you get on at the Halt, or go into town to the main station?' she asked, relishing her rôle as mastermind of Ronnie's escape. 'I should go into town. You're less likely to be seen. You only want a single, you know, then you might have something left for a cup of tea.' The idea of Ronnie sitting drinking tea in the buffet like a real traveller was most incongruous. 'I'd come with you,' she said, 'but the two of us are more noticeable than one.' The railway station with its noises of escaping steam and shunting engines frightened her. 'It's platform three, you know.' He was stupid enough to get on the wrong train.

'OK,' he said, pocketing the money. 'I'll let you have it back. Me mam'll send you a postal order.'

She watched him down the road, round the corner and out of sight. His bravery, his boundless optimism, astounded her. How did he know that his mam was still in the same place, let alone that she would willingly buy and send a postal order? It was the most courageous act she'd ever witnessed.

Chapter Thirteen

THEY HAD HIM hemmed in a corner. He was the prisoner in the dock without defence counsel. He was accused, tried and condemned before ever he set a foot inside the room. Running away was a terrible crime, no matter what you had to put up with. No circumstances could detract from the terribleness of the crime.

'What's the matter with the lad?' Mr Spencer appealed to the assembled company. 'He'll be up before the Juvenile Court again, and then where will we be?'

Mrs Spencer pulled her kimono around the bones of her frame. Yes, she had struck him, but not with the iron, never with the iron, the little liar. He drove her to distraction with his defiance, his sulky ways, his jealousy of Margaret Rose.

'You know where you'll go next time, don't you?' Mr Spencer said. 'You'll go to an approved school, or Borstal, that's where. And that'll be the end of you.' He spoke these words with a kind of relish as though sorrow and retribution and the knowledge of them lay well within his experience. 'I wouldn't mind,' he said, as though wishing to be thoroughly impartial, 'but his mother isn't even in Manchester any more. Nobody's heard of her for over six months.'

'But, Ronnie,' her mother said, 'when you lived with

your mother you were always running away. Why go back there?'

The child was ashamed of her mother's lack of perception. Ronnie had run away from his mother *before* he knew how very much worse it would be at the Spencers'. You had to have somewhere to run *to*, and so you chose the lesser of the evils.

'Where did he get the money from,' Mrs Spencer said, 'is what *I* should like to know?' The incriminating train ticket had been found in his pocket when Mr Spencer collared him beside the speak-your-weight machine in the station foyer. Mr Spencer had been taken short on his way home and made a detour to the station Gents to empty his bladder. If it hadn't been for Mr Spencer's bladder and the ill-timing of the trains, Ronnie would have been away – to nothing.

'If you ask me,' Mrs Spencer said, 'I think he stole that money. Now I come to think of it, I've noticed that coppers have been missing from my purse for a long time.'

The child's heart began to beat to the same rhythm as it had done when she'd seen the face at the back of the shed. She must own up. If she didn't then Ronnie would be suspected of stealing and Borstal would be inevitable. There was one on the outskirts of the town. It contained what her father called the real hard cases. Compared with that establishment, the Farm School was kindergarten.

'Where did the money come from, lad?' Mr Spencer asked.

He said nothing. The puffiness on his cheek had diminished. The bruise was turning yellow. Ochre.

'I've told you,' Mr Spencer said. 'It'll be more trouble. And then where will we be?' he repeated.

Up the creek without a paddle, Charlie would have said. Why wasn't Charlie *here*? He was the one person who would have spoken up, who would have dared to accuse Mrs Spencer to her face of child cruelty.

'Well?' Mr Spencer said.

The child opened her mouth to speak.

Ronnie looked straight at her and said, 'Charlie give us the money. I ran errands for him and he give us the money. I saved it up.'

'Ah,' Mrs Spencer said. This syllable stood for: 'I might have known he'd be at the back of it.' Her mother's already red face reddened more. She had developed a sort of rash thing on her chest too, as though she'd been scratched by hundreds of little bristles. 'I'm sure Charlie didn't intend you to use the money for running away,' she said. 'I'm sure he gave it to you with the best of intentions.'

The child and Margaret Rose sat next to each other on the window seat. Margaret Rose hummed the *Teddy Bears' Picnic* and snapped the blind cord back and forth against the window. She couldn't understand why they hadn't simply let him run away and good riddance. All the wrong people were allowed to breed, the child thought. They should have tests for it, like the eleven-plus. Unless having babies was something that happened of its own volition. And Margaret Rose had said that it wasn't, had said that men and women had to do things to each other first. Why then didn't they make sure that they really wanted a baby before they did those things?

'I think he's sorry for the worry he's caused, aren't you, Ronnie?' her mother said. No worry had been caused. Until Mr Spencer found him, no one had noticed his absence. He stood in the corner, silently, at bay, refusing to move a muscle even to sniff up his catarrh. She was overwhelmed by his honourable refusal to implicate her. She had not come across such uprightness outside the pages of literature: Sydney

139

Carton doing a far, far better thing; Sir Galahad, his good blade carving the casques of men.

'Shall we call the matter closed then?' Mr Spencer said 'Depending on future good behaviour?'

Mrs Spencer tied three knots in the cord of her kimono. Nothing had been resolved. Things stood as they did before. Her spirit yearned for the Weston-super-Mare of twenty years ago: the stained glass in the fanlight above the door, the bell-pull, the little maid coming to answer it, Mother with her petit-point, Daddy reciting *The Lays of Ancient Rome*, Reginald and Gwen in a duet at the piano.

'Why don't you get the doctor to give you something for your nerves?' her mother said. Mrs Spencer had once confided that her nerves were largely due to Mr Spencer, who couldn't perform adequately any more. 'He is no longer a proper husband to me, she had said.

'I've asked him,' Mrs Spencer said. 'He tells me to take things easy, take a holiday, take up a new interest. I used to have my eurhythmics, but I can't seem to concentrate these days. Too many worries intrude.'

Mr Spencer studied his hands. He might get a job, just to spite her, on the refuse wagon. They were crying out for men. That would be more of a disgrace than the dole every Friday.

'Well, if everything's settled,' her mother said, 'We'll be off.' The street lamps had come on all along the road, somebody's night-scented stocks wafted in through the window, the child – who seemed to know more than she was telling – yawned and exposed her tonsils.

They walked home to resume the meal they'd just begun when Margaret Rose came round on her bicycle to say, 'My mum says will you come? There's trouble.' Her mother had collected her from Aunt Mu's, un-aware that she had been there a shorter time than she should have been. She asked the child questions, but didn't listen to the answers, opened a tin of sardines, said she couldn't be bothered with cooking. Some of the curls had fallen out of her hair and most of the cosmetics had worn off her face.

'The nights are drawing in,' she said as they walked home. Distant cars hooted, and the local diesel train clattered along the embankment. The child thought that phrase, the nights are drawing in, one of the most melancholy in the language. It meant the end of the summer, the end of the year. For the year didn't begin in January; it began in September, when you moved up a form in school, wearing a fresh uniform and carrying a new satchel.

'How was Carrie Mortimer?' she asked. However she was, she seemed to have had a most favourable effect on her mother's demeanour.

'Fine. We had a good long talk about old times. I shall probably see a lot more of her now.' Her mother had unconsciously picked up the tune that Margaret Rose had been humming: 'If you go down to the woods today, you're sure of a big surprise.'

'I thought you said her husband was horrible and that's why you didn't see her so much.'

'Oh he's improved a lot. Settled down. They're quite happy now. She's looking a lot better in herself.'

There was a Charlie-type retort to that one, something about looking a lot better out of yourself. Sometimes he strung together a series of idiot phrases: 'Speaking myself, personally . . . I turned round and said to him and he turned round and said to me . . . of a Saturday I go to the flicks . . . of a Friday I wash my hair.' Her mother said he was wicked, and anyway, what was so funny? Everybody talked like that.

'Poor Ronnie,' her mother said. 'Something should be done about that child. Surely there must be foster homes where he could stay during the holidays?'

'He's been in two, and the National Children's Home.'

He'd imparted this information in between struggles with the breast stroke in the mornings on the beach. As well as running away from his mother, he had run away from two foster homes *and* the National Children's Home. 'Absconded,' he called it proudly. 'Where did you abscond *to*, old son?' Charlie had asked him. Once to Blackpool, he'd said, where he'd helped a man with the donkeys and slept in a shelter on the South Pier; the other times only as far as the local park. He'd fed the ducks with bread that people had discarded and, at dusk, the keeper had asked him his business. The same keeper each time, who'd brewed a pot of tea in his hut and given him a cup before calling the police.

The child stuck close to her mother. Shadows loomed from the gateways, a little breeze shuddered in the tree foliage around the gas-lamps. 'For all the bears that ever there was,' her mother sang, 'de dum de dum de dum de de dum, today's the day the teddy bears have their picnic.'

It was a catchy tune and her mother couldn't get it out of her head. It made a pleasant change from the foreign gentlemen with sobbing voices on the 78 records, bringing little white gardenias, dreaming they dwelt in marble halls, leaving flowers on the grass.

'I dreamt that I tickled my grandfather's balls with a little sweet oil and a feather,' Charlie sang, and her mother said, 'Will you *please* hush? Honestly!'

'What's the matter? My old lady used to sing me to sleep with little ditties like that: I'd like to sleep with Nazimova, I'd dum-de-dum all night and then roll her over.' He took the records out of their paper covers and squinted at them. 'Mama mia,' he said, 'Count John Macormack! Cavan O'Connor! Really up-to-date, aren't you? Why don't you donate this lot to the museum? They'd go a treat on the Edison phonograph.'

'You talk a lot of nonsense,' her mother said. She bent her head over his shirt. She was sewing little pearl buttons on the cuffs. He looked like nobody owned him, she said.

'I wish we had Venetian blinds,' she said. Venetian blinds were the latest thing; all the houses in Highview Road and Westmacott Gardens had them. The sun illuminated every patch of dust, every smear. The leaves of the geraniums on the window sill turned red and then brown because each person in the house assumed that another had watered them. In the larder a square of butter melted into a rancid pool, despite the bowl of water beneath it and the cover of muslin above it. The top of the milk yellowed from cream to cheese. The weight of the dead threatened to dislodge the fly-paper from the drawing-pin that held it to the ceiling. 'Dolly says we need a thunderstorm.' Her mother pulled the fabric of her dress away from her armpits. She was going through sticks of Odorono at a tremendous rate. 'She says we'll end up with cholera if this goes on.'

'Dolly's a sado-masochist,' Charlie said, opening the paper at the racing page.

'What's a sado-masochist?' It sounded to be along the lines of scrofulous and pestilence.

'Somebody who isn't happy until she's unhappy and everybody else with her.'

Yes, that was Aunt Dolly, to a t.

'Come and pick me a winner.'

She chose *Garden of Paradise*, eleven to two, in the two-thirty. He said that he would include it as part of his Mug's Double; the other horse was called *Paradise Island* and the odds against that one were quoted at fifteen to one. Charlie said that if they both came up he'd be away and laughing. 'When the bell goes,' he said. 'they're racing. Do you fancy a stroll?'

A stroll as far as Sydney Barnes, Turf Accountant, and Yates's Wine Lodge. A turf accountant was not a person who measured the land, that much she had learned, any more than Yates's Wine Lodge was a temple for the conversion of the heathen, a place where people gathered to sign the pledge against the demon drink, as Charlie had pretended.

He brought her out a packet of crisps. She searched for the salt and suddenly felt a hand yanking her urgently into the adjacent amusement arcade. 'Sorry about that, Princess,' Charlie said, 'but there's somebody over there I could do without seeing at this particular moment.'

She knew the feeling; she could have lived quite happily without seeing Margaret Rose. She had spilt her crisps over the floor. She bent to pick them up; it was clean dirt; her mother worried too much, but he told her to leave them. He had his back to the road. He was feeding a machine with pennies. A mechanical grabbing hand hovered above an assortment of hideous plastic rings and tie-pins and balls of bubble-gum. Every time he delivered a penny into its depths, the machine rewarded him with a gew-gaw which he swept out of the tray and into his pocket without pausing to inspect it. He didn't notice the man whom he had not succeeded in avoiding until the man put a hand on his shoulder.

'Charlie,' the man said, 'you need glasses?'

He was a big, heavily-built man wearing, despite the heat, a thick overcoat with shoulder-pads and a dark blue trilby.

Charlie didn't take his eyes off the feast of rubbish and the device that obligingly captured pieces of it for him. 'What happened to Norwich?' he said.

'Got moved, didn't I?' the man said. 'We do, you know.'

'Oh I know,' Charlie said. 'Got the stripes up too, I dare-say.'

The man put a penny into the machine and won a badge that said 'Forever True'. 'Here you are, girlie,' he said, handing it to her. 'Pin it on your frock. Yours?' he said, looking from the top of her head back to Charlie.

'Christ, no,' Charlie said.

'You always did pick 'em with kids,' the man said. 'Like to be a father-figure, is that it?'

'I wouldn't know,' Charlie said, banging the glass on top of the machine, 'what a father-figure was.'

'Mine's coming on ten,' the man said. His short blunt fingers were stained tan with cigarette smoke, his nails were bitten to the quick. 'Upheaval, you know. New school, new friends. The wife's none too pleased about it either. Having to leave the relations.'

Charlie put his hand over his heart. 'I'll be needing me handkerchief shortly,' he said.

The man took off his hat, scratched at his bald patch, and replaced it. 'Yes, well,' he said, 'just so long as we know where we stand.'

'I know where I stand. And it shouldn't be here. It should be at home for my dinner.'

'Cosy,' the man said. 'Thought you might be going to work.'

'I don't have to, do I?'

'Never thought that was your style, Charlie.'

'That's one thing you wouldn't know about – Mr Davidge – style,' Charlie said. 'Now, if you'll excuse me.'

'Certainly,' the man said, 'certainly,' and stepped back. 'Don't let me detain you.'

'You should be on the halls,' Charlie said. 'Nobody ever told you that? The Stooge. You were made for it.'

'Don't insult me, Charlie.' The man had a hurt look in his eyes. 'I'll be seeing you around then?'

'I wouldn't bank on it,' Charlie said. H took hold of the child's hand and hurried her away. He left his latest winnings in the metal tray. He didn't even say goodbye.

'I needn't have bothered, need I?' her mother said after they'd got home and he'd left most of his meal on the side of the plate. 'Too much liquid refreshment, is that it? Or are you sickening for something?' Her lips were very pink and shiny. She owned three lipsticks now, hidden at the back of a drawer, together with a round thing wrapped in tissue paper that the child had not yet had the chance to unwrap.

He lit a cigarette, tapped his ash on the edge of the plate. 'Have you ever had that dream,' he said, 'where you're running hell for leather and getting nowhere, where your legs seemed weighted down?'

The child had had it, often.

'Well, I feel that way just at the moment,' he said.

'Somebody's walking over your grave,' her mother said.

'What exactly does that *mean*? I've always wondered.'

'I've no idea, come to think of it. Oh, don't let's be *morbid*. Not when I've never been so happy since I can't remember when.'

'You're right, Nancy,' he said, 'it behoves us to make the most of it. Something about wine and roses. I remember that from one of the days I went to school.'

Mr Davidge, the child thought, looked exactly the sort of person who would walk over your grave – in great big boots.

Chapter Fourteen

SHE HAD EXHAUSTED the contents of the shelves in the children's section of the public library. She wanted to ask if she could transfer to the adults', but she didn't dare. In the adults' were books with stuff in them that children under fourteen weren't supposed to know about. That wasn't the attraction – even though she was anxious to explode the myth about men and women and bouncing around – the plain fact was that she knew a good deal of the children's section almost off by heart.

Margaret Rose selected a Famous Five and a Secret Seven. She'd probably had them both out before, but she never read enough of a book to be certain. 'Come *on*,' she said impatiently, as the child hesitated between *The Master of Ballantrae* (again) and *The Black Tulip* (again). A book was a book: two stiff covers containing pages of writing that you read in bed for ten minutes or so before you fell asleep.

The assistant stamped the date on the books and they went out to the foyer where Ronnie was staring at the public notice board: announcements of meetings, the Scottish Dancing Club, the Theosophical Society, the Townswomen's Guild, extension lectures at the Witnesses Hall: 'King Arthur: Man or Myth'; 'The Spinning Jenny: A History of Mechanization'; 'Druidical Stones in England and Wales: Their Significance'.

'They have those books with pictures and big letters,' Margaret Rose said loudly, 'for dopes who can't read.'

It's always those with the least upstairs that shout the loudest, her father often said. It was his own version of empty vessels making the most sound.

'He hasn't got a library ticket,' the child said, 'so he can't get books anyway.'

'No,' said Margaret Rose triumphantly, as though failure to own a library ticket stamped one as a complete social inadequate.

They came out of the door, skirting the padlocked bicycles and the dogs tethered to dog posts. A faint breeze carried with it the odour of rotting shellfish. A group of small children, naked to the waist, played In and Out the Dusky Bluebells. The sun blazed.

'You'll miss your precious Charlie, won't you?' Margaret Rose said. 'When you go on your holidays? My mum says it's a funny business. She says people have eyes in their heads. She says there's no smoke without fire and it doesn't take much to put two and two together.'

'My mum' talked in riddles, like the Sphinx. 'What does she mean?' the child asked.

'Ask me no questions and I'll tell you no lies,' Margaret Rose said smugly. That was pure Mrs Spencer too.

Somehow, one couldn't say 'On your bicycle' to Margaret Rose; either she was totally impervious to insult, or she would be sure to get her own back, ten-fold. Charlie had hurt her pride and Charlie would suffer for it. He was a grown man and Margaret Rose merely a child, but she would find some way. In matters of vengeance and retribution she was all powerful. Little dried-up leaves shivered on the trees, and the child shivered too. She hadn't a clue as to what Margaret Rose could *do*, but do she undoubtedly would. She was biding her time, spying on the swimming lessons from the shelter of a sand dune, waiting her opportunity. When she did strike it would be suddenly, and at the moment you least expected it.

'Are you coming to the pictures this afternoon?' she said.

'No. Not this afternoon,' the child replied.

'Why not?'

'I'm going somewhere else.'

'Where?'

'Never you mind.'

'You might as well tell me,' she said. 'I'll find out anyway.'

This was true. One might as well try to keep a secret from God, or the Devil.

'We're playing pitch and putt.'

'We who?'

We who. Are about to die, salute you. It said that at the beginning of chapter seven in the Latin primer, above a picture of a gladiator engaging in an unequal struggle with a lion. Margaret Rose's knowledge of correct grammatical construction was nil.

'Ronnie and I and my mother. And Charlie.'

Margaret Rose tore a privet leaf into shreds. 'Why didn't you tell me? What a mean and rotten thing to do.'

'I didn't think you'd want to come. You never want to come swimming in the mornings. And, besides, you play it in pairs, pitch and putt. You can't have an odd number.'

'Come swimming!' Margaret Rose said scornfully. 'As if I want to be with you two babies, splashing about and paddling.'

'Charlie can swim. Better than you.'

'Charlie, Charlie, Charlie. I wouldn't want to go anywhere with *him*. My mum says he's a shady

149

character, nobody knows anything about him. She says your mum's getting herself talked about and she should be more concerned for your welfare. She says a man took two little girls out to the headland not long ago and did things to them.'

'What things?' Don't tell me. Don't *tell* me.

But she did. In detail. Using ugly colloquial words to describe anatomical parts. They were the same things that the imaginary boyfriend had done to Margaret Rose. Except that in that particular case they had been pleasurable; when men took little girls to the headland and engaged in the same activities, they were not.

'Quite frankly,' Margaret Rose said, 'I couldn't care less.' In her voice you could hear echoes of the upper echelons of Weston-super-Mare, the cups and rosettes on the bedroom walls, the garden parties and golf dinners, the dog shows and Blue Bird balls and Auntie Gwen playing *Für Elise* on the baby grand. And the child had an inkling of how Mrs Spencer had come to be so wicked. To come down from all that to Mr Spencer shuffling his feet in the dole queue would be enough to turn anyone wicked.

'I couldn't care less,' Margaret Rose said, 'but, quite frankly, if you think that I shall ever associate with you again, you must be raving mad.'

'Is that a threat or a promise?'

But she wasn't feeling nearly as insouciant as she sounded.

'Fore!' Charlie shouted at the top of his lungs. 'Fore!' And she and Ronnie closed their eyes and cringed because the last time that her mother had swung her club she'd missed the ball entirely and narrowly missed doing Charlie what he called 'a terrible mischief'.

'Ugh,' her mother said, swung wildly, sent a shower of sand flying down the fairway, missed the ball again, and collapsed with laughter, bent double, tears streaming down her cheeks, making channels in the Creme Puff.

Henry Cotton, Charlie called her, said she was as much use as a one-legged tightrope walker, said that, with her mother as his partner, he should be given a three-hole advantage. Ronnie and the child were leading by forty-three strokes. Ronnie pitched straight and true; the child putted with a deadly accuracy. During the long peaceful afternoon, with the sun beating through her tee-shirt and blisters forming on her hands and heels – she had potatoes in both socks; her mother hadn't done much darning lately – she could overlook his appearance, his catarrh and his habits and accept the fact that, in the sphere of golf, they made a perfect team.

'Let's change over,' Charlie said. 'Let somebody else be lumbered with my partner. Come on, somebody, play the white man.'

'No, no,' they remonstrated. There were only three more holes to play. Her mother trod on one of his feet with both of her own. He howled. 'Not content with endangering me manhood,' he said, 'she tries to cripple me into the bargain,' and grabbed her round the waist and held her tight.

'Come on,' Ronnie said, dancing up and down beside the tee. He was anxious to demonstrate his newly-discovered prowess.

Charlie's hands fell slowly from her mother's waist. 'All right, Colonel,' he said. 'You're a real slave-driver, aren't you? The rest of this exercise has become what they call a mere formality, a foregone conclusion. Just as well I didn't put me money where me mouth is.' He'd said they'd murder the opposition; he'd said there hadn't been a better partnership since Alcock and Brown, since Debenham and Freebody.

She and Ronnie handed in their clubs, tucked their score cards into their shorts pockets, grinned and swaggered through the turnstile. Charlie tore *his* score card into tiny pieces and threw them into the air. He said to her mother, 'I think we'd make a better twosome at some other activity, don't you?'

Her mother had packed a picnic tea. They carried the basket across the beach to the headland. The child peered fearfully around the sandhills, but there were no men doing bad things to little girls to be seen. The tide rippled in slowly. The sky along the horizon line was violet-coloured. 'Your Dolly's dismal premonition looks like being fulfilled,' Charlie said. 'There's going to be the mother and father of a storm. You should see Myra's barometer. Not to mention her seaweed and her pine-cones.'

Her mother spread the rug over the spiky grass, began to unpack the food. 'Like I said, I knew it was too good to last.'

'We've had a good innings.'

'That's how we have to think of it, is it?' she said, distributing paper plates and cups, unscrewing the Thermos flask.

He opened a bottle of Worthington. Foam frothed over the top of it and ran on to his arm. He licked it off. 'I was talking about the weather,' he said, 'the old currant bun.'

'Oh. I wasn't.'

He leaned his head back and raised the bottle to his lips. You could see a series of swallows taking place in the brown column of his neck. He wiped his mouth with his hand. 'I wasn't thinking of scrubbing round it,' he said. 'I didn't think you were either.'

'Not us,' she said. 'Other people, other things.'

'Sod them.'

'It's all very well to talk like that. As Dolly says, closing your eyes doesn't make it go away.'

'Give us a sandwich and stop your miseries. What

will be, will be, as my old lady used to say. And she ought to have known.'

There were egg and cress sandwiches, a packet of marshmallows, slices of what Charlie called funeral cake (any kind of cake that wasn't wedding cake, he called funeral cake), two Mars Bars, beer for Charlie and a Thermos of lemon barley water for the rest of them. Ronnie pushed the sandwiches whole inside his mouth and masticated furiously. No one admonished him. They had realized that, both in the Farm School and at the Spencers', it was a case of grab it fast before somebody else grabbed it first. He took off his plimsolls and dug his feet into the cool damp sand. His toenails were long overdue for cutting; they had grown yellow and horny, like those of an animal. His fingernails were short enough. Like Mr Davidge, he bit them to the quick. She wondered what he would look like when he was grown up. Not so ugly. Surely? Maybe, with age, his features would level themselves out, match themselves up; he would not be afflicted with catarrh; his scrofulous sores would heal. She detached the chocolate coating, bit by bit, from the Mars Bar, delicately, with her teeth, until she was left with the perfectly rectangular centre of it. She took all her pleasures slowly, spinning them out, making them last. Not like the rest of them. Ronnie ate his Mars Bar in four bites, Charlie emptied his beer bottle in three swallows, even her mother had worn the new blouse so often that she was sick of the sight of it.

There was now a greenish tinge in the violet skyline. They were aware of sounds ceasing gradually: the breeze through the dune grass, the rustle of insects, the harsh cries that seemed to be ripped out of the throats of the circling seagulls.

'A deathly hush,' Charlie said. He made a crater in the sand and buried their litter: bottles, wrappings,

153

greaseproof paper. There was a big notice on the Esplanade telling you to take your litter home with you. The child obeyed it. Her blazer pockets were filled with sweet wrappers and bus tickets and pieces of break-time school bun. What was it you had to develop in order to disregard the orders of officialdom so blithely? As Margaret Rose did. And Charlie. 'Aren't I wicked?' he said. 'I'll be writing bum on the wall next.'

Ronnie found this remark highly amusing. Tears of mirth made clean channels down his face. 'Go on, laugh,' Charlie said. 'You'll wee less.' Which the child thought a pretty tasteless remark in view of the circumstances.

Charlie stretched back against the sandhill, screwed his eyes up against his cigarette smoke which rose perpendicular into the air. 'Well, Colonel,' he said, 'When's the big day? When do you have to report back?'

And, as the sun had disappeared from the sky, leaving only its shimmer to veil a glassy and ominous expanse of whiteness, so the laughter departed from Ronnie's face; all the little upward-turning lines turned downwards again, his eyes which had, for a moment, sparkled, dulled, like the sky. 'September the seventh,' he said and dug at the ribbed sand around his feet with a piece of driftwood.

'Oh-oh. Like that, is it? The devil and the deep blue sea. The frying pan and the fire. What's so bad about it?'

His words came in a torrent, as though the dam created by adenoids and catarrh and difficulty of expression had been sundered at last. She'd never heard him say so much at one go.

'They take the mickey out of us, the big lads, call us names and blame us for what I've never done. They make us write it out a hundred times and go up to the head and tell us your mam's a tart and miss supper and say you can't read nor write, you're daft and you want a knot tying in it. Cronshaw and Briggs, they punch you in the stomach and make you get them things. I don't give a sod.'

He paused for breath, blinked rapidly, moving his tongue around the inside of his mouth as though relishing this unfamiliar activity: speaking words one after the other to form a sentence, stringing the sentences together, in sequence.

'Oh surely, Ronnie,' her mother said, 'it can't be *that* bad. If you're bullied, you should report it to your teachers.'

In some ways her mother was mentally defective.

'And the animals!' her mother said. 'The countryside! Surely you enjoy all that?'

He didn't reply, just bent his head until it rested on his knees and scratched with his stick.

'Where is this place?' Charlie said. 'Stalag Nine?'

'In Cumberland.'

She closed her eyes and pictures formed behind her eyelids: a gaunt grey building with barbed wire around it in the style of the photograph of Dachau that she'd seen in a magazine; rows and rows of grey-suited urchins pacing the edges of its perimeter; green-grey fields and fells and sky and water, and sheep bleating an endless doleful chorus in the background.

'How would you like us to come up and visit you some weekend? We could hike across the moors. Very healthy. We could have a farmhouse tea: scones and cream and strawberry jam. You could show us around, introduce us to the landmarks.'

He raised his head an inch or so from his knees, swivelled his eyes in Charlie's direction. Charlie smoked calmly. 'It's not the end of the world, is it, Cumberland?' Charlie said. 'Some weekend. Square it with your old feller. Not that there'd be much squaring to do, is my guess. How does that sound?'

Glimmers of incipient expressions chased themselves across Ronnie's face: disbelief, incredulity, faint hope. Charlie continued to talk: 'Me and Nancy and the Princess. And Jack, too. Though Jack usually works on a Saturday, doesn't he? Still, there'd be the three of us. We could put up at one of those farm-houses.'

Her images of Cumberland altered drastically. Now she saw white stone, rose-smothered cottages, stretches of blue sky dotted with cirrhus clouds, huge bees with black velvet backs humming among clumps of heather.

Her mother's eyes were closed. All the muscles of her face had relaxed. Her mouth had fallen open: you could see two grey fillings and some bridgework among her teeth. She was not asleep, though. Her hands moved slowly, plaiting blades of grass, as Charlie's voice continued, talking of farmhouses and weekends away and the healthy air up on the moors.

'Do you mean it?' Ronnie's mouth was a straight line, but his eyes were eager.

'Course I mean it. What are friends for? You've not joined the French Foreign Legion. It's only a spit away, Cumberland.'

It was so simple. Charlie ironed out the complications, scorned them. All the 'what ifs' were knocked down at one blow. Friends could accomplish anything.

Her mother slipped the plaited bracelet of grass over her wrist, looked up at the sky under the shelter of her hand. 'D'you think it'll hold off?' she said anxiously. You could tell that her head was still filled with pictures of Cumberland, but her face was worried with more pressing problems. She had promised to visit Carrie Mortimer in the evening. Carrie Mortimer had summer 'flu and only her reprobate husband to look after her.

'I reckon so. Let's get back anyway, just in case. If you've got to go out tonight.' He jumped to his feet in one movement, clapped his hands together. 'Chop-chop, you lot. On your feet. Time to fold up our tents and steal away.'

The brilliance of the colours in the gardens hurt one's eyes: hard yellow laburnum, bright blue lobelia, green, green grass. Clouds were massing behind roofs and chimneys. The leaves on the trees curled inwards. Their footsteps echoed along the empty pavements. The child felt a headache forming, the pain small and compact between her eyebrows. Ronnie swung the picnic basket and dreamed of saying, 'My visitors are coming,' at the Farm School. Charlie whistled the repetitive and melancholy notes of the Harry Lime theme. Her mother walked agitatedly, darted little glances to the right and to the left. Aunt Dolly, in her kitchen, rubbed her feet, took two aspirin tablets, said, 'It's coming at last, thank goodness. I told you we needed a storm to bring it to a head, to clear the air.'

Chapter Fifteen

'YOU CAN'T BE right in your head,' her father said. 'It's going to throw it down. You'll get soaked. I thought you were afraid of the thunder, anyway. She's not paralysed, is she? She's only got the 'flu.'

Her mother's mouth was pursed as she applied the lipstick: Alexandra Rose. She pressed her lips together, said, 'She's feeling very ill. If I can't help a friend, it's a poor look-out. She'd do the same for me. Besides, it might not thunder. It might stop like this until morning. And a drop of rain never hurt anyone.'

Except me, the child thought. Rain must not be allowed to fall upon me for fear of bronchitis and pneumonia.

Her father sugared his tea. 'Just don't expect me to come and meet you when it's chucking it down cats and dogs,' he said.

'I expect no such thing. Don't you dare leave that child on her own in the house.'

'Don't talk wet. What d'you think I am? You delight in putting me in the wrong, don't you? You've a real hard nature, Nancy.'

'Good God, can't I go out for the evening without a song and dance? Do I have to ask permission? It's all right for you to spend every minute in the pub but when it comes to me and my friends, it's a different story, isn't it? You should have been around in the Middle Ages, then you could have locked me up and thrown away the key. Talk about the goose and the gander! I'm stuck in this house all day and every day. I never get a break.'

You story-teller, the child thought. You spent all afternoon playing pitch and putt.

'Oh, go if you're going,' her father said, 'and leave us in peace. Go and make Carrie Mortimer's life a misery.'

He looked towards the child for a word, a gesture, of support. The child ignored him, turned over a page of the *Junior Encyclopaedia*.

Her mother opened her handbag again and fiddled inside it. Her father rustled his newspaper and cleared his throat loudly and unnecessarily. Go, the child thought, go. Before the silence is exploded as the storm is about to explode the sky apart outside.

She went eventually, as though she would rather have stayed but something beckoned her out into the waiting streets.

They were making cocoa in the kitchen when the storm began. She closed her eyes while the first rumble of thunder gained momentum, rolled towards them and crashed directly above their heads. The cups rattled on their hooks. The fly-strip vibrated and twirled, its black cargo describing a full circle in the air. 'Told her, didn't I?' her father said. 'She always knows best. A deaf, dumb and blind man could have told you that it'd thunder before dark.'

She removed the metal clips from her hair, turned the mirror's face to the wall, took off her wristwatch and put it in the drawer, and, having divested herself of all these lightning-attracting objects, she joined her father at the window. The sky had now turned a full, rich purple. They watched sheet lightning flashing on and off like neon, a background to the jagged stabs of forked lightning that ripped through the clouds. The focal point of the storm crept closer. Between the lightning and the thunder they held their breath. A million mad drummers beat a frenzied tattoo above the rooftops.

'She won't set out in this,' her father said, 'not if she's any sense.' Little droplets of sweat had formed behind his ears and run down to the fold in his neck. 'I *told* her she oughtn't to go out.'

There was a moment of silence, and then a sound like a long-drawn-out gentle sigh, as though the world were exhaling its breath, and a second or two afterwards, with a noise like pistol shots, the rain hurled itself against the corrugated iron roof of the coal-shed.

She stepped back from the window. The force of the downpour was such that she felt it might stave in the glass. 'My!' her father said admiringly. The garden was awash; pansies and carnations were beaten to the ground; the scorched grass absorbed all the moisture that it could and then was defeated, waterlogged; the gutters over-flowed.

She wiped a clear patch on the steamed-up window. Her mother would be terrified. She wouldn't be much use to Carrie Mortimer in her hour of need. It would be Carrie Mortimer who'd have to apply cool hand to fevered brow and so forth. As she was thinking about Carrie Mortimer rising from her sick bed to minister to her mother, a white blurred shape flashed past the window. Whatever, whoever, it was banged on the back door. 'Who the hell can that be in this weather?' her father said and went to answer it. Into the scullery, dripping quarts of water on to the floor, stepped Mr Spencer. He was wearing a vast rubberized macintosh that had holes punched under the armpits, for sweat to escape, she supposed. His hair was plastered to his narrow skull and looked more grey than black, more in keeping with the colour of the stubble on his chin. As he entered the kitchen, his feet squelched in his patent shoes and his white hands hung at his sides, two appendages that had an alien, twitching life of their own.

'She's not here, is she?' he said, looking into each of the four corners of the room, shaking the rain out of his eyes.

'Nancy?' her father said. 'No. She's gone to that stupid Carrie Mortimer's. I told her, I said . . .'

'No, not your wife,' Mr Spencer said. Margaret *Rose*.'

'No, she's not here. What's up?'

'She went out,' Mr Spencer said, 'on her bicycle. Above an hour ago. We begged her, pleaded with her, the wife and I, not to go. We said there was going to be a storm.'

The child pictured the pathetic spectacle of Mr and Mrs Spencer pleading with their only begotten eleven-year-old daughter.

'I've sent young Ronnie over to the recreation ground,' Mr Spencer said, 'told him to scout around there. I was wondering if you would give me some assistance. The wife is going spare. God alone knows where she's got to.'

The water in his eyes wasn't all rainwater. The hands that fiddled and poked were now raised, palm-upward, in a gesture of helplessness.

'I'd come like a shot, her father said, 'but Nancy's out and the child here . . .'

'Bring her round,' Mr Spencer said. 'She'll be company for the wife. She's out of her mind, practically.'

'I'm all right here,' the child said rapidly. 'I'm all right here. I have to be in bed for half-past eight. I'm all right here.' She dreaded the thought of being left in the company of Mrs Spencer, who was going out of her mind, practically.

'You're not all right here,' her father said, 'and a late night won't hurt you for once.' He picked up his jacket from the back of the chair, took a stub of indelible pencil from his pocket, moistened the end of it on his tongue. 'Better leave a note for Nancy.' He took the gas bill envelope from behind the clock, wrote 'Nancy' on it in big uneven capitals. 'Here, you do it,' he said to her.

She wrote: 'We have gone to the Spencers' because Margaret Rose is missing, love Jack.' She didn't know why she'd written 'love'; except that 'yours sincerely' would have seemed silly.

'I'm not supposed to go out when it's raining,' she said, making one final forlorn attempt at resistance, but her father just said that she'd have to chance it for once and to get her outdoor clothes on.

'She's so adventurous,' Mr Spencer said, as they made their way round the corner, 'so high-spirited. She doesn't see danger.'

'She wants a kick up her pants,' her father said. He was wheeling his bicycle, wearing his yellow cycling cape. He'd have to dry it thoroughly – the bicycle – when he got home, or it would rust up to hell.

Lightning tore from the top of the sky, between them, to the ground. The rain ran over the rim of her wellingtons and down her legs. 'Adventurous,' Mr Spencer said. 'High-spirited. At her age I was just the same. Thank goodness I hadn't left for the Palais. My partner will be wondering.'

Mrs Spencer leapt out at them from the shadows of the hall. Her face was broken up into planes of chartreuse yellow and green as it caught reflections from the coloured glass in the top of the door. 'Have you got her? Have you got her?' she said. Her kimono

162

hung open. You could see an off-white petticoat underneath it, and a long sweep of bone thinly covered with flesh down the front of her chest. She beat her fists against the stiff frontage of Mr Spencer's white macintosh, made a sound like a series of bleats. The child turned her face away, embarrassed beyond measure. Mrs Spencer was acting mad, and acting very badly.

'Leonora,' Mr Spencer said, 'Leonora.' But she pushed him away from her.

'We're going out now, Mr Bell and I. We'll find her. She can't be far away. She's perhaps sheltering. She's got a head on her shoulders.'

'Go then,' Mrs Spencer said, 'go. Don't dither about here. You're useless,' she said, suddenly matter-of-fact, 'quite useless.'

'Come on, then,' her father said. 'let's get her found.' He shared Mrs Spencer's opinion of her husband.

She took off her gaberdine and her wellingtons and followed Mrs Spencer into the sitting room. The single bar of the electric fire gave out a meagre glow of heat. Mrs Spencer pulled the sofa towards it, sat down and rubbed her knees. She no longer wore her wedding ring. Perhaps it *had* rolled through a crack in the floorboards. Or perhaps it was with Charlie's uncle, together with the pair of candlesticks that Charlie had seen Mr Spencer depositing there. At intervals she raised her naked, bony hands to her temples and swayed the upper part of her body from side to side. She was *exactly* like the inept actress who'd played Ophelia in the Witnesses Hall; one couldn't quite believe in her despair; she laid it on too thick.

The child sat stiffly on the edge of a hard chair. Sometimes Mrs Spencer's wandering gaze came to rest upon her and was, for a second or two, full of pure hatred. She, the child, had no business to be sitting on

163

the edge of a hard chair, alive and well, while Margaret Rose was out in the flood, in the night that teemed with menace.

Half an hour passed. The child watched the pendulum's swing on the wall clock and massaged her legs when they got pins and needles. Then they heard feet slap-slapping along the passage beside the house. Mrs Spencer was on her feet and at the door in less time than it took to blink your eyelid. It was Ronnie. In his plimsolls. He wore a windcheater, but the rain had penetrated it, had penetrated to his skin; it dripped from the edges of his shorts, ran out of his shoes where canvas had parted from rubber. He shook his head. He had been to the recreation ground and right along the marsh road from the headland to the site of the old defunct ferry. He hadn't seen hide nor hair of her. He tried to unwrap a boiled sweet that he'd found in his pocket. It was a very old boiled sweet, and the wrapper wouldn't peel off, so he ate it wrapper and all. He smiled a little smile that was full of malicious glee. He was drenched through, but he didn't care. What he had hoped for so many mornings, lying in his wet bed, had come to pass. The child wondered if he'd really looked for her or if he'd simply stood out in the storm and gloated, imagining the dark bundle of her corpse at the tide's edge, her torso on the railway line.

'Get out, get out again,' Mrs Spencer cried, 'and go into town. Look everywhere.'

And he sucked loudly on his green sweet, smirked, and left, leaving little pools of water behind him on the carpet.

The footsteps that collided with Ronnie's at the front gate couldn't be mistaken; they belonged to her mother, quick, light and agitated. She took off her Pac-a-mac and her rainhood in the porch. She needn't have bothered putting them on in the first place, for her dress and her cardigan and her stockings were wet. There was a big ladder running down her stocking from thigh to ankle, and her face and neck were mottled with red patches as they always were when she returned from Carrie Mortimer's.

The child forestalled her in the hall. 'Margaret Rose went out on her bicycle and hasn't come back. Dad and Mr Spencer are out looking for her. Weren't you scared of coming home in the thunderstorm?' she asked curiously. 'Weren't you afraid of being struck?'

Her mother didn't answer, just glanced at herself in the hall mirror, patted a few wisps of hair back into position, and went through to receive the full onslaught of Mrs Spencer's woes.

Mrs Spencer wept, pulled at the loops of her hair, accepted a glass of Empire port out of the cabinet. 'The police,' her mother said. And Mrs Spencer said, 'I wanted to, but Ronald doesn't like being involved with the police. The procedure, you know . . . He says they'd only laugh at us. She's not been away long enough.'

Ronald. Ronald and Leonora. The child looked at the photograph on the sideboard, which showed them against the background of a promenade. At Weston-super-Mare, probably. They were looking at each other with daft expressions.

'But it's quarter past ten,' her mother said, shaking her wrist in case water had seeped into her watch. 'I'll go to the phone box.'

'Yes, yes,' Mrs Spencer said. I've given him time, haven't I? He couldn't say different.'

So her mother dressed herself in her rain-clothes and went round to the red telephone kiosk on the corner of Wellington Road and Birchwood Avenue. And the child shifted her position on her chair. And Mrs Spencer scratched at the skin of her chest until she'd raised a rash to rival her mother's.

The thunder was receding, the lightning becoming less violent and frequent. It was now quite dark. The procession that entered through the front gate while her mother was fitting her finger into the 'nine' hole on the telephone dial and preparing herself to speak, looked like a line of black-clothed, hooded monks, heads bent, contemplating their feet. The only splash of colour was a bright yellow patch in their midst. 'They're here,' the child said, and Mrs Spencer pressed both hands to a spot midway along the length of her chest.

It was her father who carried Margaret Rose, grunting with effort, while Mr Spencer wheeled the bicycle. It was her father who laid her on the hastily-vacated sofa. It was her father who wiped his handkerchief over his bald patch, readjusted his cycling cape, and went off to locate Ronnie. She heard him saying, 'Jesus wept,' as he let himself out of the front door, and prayed that lightning would not strike him as a punishment for blasphemy.

She peered over the back of the sofa. Mrs Spencer had flung herself full-length across Margaret Rose, so it was difficult to ascertain whether Mrgaret Rose was dead, dreadfully injured, or merely alive and well.

'In the park,' Mr Spencer said. 'Behind the bowling pavilion. Crying her little heart out.' He addressed his remarks to the child because it was pointless attempting to communicate with his wife who was weeping and shuddering in an ecstasy of grief, or relief. His hair was whitish-grey. She wondered if it had turned that way due to shock, just like the person who had spent the night in Doctor Carpenter's house.

'Oh, no,' her mother said when she came in, as though Margaret Rose could have had the good grace to stay missing now that she'd rung the police. 'Where on earth has she been? I'd give her something she wouldn't forget in a hurry, if I were you.'

'Ssh,' Mr Spencer said, putting a finger to his lips. 'We don't know what happened yet. She's too upset to speak.'

'Well, wouldn't it be an idea to get those wet clothes off her before she gets pneumonia?' In her mother's view nothing could be *that* bad as long as it didn't lead to pneumonia. She pulled Mrs Spencer away from her child none too gently, went upstairs and came down with a frayed towel and an assortment of clothes. 'Get some coal and make a fire,' she told Mr Spencer. And, to the child, severely, 'I expect you're wet through, too, aren't you?'

'I'm not sure,' Mr Spencer said, meaning, 'I'm not sure if there *is* any coal.' 'Well, *look*,' her mother said. 'Get some of ours if necessary.' He left the room, the little brass shovel in his hand. She realized that, compared with him, her father was a rock, a pillar, the epitome of manhood.

Margaret Rose allowed herself to be undressed, dried off and dressed again without ever once opening her eyes. Her hair was frizzed tight to her skull. There were scratches on her arms and legs. Little beads of blood seeped from them. Mrs Spencer saw them and moaned low in her throat. 'Go and make a hot drink,' her mother said, struggling to pull a vest over Margaret Rose's inert head. 'Make everyone a hot drink before we all pass out.'

But Mrs Spencer couldn't stop wringing her hands for long enough to do so. It was Mr Spencer, after he'd returned with five lumps of coal on the brass shovel, and the child who went into the kitchen and poked inside musty cupboards for the Horlicks jar and the tin of condensed milk. There was very little condensed milk left inside it. 'Adam's ale,' Mr Spencer said, going to the cold-water tap with the kettle, 'corporation pop.' There was a stained book on top of the dresser, a guide to healthy eating by someone called Gayelord Hauser. The child looked in the cupboard, which contained two sticky jars of jam, a tub of beef paste, a piece of mousetrap, a packet of All Bran, some jelly cubes, two brown bananas, a tin of corned beef, two pounds of damp sugar hard as a rock, a garlanding of cobweb and a quantity of mouse droppings.

She was carryin the watery Horlicks through to the sitting-room on a tin tray that said Guinness Is Good For You when the police arrived. Lottie Law, Charlie called them. There was a policewoman in uniform with black stockings and big black thick-soled shoes. Behind her was a police constable, also in uniform. And behind him was a big, heavy-set gentleman who wore an overcoat with padded shoulders, a navy-blue trilby, and who had tarstained fingers and fingernails bitten to the quick. She nearly dropped the tray. She had been right in her assumption: with his criminal face what else could he be but a child-molester, a lurker by the headland? And now they were bringing him to justice, to a confrontation with Margaret Rose, who would identify him as her assailant.

He took off his hat. 'Hallo, girlie,' he said. 'What are you doing here? Where's Mr and Mrs Spencer?'

'Here,' Mr Spencer said, hovering behind her, as though he was answering the register at school.

'Detective Sergeant Davidge,' the man said. 'Missing child, I believe?' And the child thought, he's a complete loony, pretending to be a policeman. They'll probably grab him and put him into a strait jacket and send for the yellow van.

'Everything's all right,' Mr Spencer said. 'She's back. We found her. Hiding in the park, she was. Little

168

rogue. I shall tell her off, tear a strip, give her what for, don't you worry.'

'In here, is she?' the big man said, going towards the sitting-room door. Surely they will restrain him now, the child thought.

'But everything's all right,' Mr Spencer reiterated. 'We're ever so sorry to have troubled you. Really.' There was something about the police that seemed to make him very nervous. The big man opened the sitting-room door.

Her mother was applying iodine to Margaret Rose's scratches, and every time the cotton wool touched flesh Margaret Rose shrieked and Mrs Spencer echoed the shriek with a moan.

'Everything all right, is it?' the big man said, as though he was unwilling to believe Mr Spencer's testimony. He walked round the sofa. The child was being forced to the conclusion that, appearances to the contrary, he really was a policeman. Margaret Rose's tightly-closed eyelids opened gradually, her jutting underlip quivered. 'Now young lady,' he said, 'what have you been up to?'

She tried to look from side to side, but her eyes were drawn to his, like a rabbit with a snake. 'Getting yourself lost,' he said. 'A big girl like you.' He loomed over her. She was swamped in the shadow of his shoulders. 'Giving everyone heart attacks,' her mother said crossly, swabbing at the cuts with the cotton wool. 'Running off?' the big man said and Margaret Rose's mouth fell open. She was really for it. 'Those look nasty,' he said, pointing a thick finger at her cuts and scratches. 'Been running through the briars?' The policeman and the policewoman stood at the back of the room, silently, impassively.

'Been off on your own, girlie?' the big man said, snapping the brim of his trilby between finger and thumb. The fire hissed as rain dripped down the chimney. 'Nobody offer you any sweeties? Nobody take you for a walk?'

'Is it *necessary*?' Mrs Spencer said. 'Upsetting this child so?' 'This child' had begun to sob, to rub her fists against her eyes.

'Just have to make sure,' the big man said. 'Got to be certain. Another report last week.' The policewoman joined him. 'What's her name?' she asked Mrs Spencer. 'Margaret Rose,' Mrs Spencer said. The police-woman squatted on her thick haunches so that her face was level with Margaret Rose's. 'Now, Margaret Rose,' she said, 'nobody's trying to frighten you. We just want you to tell us if any man spoke to you, took you for a walk. That's all. Don't be afraid.'

The hairs on her mole quivered. Her hands were square, with big knuckles. She looked as though she could take on a gang of roughs single-handed. Margaret Rose's sobs caught in her throat. You could see the white all round the edges of her eyes. She was breathing very fast, as though she'd been running in a race.

'Well, Margaret,' the policewoman said, '*was* there any man who spoke to you?'

And Margaret Rose looked from her to him to Mrs Spencer and back again. 'Yes,' she shouted, 'Yes. It was Charlie,' and turned her face into Mrs Spencer's shoulder, and, as Mr Spencer would have said, cried her little heart out.

Chapter Sixteen

EVERYTHING THAT happened during the rest of that night passed in a blur, a series of rapid magic lantern slides, or as though she were looking at the world through the wrong end of a telescope: she remembered her mother's face jerking upward as though someone had pulled a string at the back of her neck; she held the iodine bottle in one hand and the cotton-wool in the other and she said, 'You little liar,' in a curious puzzled tone. She remembered the big man saying to the uniformed policeman, 'Get that child out of here. What the thump are you thinking about?' and being bundled into the hall, and, a few minutes later, her father coming in with Ronnie and saying, 'This one was sitting in a shelter at the back of the funfair. Dear God, has the world gone mad? Damn kids. Nothing but trouble from the day they're born,' and then, 'Why are the police here? She's all right, isn't she?' and pushing open the sitting-room door and saying, 'I've found him.'

She remembered sitting with Ronnie on the stairs. It was dark, but neither of them thought to switch on the light. She could see the white disc that was his face, and smell his wet clothes. She whispered, 'Did you hope something had happened to her?' And he whispered back, 'Yes,' and his head drooped towards his knees.

They strained their ears towards the sitting-room door, but all that could be heard was a low rumble of conversation and an occasional burst of weeping from Mrs Spencer or Margaret Rose.

After that there was a great deal of to-ing and fro-ing. The policeman came out and banged the front door behind him. They heard the sound of his car starting up. Mr Spencer came out, sidled between them on the stairs, came down with a green blanket, spoke never a word. Then they all emerged: Mr and Mrs Spencer with Margaret Rose between them bundled in the green blanket, her mother, clenching and unclenching her hands, Mr Davidge and the policewoman, and her father saying, 'That I'll never believe. Not in a million years.'

Mrs Spencer put a raincoat over her kimono, the big man put on his hat, her mother donned her Pac-a-mac. Mr Spencer was still wearing his white macintosh and Margaret Rose had the blanket. Their loins thus girded, they opened the front door and went out into the night. All except her father, who peered at them both from the bottom of the stairs and said, 'It looks as though we're three spare parts. I'd better take the pair of you home.'

She remembered riding on his crossbar through the silent streets. Once she fell asleep and bumped her head on the handlebars. She remembered thinking that the afternoon on the pitch and putt course seemed several lifetimes ago.

The light in the bedroom was grey when she awoke. There was a moment when she stretched her legs and wiped a thread of saliva from her mouth on to the pillow and she was genuinely puzzled: why on earth should she be waking up in that period when night is just turning into morning? And then she heard voices through the wall and remembered. One voice, mostly,

monotonous, with the occasional deeper-toned inter-
jection. Ronnie, if he was still here, must be in the
spare bedroom. She tried to concentrate on her horse
drawing on the opposite wall, to assess her technique,
but her thoughts refused to be disciplined, channelled.
Margaret Rose had said that she'd met Charlie. But
Charlie wouldn't take Margaret Rose behind the bowling pavilion at night in the middle of a thunderstorm.
She turned her hot face from side to side on the pillow.
The pillow felt coarse and grainy, with a thin and
clammy overlay of sweat. Margaret Rose had run a
terrible risk being out late at night like that. Those two
little girls, a few weeks ago, behind the sand dunes on
the headland . . . She drew her knees up to her chest.
She felt as though a hand was squeezing the bundle of
intestines low down in her body. Margaret Rose surely
had not meant to imply . . .? Could not have meant to
imply . . .? The hand tightened its grip. She couldn't
put a name to the feeling that she experienced: excitement? terror? disgust? It was similar to, but worse
than, the feeling she'd had when Margaret Rose told
her about the bleeding and what men and women did to
one another when they were in bed. The voices continued through the wall: a monologue, interspersed with
deep staccato comments. *They* never did it; she'd swear
it on the Bible. And neither did Charlie. And never,
never to Margaret Rose.

She fell asleep. And the terrible figures moved
through the grey mist of her dreams: Mrs Rochester
rending the wedding veil; the Phantom of The Opera
pursuing her along the tide-line of a purple endless
beach where there was no refuge, no sanctuary; Mrs
Spencer, waiting for her in an upper room of Doctor
Carpenter's house where fungus grew on the walls and
torn curtains fluttered and the Four Horsemen bran-
dished their steel-grey swords and lances; Mrs Spencer,

laughing and opening her kimono. And Charlie and her mother, dancing the polka: and *one* two three, out in the garden among the ruined roses and the moon-faced marguerites, ignored her screaming, lost in their own hectic private rhythm. And although the house, which she could see clearly from the outside, was gashed with doorways and windows, the room that she cowered in offered no means of egress, and she knew that she was done for.

'Wake up,' her mother said, 'wake up. You were dreaming. It's all right now, it's morning and you've woken up.'

It was and she had. Her mother's eyes seemed sunken. Little lines criss-crossed the lilac-coloured skin beneath them. 'At our age,' her father said, 'you can't do without a proper night's sleep. You suffer for it.' His chin was rough; his sparse hair stood on end.

Only Ronnie seemed unaffected by the happenings of the previous night. He ate three bowls of corn-flakes, in rapid succession. He wore a pair of her father's trousers and one of his shirts, rolled up at the wrists and ankles, because his own clothes were drying on the clothes-maiden in front of the fire. Her mother closed her eyes and stepped back from the spitting fat in the frying pan. An egg yolk broke and ran in a yellow river over the albumen and the streaky bacon. The child retched. Ronnie poked with his fingernail between his molars and dislodged a wad of damp cereal. Her father scraped his fork along the edge of his knife and cut the fat white rind off the bacon, dipped a piece of bread into the jelly-like, not-quite-set top of his egg. The child leaned sideways and vomited on to the floor.

'God!' her father said. 'That's all I need,' and went wearily for the floorcloth and soaked it with San-Izal and mopped at the frothy white stream on the linoleum. 'It's the upset,' he said, crossing his knife and fork, pushing his plate away. 'Feel better now?'

She nodded. She said, 'What happened last night? Was Margaret Rose telling a story?'

'That's about the strength of it,' her father said. 'They had to check up on it, you see, because there's been one of those strange men around recently, talking to little girls, taking them for walks. The kind we've warned you about.'

'Have you finished?' her mother said, snatching his plate away and banging it into the sink. 'Because I want to get on.'

'Don't get your hair off. You ought to get to the doctor too. Get something for your nerves.' He put on his jacket, adjusted his cap, said, 'Keep her away from there,' nodding his head in the child's direction, and was gone.

Her mother washed the dishes very sketchily, left them to drain, took off her pinafore and combed her hair. She sighed deeply all the while. Ronnie changed into his own dry creased clothes: vest, socks, grey shirt and shorts, fair isle pullover, snake-clasp belt and windcheater. His plimsolls had disintegrated totally. Her mother found him an ancient pair of tennis shoes that she used to wear, years ago, when she was a member of a tennis club, before she got married. Ronnie was delighted. They fitted perfectly, and the soles were so thick and springy that you could bounce up and down inside them.

'You'd both better come with me,' her mother said. 'I'm not leaving you on your own, not with one of those men roving around.'

'Where are you going?'

'You'll find out.'

Leaves and bushes dripped themselves dry. The cherry-blossom trees rained showers on your head

175

when you walked underneath them. The gutters gurgled and the dark earth steamed. But the blueness of the sky had been wiped away and painted from a dimmer palatte. The summer was over, she knew, the timeless days of bare legs and sand in your shoes and tar bubbling on the roadside and a few more strokes every morning while Charlie looked on and shouted, 'That's it, Esther Williams, get those old arms working,' and Ronnie withdrew a foot from the water with a shudder and Margaret Rose peered from behind a clump of dune grass.

All the curtains at Number Thirty-two Jubilee Villas were drawn together, as though there had been a death in the family. Margaret Rose certainly deserved to die. The child could not think of Charlie without also thinking of the disgusting thing that Margaret Rose had indirectly accused him of. 'You wait here,' her mother said, and went up the path to the front door. The child and Ronnie leaned on the gate; they were to be kept at a distance for fear of contamination. The bell rang inside the house for quite a long time before Mr Spencer opened the door. He was wearing his pyjamas and not wearing the bottom set of his dentures. 'Yes,' he said to whatever her mother was saying, 'yes, as you like . . . wits' end . . . the gas oven . . . the bottom of the lake . . . sling my hook . . . very grateful.'

'You're to stay with us for a couple of days, Ronnie,' her mother said when she came back. 'I think they've enough to contend with without you as well. And you're to behave yourself.'

They glanced backwards at the Spencer's house. The front door was closed. There was no sign of life.

'Smashing,' Ronnie said belatedly. 'Smashing.' And bounced up and down inside the tennis shoes.

Her mother had told a story too, though of a less serious nature. Carrie Mortimer did not live over beyond the recreation ground. She lived near the terminus of the number thirteen bus, where the town proper gave way to country lanes and market gardens and smallholdings. Hens pecked inside barbed-wire runs, greenhouses and lettuce plots stretched as far as the eye could see. It was a depressing landscape. Neither town nor countryside, the general impression was one of shoddy structure, damp walls and ramshackle outbuildings. Carrie Mortimer lived in a bungalow called The Glades, though anywhere less glade-like would have been hard to imagine. Nor was Carrie Mortimer herself as the child had imagined. Ungirdled flesh, lumpy legs, red hands and a damson-coloured mouth painted on; was this the woman who had turned heads on the Promenade, who could have had her pick of the fellows?

Eddie, the drunken sot of a husband, was out delivering potatoes on the wagon. 'Thank God,' Carrie Mortimer said, 'to get him from under my feet for a bit. Come on in. This is Veronica, is it? My! Bonny! And is this her young man?' The child stared hard at the hall wallpaper – yellow, with evil-looking green fish swimming about on it – while waves of anger and humiliation radiated through her body. Inside, the house smelled of cooking fat and cats' mess and cigarette-smoke and bodies and urine. 'I'm just rinsing the nappies,' Carrie Mortimer said. 'Come through to the kitchen. You don't know how lucky you are, Nancy, just the one. I swore after our Kevin . . . I still don't know how it happened. I said to that lady doctor at the clinic, "All I need is a pair of pants on the end of the bed and that's it, another one on the way."'

In the corner of the kitchen a baby lay asleep on a sofa. Last night's ashes filled the grate. A cigarette burned a mark on the edge of the mantelpiece. A tin bucket full of soaking napkins stood beside the sink.

A fly staggered around the rim of an open jam-jar. A small, large-headed child sat at the table and pummelled a grimy piece of Plasticine into a sausage shape. A black-and-white fox terrier rolled on the rug and shed its hairs all over the furniture. Carrie Mortimer moved ponderously around the room, removing newspapers and magazines and children's toys from the seats of chairs so that they could sit down. 'A mess as per usual,' she said. 'Can you believe it, Nancy, when I used to be so particular?'

The child had observed squalor at close quarters before: the Spencers'; but theirs was a cold, dreary and hopeless squalor; here at least the dirt and disorder was the residue of human vitality.

'She takes after you, doesn't she?' Carrie Mortimer said, sinking down into the sofa and lighting another cigarette although the first one still burned on the mantelpiece. 'She really puts me in mind of you at the same age . . .' She strove for the appropriate adjective, '. . . ladylike.'

'Oh yes,' her mother said, laughing without humour, 'Ladylike, that's me. Ever so.'

'What's up, kid?' She pushed bits of auburn hair back under her turban, slapped away a fly, drew on her cigarette, withdrew it from her mouth, its cork tip rimmed with damson. She seemed remarkably recovered for one who had been on her sick-bed only the night before.

Her mother gave a series of small, meaningful glances. Carrie Mortimer got to her feet, opened a cupboard, took out a packet of ginger nuts. 'Kevin,' she said, 'take Veronica and this young man into the garden and show them the swing and the sandpit. Here's some biscuits for you. And mind you share them around.'

'Garden' was not an accurate description for the wasteland outside. Three bigger, but similarly large-

headed children dug in a sandpit. A few scraggy
aphid-infested roses bloomed among the nettles and
ragwort and chickweed that covered the earth and grew
up and over a rubbish-tip in the corner that glistened
with bluebottles. 'Want one?' Kevin said, tearing at the
cellophane on the biscuits. 'No, thank you,' she said
politely, fearing that they would be impregnated with
the same smell that permeated the rest of the house.

'I'll have hers,' Ronnie said, jumping on to the seat
of the swing that hung on rusted chains from the limb of
an ancient pear tree. At the mention of food, the other
children gave up what they were doing and approached, hands outstretched. Their ages ranged from
about four to seven. They looked like the same child at
different stages of its development. Except that one
was a girl. Ronnie worked his legs vigorously, and
swung higher and higher. The branch groaned. 'Smashing,' he said. 'Want a go? I'll push you.' They shoved
one another aside in their eagerness to be first. He
lifted the one called Kevin on to the seat, very gently,
and arranged his hands on the chains. He liked little
kids. She left him to it. She sat on an upturned
wheelbarrow, which was out of view of the kitchen
window, but within earshot of the kitchen's interior and
the conversation of its occupants.

'My God,' Carrie Mortimer said. 'And here's me
thinking it's the usual trouble.'

'What do you mean,' her mother said, 'the usual
trouble?'

'When I say the usual trouble, I mean the usual
trouble.' She laughed; you could hear loose phlegm
rattling around in her throat. 'I thought you'd slipped
up. Or he'd slipped up. Whichever.'

'Don't be daft,' her mother said.

'Who's being daft? It can happen to the best of us,
duckie. At least it can if you're married to a silly sod

like I am. I'll chop it off some night, I swear to God I will.'

'Well, I'm not. It isn't,' her mother said. 'It's worse than that.'

'Nothing's worse than that. Believe you me. Well, go on. What happened?'

'I told them I'd seen him,' her mother said, 'on my way home from here. I told them he couldn't have been anywhere near the park.'

'And did he say the same?'

'I don't *know*. He was in a different room. I don't *know* what he said. I daren't go round there, Carrie, to find out.'

'But anyway.' Carrie Mortimer cleared her lungs into her handkerchief. 'Anyway, this kid finally admitted she'd been telling a tarradiddle?'

'They examined her.' Her mother's voice went low and grave, as though she were speaking in church. 'After what she'd said, they had to. Dear God, she screamed blue murder. Even I felt sorry for her, the little madam. She'd never been touched, of course. But you should have heard what she came out with! Lord knows where she'd picked it up from.'

'Oh, they pick it up,' Carrie Mortimer said, 'from the time they're that high. These days they know the ins and outs of a duck's whatnot. When we were their age – I was as green as the grass. So, anyway, she told them then she'd been making it up?'

'She kept changing her story until she finally confessed it had all been a fairy tale. I don't think they'd really believed her from the start, but what with this child-molester on the loose . . . That sergeant said you'd be surprised how many they had, little girls with too much imagination, he called them.'

'So how had she got scratched like that?'

'Some boys had chased her and she'd run through those brambles – you know – on the edge of the park.

There was the sound of a match being struck and a curl of blue smoke drifted outside. 'But why?' Carrie Mortimer said.

'Jealousy, I suppose. Desire for attention. She's been spoiled to death and she resents this Ronnie – the half-brother - even though he has a dog's life. So she thought she'd stop out and frighten them a bit. But of course it all got out of hand when the police showed up. I wouldn't mind,' her mother said, 'but it was *me* that called them. My God!'

'How did he take it, Charlie-boy?'

'He was as white as that wall.'

That wall wasn't white, the child thought; it was a sort of dirty cream colour.

'I don't wonder,' said Carrie Mortimer. 'It's not a nice thing to be accused of, is it? It'd be funny really . . . if it wasn't tragic,' she added quickly, 'I mean, him supposed to have been . . . while all the time . . . Where were you?'

'Over by the golf links.'

'You know, Nancy,' Carrie Mortimer said, 'you could have knocked me down with a feather. You, of all people. I'd never have believed it. You were always so prim. I always thought it'd be *me*, you know, a bit on the side.' She sighed deeply. 'Fat chance!'

'It's not that,' her mother said. 'Don't call it that.'

'Oh, love, it's never that. It's always the big thing. You're romantic, you are. Always were. Why don't you just accept it as a nice healthy exercise? Don't try to tie ribbons on it. Take it while it's going.'

'I can't be like that,' her mother said. Her voice was tearful. 'I've got feelings. I've got a conscience.'

'Aye,' Carrie Mortimer said, 'But has he? One thing that's got no conscience is a standing whatnot. As we all know to our cost.'

'I was trembling. I couldn't hold still. I thought they might come round here . . .'

'So what? I'd have said the same.'

If I listen hard enough, the child thought, I will eventually discover the kernel of logic that makes sense of it all. Just as when you're faced with a page of French, you remember the meaning of one word and that word leads you to another, and so on until you've translated the lot.

'It's Jack you want to worry about,' Carrie Mortimer said. 'Hasn't he noticed?'

'He wouldn't notice if I embroidered it on a banner and carried it through the streets. Last night, you should have heard him, speaking up for Charlie. You'd have thought they were brothers. It's that part of it I hate,' her mother said, 'the sordidness.'

'Oh, come off it. Sordid! It's the fact that it's on the sly makes it all the more exciting. Like when you're courting. Back of the car. Behind the golf links. You can't get enough of it. When we're married, you think, we can have it every night, legal, in bed. It's like everything else: when you can have it, you don't want it any more.'

Silence fell. The child raised her behind from the edge of the wheelbarrow, ready to flee if necessary. Then her mother said, 'It's love I'm talking about, not just that.'

'Oh yes? You just sit and hold hands?'

'No.'

'What's happened is: he's shown you what a good jump can be like and you're so grateful that you start talking about love. That's all.'

'Carrie!'

'I'm telling you. Love's in the library books.'

Was jumping anything to do with bouncing? And if so, who were they talking about? 'One, two, three, you're off,' Ronnie shouted and sent the female child hurtling into space.

'Why don't you stop for a bit of dinner?' Carrie Mortimer said. 'I can always open a tin. And he's away all day, praise the Lord.'

'No. I must get back. In case.'

'In case he comes round? If I were you I'd cool it down a bit. I'll bet your Dolly's big nose is twitching as it is. God, she used to give me the creeps. Like the hanging judge, she was. Yes, slacken it off a bit is what I'd do if I were you. I should be so lucky!'

'I can't, Carrie, I can't.'

'Well, if you can't, you can't. But you're laying up a whole lot of grief and heartache for yourself. You know that?'

She gave the child and Ronnie a packet of fruit-gums each when they were leaving. She was what Aunt Dolly would call a big, blowzy woman, but good-hearted. You could tell that trials and tribulations which would fell frailer mortals would simply roll off her; she would clear herself a space among the household débris and sink down with a romantic book and a box of soft-centred chocolates.

'You can have mine.' She handed the fruit-gum tube to Ronnie.

'Don't you like them?' He stuffed them into the pocket of his windcheater. She suddenly envied him enormously: that he could be happy because of an extra tube of fruit-gums and a few little kids to play with and two days' reprieve from the Spencers.

They sat together on the front seat of the bus. Her mother sat at the back, her chin on her hand, and the conductor had to tap her on the shoulder to remind her about the fares. Low-lying gardens were flooded, and small children in wellington boots sailed paper boats

183

over the grass. Overhanging branches of sodden trees scraped against the bus windows and released gouts of rain. The sea glittered under a pale, water-colour sky. In the town, holidaymakers carried transparent plastic macintoshes over their arms and forsook the ice-cream stalls for the fish-and-chip shops. The bus passed the end of the boarding-house street and the child craned her neck for a glimpse of the Marlborough. The only human figure to be seen was a woman, possibly Myra, shaking a mat on the front step. Half of her longed to see Charlie, the other half dreaded it. Today's Charlie was a different proposition from the Charlie of yesterday, on the pitch and putt course, yelling 'Fore!' and making plans for weekends in Cumberland. He had been sullied. He had been shown to be as human and vulnerable as everybody else. And she had believed him to be special, to live in a world governed by rules that he had fashioned for himself.

'Come on, you two,' her mother called. 'It's our stop.' Her chin was still cupped in her hand. She looked, as Aunt Dolly would have said, like somebody who'd lost a shilling and found sixpence.

Chapter Seventeen

IT WAS THE Saturday afternoon of the local carnival. The previous summer the child had walked in the procession wearing a long white dress and carrying a white porcelain dove; she was meant to represent 'Peace'. Aunt Dolly had kept pace with the parade throughout its duration, from the parish hall to the recreation ground; the dove was her property and she was afraid that it would be dropped and broken *en route*.

'Are we going?'

Normal procedure was for her mother to meet her after the procession and the tableaux had broken up, bringing her ordinary clothes, which she would change into inside the stuffy and smelly wooden ladies' toilet. Then they would wander around the handicraft stalls, the white elephant stall, the coconut shies, the bran-tub and the wishing well. They would buy an ice each and watch the children's sports. Margaret Rose always won every section of the girls' races, just as an extremely rough council school boy with a body like a whippet and a reading age of five always won the equivalent boys' races. The child did not compete. She never entered competitions unless she was certain of winning.

'You can go if you want to,' her mother said. She took her purse out of the drawer, opened it and pushed a two-shilling piece across the table.

'We always go,' the child said stubbornly. 'You *always* come to watch me.'

'You're not in it this year, are you? We can watch through the window when they come past. Or you can go with Ronnie.'

'Why don't you want to come?'

'Because I don't feel like it, that's why. Don't nag. I'll be glad when term starts,' she said, not entirely irrelevantly.

'I'd rather stop in,' the child said. 'I'd rather do a jigsaw.'

Ronnie came down from the bathroom, where he had been making faint inroads upon his grime. 'Do you want to do a jigsaw, Ronnie?'

He nodded. He was unaware that there was an alternative. They cleared the table and set upon it the big baking board as a base for operations. The jigsaw was composed of five hundred pieces: 'Tarzan in the Jungle'. It was very difficult. When you'd eventually completed it, you were loath to break it up and shovel it back into the box. Her mother banged cups on the draining board and ran the tap so fast that it sounded like Niagara. 'You ought to be outside in the fresh air,' she said, 'in the bright sunshine.'

'It isn't bright sunshine.'

'Don't answer back.'

'I'm just stating a fact.'

'Then keep your facts to yourself.'

Ronnie looked wary. He thought he'd escaped from all that for a couple of days.

'If I can't state a fact . . .'

'Seconds out. Break for the bell.'

He stood in the doorway, just like before. And the sight of him, just like before, his daft comments, cancelled out the previous night and its nasty-tasting aftermath entirely. She could feel her heart through her

186

tee-shirt, feel her mouth go dry with excitement, her legs go weak with pleasure.

'You're perky,' her mother said, wringing out the dish-cloth as though her life depended on it.

'Yes,' he said, 'Well, it's how I always am, isn't it?'

'Not always.'

'Have you got any aspirins, Nancy?'

'Have you been propping up a bar?' she said, taking off her apron, stuffing it behind a cushion.

'Perhaps I have. That's not against the law, is it?'

'Oh, sorry I spoke. It seems as though everybody's got the miseries this afternoon.'

You included, the child thought.

Charlie sat down at the table while her mother went upstairs to the medicine cabinet with her nose in the air. 'Hello, Colonel,' he said. 'Have you changed your address?'

'He's staying here,' the child said, 'until . . .' She was too embarrassed to continue.

'Until the fireworks die down,' Charlie said. He fitted a piece of blue sky into a crucial gap in the jigsaw.

She leaned across the table, whispered, 'She ought to be put in prison.' To do this, to acknowledge that she knew of the horrible allegations, demanded an enormous effort. She felt herself blushing. But it was necessary that he should know that he had at least one champion. My mother seems to be unsympathetic, Ronnie is too thick to comprehend fully, but I will stand by you, for all the years until I'm old enough for you, for ever.

'Maybe so, Princess. There's a lot outside that ought to be in. And vice-versa. Thanks Nancy. You've saved me life.' He took the two white tablets from the palm of her hand and swallowed them down without milk, water, anything! The child was tremendously impressed. 'Perhaps that'll do the trick,' he said. He pressed his hand against his forehead. 'They're playing the Anvil Chorus inside there,' he said, 'with encores.'

Her mother made the kind of face that meant: over-indulgence invariably ends in tears, so it's no use feeling sorry for yourself or expecting anyone else to feel sorry for you.

'I was expecting you,' he said, 'this morning. Round the boarding house.'

'I thought you'd have had enough notoriety for a while.'

He grinned. 'You should have seen Myra. Horatius holding the bridge wasn't in it. "I don't care who you are," she says, "this is private property, and you don't cross my threshold without a warrant." I practically had to defend him, big feet and helmet, from her. She was a real peach, Myra.'

'Good for Myra. We all did our bit, you know.'

'You didn't say anything daft?'

'I said I'd seen you on my way home from Carrie's. Which is perfectly true,' her mother said in italics.

'Oh, Christ Almighty,' he said, putting his hand to his forehead again. The child drew in breath, hoped that God suffered from deafness, like her father.

'What did *you* say?' The colour drained from her mother's face.

'Told them the truth, didn't I? I was at the pictures: *Easter Parade*, starring Judy Garland and Fred Astaire, glorious Technicolour, choc-ice in the interval.'

'Oh God,' her mother said, 'God.'

'Don't worry. They'll only be splitting their sides. They'll have cottoned on all right. They get it every day of the week: "And where were you, Mr Bagshot, on the night of the murder?" "Oh, I was in the potting shed attending to the dahlias." "Come off it, you were attending to Mrs Cholmondely in the back of your Bentley." They've heard it all before, love.'

188

The child slotted Tarzan's face into place above Tarzan's body. Usually she reserved this part, the easiest, until the last; it gave one the greatest amount of satisfaction to do it that way. This afternoon, however, she simply hadn't the patience to figure out all that look-alike undergrowth and creeper.

'Don't worry,' Charlie said again.

The truth, the whole truth and nothing but the truth had obviously not been told. Perhaps it wasn't only Margaret Rose who stood in danger of prosecution for perjury. Something was going on, *sub rosa*, as Aunt Dolly called it, something you couldn't fathom. Her mother had been telling lies in a misguided attempt to shield Charlie, whereas Charlie, entirely innocent, had not needed shielding. Her mother was an awful fool sometimes; Aunt Dolly said that too.

'A band,' Ronnie said, cocking his head on one side like a dog, 'a band,' and got up and went to the door, happy to abandon the fiendishly complicated jigsaw puzzle.

They went through to the sitting-room and grouped themselves at the window. The same short fat man with cheeks like Cox's Orange Pippins played the big drum. She always looked forward to the little man especially; he was so obviously conscious of the importance of his position in the band and beat the drum with such proud gusto. They played 'Blaze Away' and 'The British Grenadiers', supplemented by members of the Boys' Brigade who blew bugles, their cheeks popping, and looked straight ahead of them, embarrassed in case their friends or relations might be watching.

'I shall never dare to walk past that police station again,' her mother said. 'I shall never be able to hold my head up.'

You and Mrs Spencer, the child thought, both bowed with shame.

189

'Small town,' Charlie said, 'small minds. Nothing else to do with their noses except poke 'em into other people's affairs. Doesn't it drive you barmy? You ought to get out. The world's a big place.'

'Oh yes. Just like that.'

'I bet you thought you would, once.'

'I did. Once.'

Her mother had been to business school and had become a private secretary to a solicitor. She had worn a clean blouse everyday and kept her fingernails filed down short, because of the typing. Her stocking seams had always been positioned dead centre, and Mr Parkinson, the solicitor, had thought the world of her.

The parade passed slowly by: little girls and boys tricked out in finery that their female relations had stitched at painstakingly for months. Tinselled fairy wings glittered, Britannia waved a cardboard sword and clutched a papier mâché shield to her chest, cotton wool bounced from the skirt of the Snow Queen.

'Peggy O'Neill's "Peace" this year,' the child said. It wasn't even a dove that she carried; it was one of those plaster duck things that people had flying on their walls.

'Peggy O'Neill,' Charlie sang, 'was a girl you could feel.' And her mother said, 'Hush' automatically. Ronnie stared avidly at the multicoloured cavalcade, drinking it in. It was so different from the green-grey and the sheep of Cumberland, the drab grey of the Manchester back streets, as to be almost incomprehensible to him. 'Where do they go to?' he said, his nose against the window-pane.

'They go to the recreation ground. They form tableaux in the arena and a band plays. Then there's a fête and races for the children.'

'Couldn't we go?'

Or was there yet another rule, among the many others with which he was not conversant, forbidding his attendance at local carnivals? He would not have been in the least surprised; life, for him, had always been a puzzlement.

'Course we can go, old son,' Charlie said. 'There's nothing we can't do if we really set our minds to it. Isn't that so?'

It wasn't so, the child thought regretfully. One had to recognize one's limitations: develop those things one *could* do, abandon those one couldn't. Some people found this hard to accept: Margaret Rose, imagining that one day she would be able to spell correctly without ever having to learn; her mother listening to the old-fashioned records and believing they would lead her to some dark enchanted place where people drank wine from crystal glasses and danced in swishy dresses and never had to wash the dishes.

'You take them,' her mother said. 'I'll get on with my work.' She took the tin of silver polish and a soft cloth out of a drawer, lifted down a canteen of cutlery that was never used from the shelf.

'Get your coat on,' Charlie said, 'and don't be so damn silly.' It was the first time that she had seen him look really annoyed.

'You said it: small minds, nothing better to do with their noses . . .'

'If you don't come,' he said, 'I shan't budge from here. And the kids can go on their own. And that'll give 'em all something to chew on, won't it?'

Her mother shrugged her shoulders, put on her cardigan. She didn't even bother with the Creme Puff or the Sugar Plum lipstick. The corners of her mouth drooped downwards. The child wanted to pummel her, to shake her by the shoulders, to rouse her from her determined apathy. Last night's all finished, she wanted to say, everything's as it was before. Smile! Laugh! Even if doing so gives you crease marks round your eyes. Be as you were on the golf course: a happy woman, not just my sighing mother.

On the recreation ground he gave them two shillings apiece and told them to lose themselves.

'Aren't you going to roll pennies or throw coconuts?' she said, disappointed.

'Not today. I've got housemaid's knee and tennis elbow.'

'That doesn't affect your hands,'

'Writer's cramp then, smarty.'

'What have you been writing?'

'Betting slips. And me memoirs.'

'In the war,' Ronnie said, turning the florin over and over in his hand, 'In the war, weren't you scared?'

'What brought that on?'

But, by now, the child thought that she understood Ronnie's tortuous mental processes: the fête had reminded him of the funfair, which in turn had reminded him of the Big Dipper and the fact that he was too scared to go on it; now he was wondering if men like Charlie experienced cowardice, or was it yet another shameful characteristic exclusive to himself?

'Every day,' Charlie said. 'Bleedin' petrified. Now get gone!'

They bought warm bottles of Vimto from the refreshment stall. Ronnie was all for equipping himself with two shillings' worth of Vimto and potato crisps and chocolate biscuits until she reminded him of the delights that he would be forfeiting: the sensual ecstasy of digging deep in the bran, the satisfying physical exertion of drawing back your right arm and getting a coconut in your sights, the eternal hopefulness as you poked among the handleless teapots and silent musical boxes on the white elephant stall in case anyone had slipped in a family heirloom inadvertently.

'We'll be seeing you again in September, I hope,

Veronica,' Miss Tibbs said, laying a hand on the child's shoulder. She stood drinking a cup of tea next to her ancient father in his wheelchair. In between drinking her tea, she fed him with little spoonfuls of ice-cream. When he was ready for the next one he jerked his head forward. His crippled hands lay in his lap. His pouched eyelids were closed, his dewlaps quivered. There were little dribbles of spit and ice-cream on his waistcoat. He seemed quite unmindful of his surroundings. 'He likes an airing,' Miss Tibbs said, smoothing the white hair on the top of his head. 'He likes to be among a gathering.' Aunt Dolly said it was a disgrace, Miss Tibbs having to cope with an immobile old man like that, all the private, the *personal* things. He should be in a home, Aunt Dolly said. Or out of his misery. But Miss Tibbs loved her father. That was beyond Aunt Dolly's comprehension.

The bran-tub yielded a tiny model aeroplane which she exchanged with Ronnie for a pencil-case. The coconut shy yielded nothing except the knowledge that dislodging a coconut from its perch was considerably more difficult than it looked. The white elephant stall was, as always, a let-down. Aunt Dolly said that those who ran it picked out the best for themselves beforehand. Perhaps Ronnie was wise, she thought, to spend so much of his two shillings on food. With food, you knew exactly what you were getting; every year one approached the bran-tub and the wishing-well and the coconut shy with the feeling that this year they would come up to expectations; every year one was disappointed.

Her mother and Charlie paced the length of a hawthorn hedge and back again, just as the games' organizers paced the distance for the egg and spoon race. 'No,' her mother said, 'don't talk like that. There's no point. It's like offering a mock reprieve to a condemned man. You know as well as I do, there's no possibility.'

'You make it,' he said, 'You take it. It doesn't come to you. My old lady, she grabbed at it to the day she died.'

'And where did it get her?'

'It got her to a combined room in Stockton-on-Tees with no hot water and a lavatory she shared with six other people and the paper curling off the walls with the damp. But by Christ, she never stopped trying.'

Her mother walked right through a great puddle. In her best shoes! Charlie kept taking the scarlet Du Maurier packet out of his pocket, lifting out a cigarette, half-smoking it, then throwing it away. They were too absorbed to notice her. She watched him: his impatient gestures, his shoulders hunched against the wind, his black hair blowing away from his forehead, the rough curly hairs on the knuckle joints of his hands, the faint hazy blue shadow on his chin. I love you, Charlie, she thought, and the admitting of this knowledge rooted her to the spot. She had said the words in her head and opened a door to a flooding of sensations that she could not name. The only thing of which she was certain was that this fact could not be excluded from the other areas of her life: you discovered that a jam-jar of frogspawn became a jam-jar of tadpoles, you learned *amo, amas, amat, amamus, amatis, amant*, you were told that you added up fractions by finding the lowest common denominator, and these various bits of knowledge you absorbed and compartmentalized; they did not spill over into each other. But she knew that *this* knowledge would invade everything else, that it would be there when she was executing a *pas de chat* in the ballet class on a Friday morning, or having her teeth drilled at the dentist's, when she was reciting 'The splendour falls on the castle walls', or brushing her hair a hundred strokes every night. It was inescapable.

Ronnie came tearing along, his head down, a coconut clutched between his arm and his body. His face was split by an unaccustomed smile; his teeth needed attention. 'Look what I won!'

'Go find a heavy stone,' Charlie said, 'and then you can break it open.'

'I'm not breaking it open.' He sounded affronted. 'I'm keeping it.'

Together with the plaster dog with the tartan bow that he'd won at the funfair, she supposed. They would form the nucleus of all personal possessions that he might acquire in the future.

'I'm going in for the race, too,' he said. 'I gave them me name. Are you coming to watch me?'

'Watch you?' Charlie said. 'I should say so. Shout for you till our lungs burst. Didn't know you were on the athletic side, Colonel.'

He stood in the middle of the line of starters. He bounced on his toes inside the tennis shoes, shook each foot experimentally from the ankle, squared his shoulders and stuck his head forward. The child guarded his coconut. She wanted him to win, and dreaded the thought of sharing his humiliation when he lost. She closed her eyes, heard the starting gun, heard Charlie's voice among the general uproar: 'Go it, Colonel! Run your little legs off!' When she opened them again, the tape was broken, Ronnie was stretched full length on the sodden turf and the thin boy was looking at him with an air of disbelief. Charlie had his arms above his head, hands clasped, and her mother was smiling all over her face. But it wasn't until an official announced: 'Number one, Ronnie Spencer, number two, James Rigby,' that she could believe that against all the odds: the thin boy, his own ability, his propensity towards defeat; he had actually won.

His prize was a big box of paints. She eyed it enviously. It contained five shades of blue and six shades of red. She knew that it was no use offering him anything in exchange for it. The plaster Skye terrier, the coconut, the paint box; nothing would induce him to part with them. The thin boy looked utterly dispirited; he wasn't to know that Ronnie's victory was a mere fluke, a flash-in-the-pan. He squirmed when Ronnie went forward for his prize. The applause was thin, unenthusiastic; the local children didn't approve of strangers cornering the market in prizes; they had expected the thin boy to win, it was traditional.

'I never won anything before,' he said wonderingly. He said it all the way home, and every time he said it, Charlie replied, 'You played a blinder, Colonel. You want to get your name down for the Olympics,' or 'You ran so fast I thought you were going to disappear in a puff of smoke.'

'The weather has changed,' her mother said, looking up at the sky, as they left the colour and the shouting and the music behind them, and the inflection she put into those four ordinary words imbued them with a dozen shades of meaning.

Chapter Eighteen

THE MOURNFUL BELL of Christ The Saviour tolled away the breakfast hour; her father yawned and reduced a pristine copy of the *Reynolds News* to a crumpled mess. Sunday was bells tolling on different notes, the rustle of newspaper pages, the spastic tick of the sitting-room clock, the smell of meat roasting, the shadows moving their positions on the carpet; Sunday was the lurking possibility that other people might be enjoying themselves elsewhere. They had welcomed the Major – though they'd grumbled and complained; he was a *divertissement*, he ruptured the monotonous fabric of the day with his reminiscences and his elderly dainty fads and his determined joviality. But the Major was dead and all that was left was to read the *Reynolds News* and eat up the roast meat and curse the bells and wash your hands preparatory to going to the aunts' house for tea.

Because the weather had changed, it was back to the routine of woollen vests and liberty bodices and cod-liver oil and malt. It was her mother's only concession to normality during the whole of that strange summer. On reflection, the catalogue of erratic behaviour was endless: expensive new clothes, pots and tubes of cosmetics that promised instant beauty, socks left un-darned, the supervision of cleanliness and sufficient sleep and certainty of one's whereabouts neglected, long evenings spent winding up the quivering voices on the gramophone. Once, the child thought, I couldn't go to the lavatory without informing her of my destination. I dared not be a minute late from school or she would be pacing the pavement in front of the house; my life had to be laid open before her for her scrutiny and approval. Now she allows me to wander almost at will, to spend hours at the suspect Spencers', to overhear Charlie's vulgar remarks to my heart's content. Or, perhaps, not so much 'allows' as fails to notice.

'Are we going, then?' her father said. He tried to fold the newspaper into some semblance of order, but it defeated him and he threw it, crumpled and torn, into an armchair.

'I suppose so.'

'There'll only be a song and dance if we don't go.'

'I know. It's like a life sentence. One Sunday, can't we do something different? Take a trip somewhere? Eat breakfast at dinner time? Go mad and tear paper?'

'I don't know what's the matter with you,' he said. He sat down and tied his shoe-laces. 'I don't. And that's a fact. Unless you're on the change or something.'

'*What*?' her mother whirled round from the mirror. 'How old am I, Jack?'

'I don't know. Thirty-five, aren't you? Thirty-three!'

'I am thirty-four years old,' her mother said, 'and for nearly fourteen of those years I have been married to you, and it seems that you know as much about me as a stranger on the street.'

'Oh don't start the Problem Page,' he said. 'Not on a Sunday. It's supposed to be my day of rest. And knowing has nothing to do with caring. You'd do well to bear that in mind. I may not have a good memory but at least I'm bothered about you. Whether you're bothered about me is a different matter.'

'You're making my heart bleed,' her mother said.

Aunt Dolly opened the door to them. She still wore her cemetery hat. The child wondered if she'd eaten her lunch wearing it. 'Well,' she said, 'well, I've been waiting for you.' Aunt Mu, from the kitchen, said, 'Dolly!' in a warning voice.

'Don't "Dolly" me. You're not dealing with our Herbert now, you know. I speak my mind, as everybody knows.'

Everybody did know, to their cost. She imagined that speaking one's mind was a virtue.

'We've brought Ronnie,' her mother said. 'He's staying with us for a couple of days.'

Aunt Dolly looked him up and down. 'As long as you've got plenty of clean sheets,' she said, 'from what I hear.'

But Ronnie – as well as winning a race and a coconut – had not wet the bed, the child realized; for two nights, at any rate.

They took off their coats and seated themselves. Aunt Mu brought in cups of tea and made futile attempts to engage Ronnie in conversation. Aunt Dolly bent and massaged her knees. The hat was formidable, the sort you'd wear to pass sentence of death on somebody. 'You certainly kept it to yourselves,' she said, 'all the goings-on.'

'What goings-on?'

'What goings-on! Don't come the innocent. The goings-on at the Spencers'.'

'Not much to tell,' her mother said, drinking her tea in little sips, studying the handle of the apostle spoon.

'Heck as like!' Aunt Dolly said.

'How do you know about it?'

'You'd be surprised. There's not much I don't get to know about, sooner or later.'

If Margaret Rose didn't grow up to be like Carrie Mortimer, the child thought, she'd grow up to be a second Aunt Dolly, a determined excavator of other people's buried shame.

'Didn't I tell you?' she said. 'Right from the beginning, to have nothing to do with that family? Anyone with two eyes in their head could see that it was a funny set-up. You're a bad chooser, Nancy. Always were. No judgement.'

Nancy chewed her lip, was silent.

'What are they going to do with her?' Aunt Dolly said, 'that wicked child?'

'I'm not sure. They said something about the Child Guidance.'

'Child guidance! Give me a couple of months with her. I'd guide her all right. It's Borstal she needs.'

Ronnie pricked up his ears. Borstal was *his* inevitable destination.

'And talking of Borstal . . .' Aunt Dolly said.

'Dolly,' Aunt Mu said again, stirring her tea so vigorously that the liquid whirled round madly inside her cup. 'Dolly, please.'

Aunt Dolly ignored her. 'I've got a bit of information for you,' she said, tracking her mother's gaze along its progress around the room. 'And you're not going to like it.'

The hat had been kept on deliberately, for effect. It gave weight and awesomeness to pronouncement. It was a hat as worn by the chief witness for the prosecution in an open and shut case.

'There was a policeman, wasn't there?' Aunt Dolly said, 'who came round to the Spencers'? A detective sergeant? A Mr Davidge?'

A big man, the child thought, a bulky man who called all female children 'girlie' and whose velvet brown eyes registered no variation in expression.

'There was a policeman, yes,' her mother said.

'Yes, there was a policeman,' her father said. 'Of course there was.'

'His name I wouldn't know,' her mother said. 'We didn't get that familiar.'

'No,' said Aunt Dolly, 'you wouldn't know. And what you wouldn't know, either, is that this Mr Davidge happens to be Mr Woodham's first cousin on his mother's side.'

'Three cheers for Mr Woodham,' her mother said. 'Bully for Mr Whatsit.' That was one of Charlie's expressions: Bully for so-and-so.

'They had dinner together last night,' Aunt Dolly said, 'Mr Woodham and the cousin and his wife. Of course, what was said was absolutely confidential.'

'Of course,' her mother said. She yawned widely and looked out of the window.

'Mr Woodham,' Aunt Dolly said, 'would never have dreamed of breathing a word to me, if he hadn't thought that you were at risk.'

Her mother looked round slowly until her eyes were on Aunt Dolly's face.

'What *is* she on about now?' her father said.

'I debated within myself,' Aunt Dolly said. 'But you are my sister, after all, and I do have a responsibility towards you. You may be a pair of fools. I don't suppose that you can help that; it's nature. But I won't sit back and see you be taken for bigger fools than you are already.'

She was enjoying it enormously: the build-up to whatever climax was following. Why haven't we been sent out of the room, the child thought, why haven't we been told to run out and play? Either it's nothing so very terrible, or she thinks we're too young and dim to understand.

'If you've got something to say,' her father said, 'come out and say it.' Over the years he had made this same request to Aunt Dolly time without number. For a plain-speaking woman, she took a delight in wrapping up her information.

'Right,' she said, 'I will.' The child shivered, although the palms of her hands were damp and squeaked when she rubbed them together.

'Your pal, Charlie,' Aunt Dolly said. And the child's muscles tensed. She had known it all along. Her instinct had told her that it must be to do with Charlie. People didn't simply arrive from nowhere to illuminate your life. They had to have a background, and an explanation for their presence and a mapped-out future.

'Mr Davidge knows your pal Charlie. From way back.'

That was an expression she'd picked up from the American soldiers. There had been a hospital for them on the outskirts of the town. Great numbers of them had suffered from a disease that seemed to be peculiar to American soldiers.

'And you don't need me to tell you how he got to know him. In what circumstances.'

She paused for breath. And then proceeded to tell them in what circumstances Mr Davidge had got to know Charlie.

He had lived out the sort of future that Mr Spencer had forecast for Ronnie: approved school, Borstal, jail. 'In Norwich,' Aunt Dolly said, 'they had him up three times. He was convicted for fraud. He had a record as long as your arm: deception, false pretences, petty thievery, you name it . . . Mr Davidge got to know him quite well. He said it was a classic case, a bad start in life, a few brains and no character. He said that was why they never believed the Spencer child from the first. It wasn't his style. His style was stealing and confidence trickery. And living off women. Do you know where he'd come from, direct from, to that funeral?' Aunt Dolly said. 'Why, from jail, of course. Three years, he'd been doing. Selling, he told you? He'd been selling all right. Except that what he sold wasn't his to sell. What a pack of lies he's fed you. And you lapped it up. Just because you knew his father. And what you found out about his father should have put you on your guard against the character of the son. "A con-artist", Mr Davidge called him. "Second nature," he said. Well, he's conned you fair and square, hasn't he?'

Her mother licked her lips, gripped her hands between her knees to stop them trembling.

'Scum,' Aunt Dolly said, 'scum, his type is. A job! He was in no hurry to look for one, was he? Probably never done an honest day's work in his life.' You could see in her face all the years of aching feet and varicose veins and saying, 'Yes, madam.'

'All that talk about the RAF,' she said. 'He was never in the RAF. He was never out of England. The only war that he saw was through the prison bars.'

She cleared her throat, brushed the lap of her dress, composed herself for the reaction.

The clock ticked. Aunt Mu clattered the tea cups on the tray. Her father ran a finger round the collar of his shirt. 'I'll be blowed,' he said, 'I'll be blowed. Never in the RAF?' This piece of news seemed to have disillusioned him more than the rest of it put together. 'How come he knew so much about it then?'

'They're cute,' Aunt Dolly said, 'they pick up things quickly. They live on their wits. They leave people like you and me standing.'

'Why bother with us?' he said. 'We'd nothing for him.'

Aunt Dolly didn't answer.

Her mother looked up, gazed steadily at her sister. 'Let's have it all, Dolly,' she said. 'Now you've started. Just what else was said and why did he bother with us?'

Aunt Dolly opened her mouth to speak. Aunt Muriel stood up and said, very quietly, 'One more word, Dolly, and I walk out of this house. For good.'

The first time. In living memory. Aunt Muriel, who'd buried two babies and buried a husband and allowed her sister-in-law to ride rough-shod for the sake of a home and companionship. They couldn't have been more stunned if she'd taken off all her clothes and danced on the table.

Words formed themselves in Aunt Dolly's throat, struggled for expression. For a moment the balance of power swung this way and that, and then you knew – it was a discovery – that Aunt Dolly needed Aunt Muriel more than Aunt Muriel needed Aunt Dolly. Real power lay in knowing just when to use it.

Whatever might have been said was not going to be said. There was a little silence while Aunt Muriel sat down again and straightened the tablecloth that she'd ruffled in her rising. And then an alternative pronouncement was made:

'I said to Mr Woodham: "I thought there was something funny about that one right from the minute he appeared on the scene." I've a nose for that sort of thing. Some people do. Mr Woodham said, "No one could put anything over on you, Dolly."'

'Don't you wish that somebody would? Just once?' Her mother stood up. Her legs were quivering as well as her hands. Her voice wandered up and down the register as boys' voices did when they were breaking.

'What do you mean,' Aunt Dolly said, 'by that?'

'I mean, if it happened just once, it might prove that you were a human being instead of a damned machine,' her mother said, and walked slowly out of the room and out of the house, testing each step before her like an invalid.

One thing, only, worried her: that because of her parents' disillusionment and disapproval it would be difficult to maintain contact with him. Difficult, but not impossible. Though it would be tiresome having to manufacture alibis, she knew that she was intelligent and resourceful enough to do so. Autumn was on the way; there would be opportunities for diversions on the way home from school. No illness would complicate the issue. She knew that she had left all that behind. Fresh air and exercise and sunshine and Charlie had cured her.

She wanted to talk it out with him, to tell him that jail and all the rest of it made no difference to her regard for him, that she herself was a victim of Too Much Imagination. She wanted him to tell her his true story which could hardly have been less incident-crammed than his fantasy one. She despised all the people who thought themselves fit to pass judgement upon him, who were too limited to realize that when your life didn't come up to the expectations you'd had, it was comforting to invent another one for yourself, and sometimes the invention spilled out of your brain and through your lips, almost involuntarily.

In bed, on Sunday night, she lay awake thinking out alternative plans for the future. It was necessary to act quickly, to convince him that there was no need for him to feel ashamed.

In the event, however, her stratagems were unnecessary. The next morning, after her father had left for work, her mother put on her coat, pocketed the back-door key and said, 'Come on, hurry yourself up, we're going out.'

'Where to?'

'Never you mind.'

They sat on the top deck of the bus. It looked like rain again; not another Technicolour thunderstorm, just thin slanting monotonous drizzle. Her mother bit ragged pieces of skin from around the cuticle of her fingernail and didn't answer when spoken to. All the little lines had reappeared in her face. She looked plain, unattractive.

The child knew where they would alight, knew the route they would follow, was not, however, prepared to be told, 'You stop there and don't move,' when they reached the front of the Marlborough.

The season was dying. White 'Vacancies' signs appeared in the windows of the boarding houses. Young faces were replaced by old ones; heads, grey, silver, and bald, nodded in deckchairs on the terraces; they were the end-of-season, cheap-rate pensioners. All the hydrangeas in the ornamental stone pots were turning to russet, the striped umbrellas were furled and put to store, the clamour of children gave way to the muted, silence-interspersed conversations of the elderly.

Her mother rang the bell and a woman in a flowered overall opened the door. She shook her head a few times when her mother was speaking and then went away again. The child edged surreptitiously up the tiled front steps. By the time Myra appeared, she was within earshot of the conversation.

'Yesterday morning,' Myra said. 'Packed his bag and went.' There were purple patches under her eyes like thumb-marks. She kept wiping her nose with her handkerchief. Even her magnificent chest jutted less proudly. 'Never a word of explanation, just "Give us the bill, Myra, while I've still got a few bob to bless myself with." I said to him. "You're not going for good, are you?" "It's probably a good thing I'm going," he said. "Put it that way." I was that upset – I looked on him as a son, almost – I can't really believe it yet. It was those damn police,' she said, moving the handkerchief back and forth against her nostrils. 'It was enough to make anyone want to leave. Disturbing decent people, making rotten allegations. Him of all people! He wouldn't have harmed a fly. Or I'm no judge of character.'

The child watched her mother's knuckles whiten as she clutched on to the wrought-iron handrail that was affixed to the steps. A shrill voice, from inside the house, called, 'Do I change number twelve, Mrs Grainger?'

Myra put her hand into the pocket of her cardigan. 'One thing he did say was, "If a lady named Nancy calls, will you give her this? Tell her I meant every word I said. Not that she'll believe it." I take it, dear, that you're that lady?' Her mother nodded. A white envelope changed hands. 'Don't be embarrassed, dear,' Myra said. 'I wouldn't begrudge anybody the little bit of happiness they can snatch out of this rotten world. I have known sorrow myself. I have known what it is to cry my heart out in the grey dawn.'

She'd got that out of a library book, the child thought, one of those under 'R' for Romance. The Countess Eleonora and a Gentleman of Substance. There was always an illustration on the front cover of those books: two dopey people gazing at each other, in the manner of Mr and Mrs Spencer at Weston-super-Mare.

A seagull alighted on the gate post, opened its throat and made the tearing sound common to seagulls. *Larus canus*, the child remembered, and *perdix perdix*, and the mute swan, *cygnus olor*, the Local History Museum and Charlie saying, 'I'm not much good, you know.'

Myra's head nodded to meet her bosom. Her mother's knuckles were five white knobs of bone on the iron rail.

'Charlie,' the child said softly, 'Charlie.' And the seagull imitated the sound, distorted it, sent it soaring away into the æther.

'Children are a comfort,' Myra said, and leaned forward and pressed her mother's forearm. Her mother said, yes, and that she must be going, and, really, she was very sorry to have bothered her at what must be a busy time.

Myra looked at her, her head on one side. 'Don't worry, dear,' she said. 'I am discreet.' And then, in a different, hard-edged voice, 'You've got to be in this business. It wouldn't pay to be otherwise.'

Soon they would pull the slatted wooden blinds down over the rock shops and the oyster stalls, switch off the lights in the funfair and padlock the great iron gate. They would lift the flags out of the miniature golf course and shunt the miniature train into its winter shed. Madame Bonney would pack up her crystal ball and her Tarot cards and pursue her profession, spasmodically, from her first floor flat in Hanover Buildings. The bandsmen would play the Radetsky March for one last rousing encore and place their instruments in their instrument cases. The younger elderly men would polish their bowls and put them in cupboards under the stairs. The old, old men would disappear from the recreation ground and take to their beds, or nurse their arthritis, or die of pneumonia. Uncle Arthur would wave his hand to the last of the kiddies in the Marine Gardens Pavilion and label his trunk for panto in Newcastle-upon-Tyne, or Barnsley, or Stoke-on-Trent. The railway cleaners would sweep sand out of the final train on the excursion platform. Myra and the other boarding house keepers would slap fresh paint on their premises and take their holidays. The forecourts of the Grand Hotel and the Majestic would be crammed with cars which disgorged dinner-suited men and ladies in long frocks and elbow-length gloves for Ladies' Night Masonic Dinners and Charity Balls. The seasonal waitresses would take off their frilly aprons and return to their machines at the hosiery factory. Sea fogs would roll across the marshes and muffle the hoof-beats of the boggart horses and their wraith-riders. Dusk would come against the window earlier and earlier and the clocks would go back, and one morning you'd shiver at the door and see white frost on the lawn and, by that time, summer would have become a very hazy memory, a forgotten season.

She could understand why her mother cried, quietly, in bed when her father was asleep, why she never used the Creme Puff or the Sugar Plum lipstick any more, why she shoved the floral print dress and the new blouse to the back of the wardrobe and stopped whatever she was doing and held her hand to her chest whenever she heard a step at the back door. She could understand, because her mother was simply exhibiting what she, the child, was forced to conceal. He had gone, and it was as if someone had switched off all the lights in the world.

Chapter Nineteen

SHE WAS SULLEN, she was uncommunicative, sometimes downright rude. 'What's got into the child?' they said, and she would curl her lip and take *Kidnapped* or *The Black Tulip* to read on the bottom step of the stairs. She hated them all for their different degrees of responsibility for what had happened.

The visit to the relations in Yorkshire had been cancelled. The rain set in and the hardy annuals shed their petals and died. Nothing and nobody was proof against the pervading melancholy inside the house. One evening, on the wireless, the Palm Court Orchestra began to play, 'I dreamt I dwelt in marble halls,' and her mother ran across the room and turned the knob so viciously that it nearly came off in her hand. 'I was listening to that,' her father said. He liked a good tune. 'Tough luck,' her mother said. 'It gives me the pip.'

She opened her satchel and took out her Latin primer, for next year it was the scholarship and one must work very hard. 'Amavi, amavisti, amavit,' she chanted, 'amavimus, amavistis, amaverunt, amaveram – I had loved, amavissem – I might have loved.' The black print danced and dissolved in front of her eyes. The world was empty, bleak. The future stretched onwards to infinity, a grey plain that promised nothing. The best time was over. 'Don't squint,' her mother said. 'You'll need glasses before you're twelve.' She said it automatically; there was no conviction in her voice.

The only activity for which the child could summon any enthusiasm was the search. Opportunities were not frequent: ten minutes while her mother went to the corner shop, an hour while she washed the clothes in the kitchen, an hour punctuated by heart-stopping moments when the noise of the wringer ceased, and she froze, her hands in a prohibited drawer or a forbidden cupboard.

The wardrobe yielded nothing. Neither did the dressing table. Nor the chest of drawers. Except for the mysterious, soft, tissue-wrapped object, and she was no longer interested in discovering the identity of that. Her search, when the opportunity arose, was organized and thorough: the pockets of clothes, the interiors of stacked suitcases, the folds of winter underclothes, the cupboard high in the wall of her parents' bedroom where the Christmas decorations were stored. But a week of methodical searching produced nothing. Perhaps she was wasting her time. 'I'm going to the library,' her mother said. The books were long overdue. She was going to get her tickets out; she couldn't settle down to reading any more. 'Do you want to come?'

The child looked up from her French book, she shook her head. 'I'm learning my French.' Un jour, la famille Laborde . . . La famille Laborde was a pain in the neck: Maman was forever in the cuisine, Papa worked very hard, Jean-Paul and Marie-Thérèse and Pierre had smug round faces and raisin eyes and prefixed every sentence with 'Alors!'

'Behave yourself then,' her mother said. 'I shan't be long.' Her mother said 'behave yourself' almost as frequently as the Laborde children said 'alors!'

The door closed behind her. The child closed her French book and put it back into her satchel. It was the turn of the broom cupboard today. She moved the

211

vacuum cleaner, the wall-brush, the carpet sweeper. She shifted two tennis rackets that needed re-stringing, an ancient battledore and shuttlecock, several annuals, a raffia workbasket, a tin of marbles, a number of coat-hangers that Carrie Mortimer had appropriated from the boarding house and passed on: they said 'Property of the Bella Vista Hotel'; a flat-iron, two pictures of nymphs gazing into pools, and an abacus fitted with yellow beads. She moved a birdcage and a grey matted mop-head and the wings that she'd worn to be the Angel Gabriel in a Nativity Play, and then she was at the back of the cupboard and the only things left were two worn-out handbags that belonged to her mother.

One of them she had taken away with her on her honeymoon. It was made of black squashy leather and the inside was lined with silk and smelled of cachoux and old stale perfume. It contained two Kirby grips, some grains of face-powder and the stub of a ticket admitting one person to a performance of the Variety Music Hall at Scarborough.

The other bag was cheaper, more workaday, made of brown shiny plastic with two gold-coloured clasps, one of which was broken. She held it for a moment before she opened it. It was the last throw of the dice upon which everything depended. Sometimes hidden things gave off emanations; she had felt them, during children's parties when the rest of them hunted and she found the thimble, guided to it by some peculiar form of magnetism. This brown bag, however, maintained an impenetrable façade; it did not call out to be looked into, and when she opened it the little flutter of excitement that she'd felt died instantly, for all that it contained was a soiled white glove and an empty book of matches, a pink button and one of those plastic sticks that people stuck through cherries in drinks.

She lifted the small square mirror out of the inside flap, breathed on it, wiped it with her sleeve and looked at herself. Her face had filled out, no doubt about it. Her eyes looked less big and bright than they used to do. People called them brown, but when you looked closely you saw that they were more olive-green than brown, with little gold flecks at the edge of the irises. It was as she was replacing the mirror that she saw that in the flap of the handbag there was a zipped compartment, and it was then that her instinct snapped into action and she knew, before she opened it, that the letter would be inside.

The envelope and the writing paper were thin, cheap and lined. There was no address in the top right-hand corner, and it simply said, 'Sunday', instead of the proper date in its complete form. She was disappointed with his handwriting: it was small and unsure and backward-sloping, adorned with unnecessary flourishes and curlicues. She had thought that a man such as Charlie would write big and definite and straightforward.

When she began to read she was not especially aware that her heart was beating under her blouse. By the time she'd turned the page and reached the end she felt as though her buttons would burst their moorings under the bombardment they were receiving. She had to go back and read it all again in case her eyes had suddenly taken on a life of their own, independent of her brain; she thought of those ink blot things that meant different things to different people.

The letter said:

'Nancy —,
    I am giving this to Myra to hand on to you. I didn't know whether to bother writing or not. I didn't want you to think badly of me. Though I expect you'll think badly of me anyway. You can't help but. When you

213

hear the whole story. Which you will, sooner or later, this being a small town and people in it with nothing better to do than jaw, jaw, jaw about anybody out of the ordinary. Well Nancy I was a bad lad. Still am I suppose. Never did half of those things I told you. A big romanser my old lady used to call me. Got it from her. She could tell the tale all right. And the old fellow too I shouldn't wonder. Still, there we are, that's me, a fool to myself as they used to say at the bad lads' home.

I just wanted you to know Nancy that I thought the world of you. And if you'd of come away with me I'd of loved you till you died of it. You and me and the kid we could of been as happy as Larry. I might even of got a job. And pigs might fly, I hear you say. That's something we'll never know now. I wish to Christ I could of persuaded you. I've always been a loser at that too.

Now, you see that the kid keeps up her swimming. Tell her Charlie had to go away. She's young and tough, she won't mind. But what about you Nancy will you remember me? I won't forget you. Ever. I'll never forget those nights down by the golf course in the old clapped-out jam-jar – you said you'd never done it before in the back seat and you were so scared and I said kissing like spider's web, leads to undoing of flies and you laughed. Oh Nancy I did love you the way you felt, your breests and the way you came for me. I'll never meet another like you. I swear to God. When you think bad of me remember that, remember you said I love you Charlie just before all this blew up.

I'm off now. On the road again. I'll survive. Now you take care of yourself Nancy and stick with Jack. He's no Rudolph Valentino but he'll do right by you. Nothing surer.

Your own loving,
Charlie.'

214

His punctuation left much to be desired. He had spelled 'romancer' wrongly. 'Breests' puzzled her for a moment or two, until it dawned on her what it was supposed to mean, and then her face flamed. Breasts was one of the rudest words you could say. And to write it down on paper was ruder still. Sometimes, when he meant 'have' he had written 'of' which was the way it sounded spoken. Charlie writing was not the same as Charlie speaking. The kid, indeed! He had never called her that. It had always been 'Princess'. The letter was written with a malfunctioning ball-point pen and the creases in the paper were deeply scored and beginning to go ragged as though it had been re-read a great many times.

She thought about all these trivial points at great length because by doing so she put off having to think about the letter in its entirety, its composite meaning.

The gleeful face of Margaret Rose floated into her mind. She was saying, 'I told you so. You wouldn't believe me.' She was saying, 'Reckon you're so clever! You don't know anything. Men and women . . . Bouncing . . . Jumping . . . My mother and father . . . *Your* mother and father . . . Men and women.'

For the second time in the space of a week the child was sick, without warning, on to the floor. She leaned her cheek against the cool plaster of the cupboard wall. After a time, when the dry retching had ceased, she went into the kitchen and ran the floor-cloth under the tap and came back with it and mopped up the vomit. This caused her to retch again, painfully. She had to close her eyes and pinch her nostrils together with one hand before she could continue. She dared not use the San-Izal to smother the sour odour because her mother would smell it and ask why, so she fetched the Attar of Roses talcum tin from the bathroom and sprinkled some of the powder on to the floor and ground it in with her heel.

And then she ground her fingernails into the palms of her hands and left the imprint of a series of little red crescents on the lines that foretold your future. She hated everybody who breathed. She hated her mother and she hated Charlie who had called her 'the kid' and whose declared love for her had been, after all, just another variation on the theme of adult deception, a crueller variation. But most of all she hated herself, for her gullibility. It was an adult world. She knew that now. And whatever they said to you, and whoever said it, it all came to the same thing in the end. They conned you, they betrayed you, they never, ever, meant what they said. She threw the bag and the letter into the cobwebs in the furthest darkest corner of the cupboard. She thought of Aunt Mu and Miss Tibbs talking of trust and caring and human kindness. She thought of Aunt Dolly and Mrs Spencer and Charlie who trusted no one. They were the survivors. Trusting was for fools.

He wore his brown windcheater and his grey shorts and the snake-clasp belt and her mother's tennis shoes and he lugged his hold-all up the hill, changing it from hand to hand as he went; his outline altered as he was weighed down, alternately, on either side. She saw him a good minute before he saw her and, at first, she thought of doing his old trick in the shadow of a gatepost to avoid an encounter, but, after all, he was the only person with whom she had no quarrel, the only person who had not contributed, in however small a fashion, to the way things had turned out. So she ran, up the slope to the railway station, and caught up with him at the booking office.

'Hello, Ronnie,' she said.

'Single to Penrith,' he said. He had the exact money. The Spencers must have ascertained the price of the fare beforehand. 'Hullo,' he said. 'I can't give you that money I owe you, because I bought the ticket. Unless, you could try and get the money back on it?' She shook her head; it was the League of Pity who would go short, and she didn't much care about that. 'I'll send it to you,' he said, 'when I get my first wage.'

'OK.' It wouldn't happen. He would forget her address, or not know how to fill in a postal order even if he remembered it.

They walked over the bridge to the platform. The once-lustrous geraniums were now faded and tattered. The porter was engaged in painting the railings and warned them to shift themselves from his area of activity. The railway tracks ran parallel, onward to infinity where they would meet. Except that infinity didn't exist. They were the only occupants of the waiting room, where the floor was ankle-deep in litter and the walls were scrawled with dirty words. This was a little branch-line station, not the big one with book-stalls and confectionery kiosks and a speak-your-weight machine where Ronnie had been apprehended.

He unwrapped a packet of Beechnut chewing gum and handed her a piece. She accepted it because she was no longer worried about germs. Stories about germs were probably as untrue as everything else they told you.

They revolved the gum around their mouths without speaking for a time. She thought it was extremely brave of him to be travelling alone without even a label pinned to his front stating his name and destination. He sat with his hold-all between his feet. The zip was broken and she could see, in amongst the dirty vests and pants, a plaster Skye terrier, a box of paints and a coconut. His freckles stood out, copper-coloured, against the paleness of his skin. He had washed as far as his neck and his wrists. He looked as though he was returning for a court-martial. To cheer him up, to take

217

his mind off the impending reunion with Cronshaw and Briggs and the rest of them who taunted him with his stupidity and bed-wetting, she said, 'What's going on at the Spencers'? My mother won't let me have anything to do with Margaret Rose. And if she goes back to Burlington Court I must ask to be seated somewhere away from her. But I don't think she will.'

'It's awful,' he said. 'They cry all the time and nobody washes the pots and have to hide when the rent-man comes. We all hide. On the stairs. And he shouts things through the letter-box. *He* says he's going to jump in the lake and *she* says she's off to her sister's and that pig keeps pretending to be ill and squawking and saying she's going to die. I wish she would.'

The child nodded agreement. But she knew that although she could will horses and Ronnie to win races, all the wishing in the world wouldn't put the jinx on Margaret Rose.

He had chewed all the flavour out of his gum. He removed it from his mouth and stuck it under the bench. 'Is it true,' he said, 'Charlie was in the nick?'

'What's in the nick?'

'Prison,' he said, grinning, mocking her innocence. 'Your auntie said he'd been in the nick and Borstal and those places.'

'Yes, it's true,' she said. 'Where do you have to change trains?' She didn't want to discuss the subject.

'Preston,' he said. And continued doggedly, 'And he's not coming back?'

'Shouldn't think so.'

'So he won't be coming to see us at the school after all?'

'Shouldn't think so.'

He untied and retied his shoelaces very deliberately, his head bent so that she couldn't see his face.

'They're always pretending,' she said, 'always having you on. They all tell lies.'

'He wasn't pretending,' he said into his kneecap. 'Charlie.'

'Oh yes he was,' she said gloomily. 'He was no different. They like making fools of you.'

'Not him,' he said stubbornly. He looked up. His face was paler, as though he was facing, for the first time, the prospect of Cronshaw and Briggs and no weekend visits to alleviate the torment.

'You won't ever be coming back here for a holiday then?'

'No,' he said. 'Next year I'll be working.' His face said, *if* I can make it through the next few months, now I know there is no hope of relief, of distraction, however brief.

It was worse for him really, if you thought about it; he had pinned such a lot of hope on Charlie. 'Never mind,' she said, 'you shot down those ducks and won that race and you almost learned to swim.'

You could detect the debate going on inside his head: on the one hand, the race and the coconut and the unexpected pleasures, on the other, the beatings and the iron at his head, the unsuccessful attempt at flight towards his absent mother, Charlie's defection. His eyes flickered and he decided, to come down on the side of cheerfulness. After all, memories were forever; they proved that events *had* happened, and he had them in concrete form: the coconut, the Skye terrier, the box of paints.

'Your train is coming.'

The porter balanced his paint-brush on top of his paint tin and fetched the green flag out of his cubby-hole. The steam lay back, a white plume against the still, dun-coloured sky. He selected an empty compartment, threw his hold-all into the luggage rack, pushed the window down to its fullest extent.

'Goodbye,' she said. It was as if saying goodbye to him made an end to everything. She wished that there was

219

some profound remark she could make that would convey to him the special relationship that they had all shared. She wished that he was intelligent enough to understand it.

'Bye,' he said and put the last rectangular tablet of chewing gum into his mouth. The porter shouted, 'All right, Percy,' and waved his flag. The carriages began to move slowly along the platform. 'He wasn't, you know,' Ronnie said.

'Wasn't what?'

He leaned out of the window at a most perilous angle. 'Silly young devil,' the porter shouted, 'get inside.' The train slid away. The steam blew back and enveloped him. 'Wasn't what?' she cried.

'Pretendin',' he called and the word was stretched out the length of the train, echoed thinly through the steam, hung in the still air above the shabby geraniums.

'I saw Ronnie,' she told her mother when she reached home, 'going back.'

'Oh yes,' her mother said without interest. She had no sympathy to spare for anyone else. 'I'm going upstairs to lie down. Can you keep yourself occupied for a while?'

She was going upstairs to cry. She had to take the opportunity for a private weep whenever it presented itself. The child heard her through the wall. All day she drooped around – 'Leave me alone and let me die,' Aunt Dolly called the expression on her face – and in the afternoons or at night, after her father had gone to sleep, she wept into the pillow. The child despised her. All the tears in the world couldn't alter the situation, so why cry? You had to continue, the child had discovered, you had to regain your equilibrium by convincing yourself that, whatever Ronnie chose to believe, he *had* pretended, that it was in the nature of all human beings to let you down when it came to the point. You had to put your faith in yourself and what you could do, unaided.

She gazed at the picture of the horse above the mantelpiece. The fetlocks *were* all wrong. The withers were too narrow. She had not caught the flow of the mane. And the feet were at a quarter to three. She opened her desk, brought out a sheet of cartridge paper, an HB Venus pencil, and a soft rubber. She pulled a stool up to the desk, placed the paper neatly and symmetrically upon it's surface, sharpened the pencil to a fine point. The time was ripe for another attempt. A year hence she knew that she would look at it with a similar dissatisfaction. But one day, eventually . . . Eventually.